FORCE THREE RISES

An Amos Mead Adventure Novel
by

Tom Gauthier

Published by *ToMar Associates*
Publishing

P.O. Box 362, Janesville, California 96114
United States of America

First Edition Printed 2015
Copyright © 2015 by Tom Gauthier
All rights reserved.

ISBN-13: 978-0692403396

Cover Design: Dr. Ray White

Author's photograph by: Pam Woodworth

This is a work of fiction and is not intended to refer to current
places, events, or living persons, however, some events,
characters and locations are based on historic records.
The opinions expressed in this manuscript are solely those of the
author.

Dedicated to the Warriors Who Fought

Bravely Against All Odds on the

Korean Peninsula: 1950-1953

ACKNOWLEDGEMENTS

Though the Korean Conflict is the background for this story, my thoughts are never far from the cadre of veteran soldiers who trained me in Basic Combat Training at Fort Ord, California in 1959. From our commanding officer, who was awarded the Medal of Honor as a PFC in WWII and earned a battlefield commission in Korea, to our First Sergeant also a decorated combat veteran, these men showed me why we honor the service of those who choose to step up when our country calls. Thanks for your service, gentlemen.

My own family has worn our uniform in every American conflict from King Phillip's War in 1675 to the Iraq War, and grandsons are still in active service today. They are part of my motivation to write in honor of their history.

But one does not create alone. The constant support of my wife, Marlene, has kept me going through the recent bouts with health issues. She's also my best marketer and cheerleader! Thank You is a weak response for unselfish love like hers.

My military advisor, WWII bomber pilot and good friend Don Sokol keeps my technical side in order. When he's teamed up with former LTC Peter Clark, US Army (Ret), I can be assured that technical details in my stories are true and accurate. (Peter Clark is author of the award winning book, *Staff Monkeys: A Stockbroker's Journey Through the Global War on Terror.*) Thank you, gentlemen, especially for your service.

A special thanks to my friend Liudmila Mullin from St. Petersburg, Russia, for editing my Russian Cyrillic dialog for realism and accuracy.

Finally, to another talented friend, Dr. Ray White, who knows his way around the digital design world, providing the great covers for my books, my continued gratitude for your work and your friendship.

"The basic difference between an ordinary man and a warrior is that a warrior takes everything as a challenge, while an ordinary man takes everything as a blessing or as a curse."

Don Juan Matus

Don Juan Matus is a major figure in the series of books by the late Carlos Castaneda

FOREWORD

Tom Gauthier again demonstrates that he is a natural and highly entertaining story teller. One of the pitfalls that some authors, and unfortunately readers encounter with sequels is excessive repetition and a failure of the characters to develop beyond how they were described at the start of the series. Gratefully, Dr. Gauthier avoids that mistake. His characters continue to develop, so there is no chance of the reader being lulled into an obvious conclusion based on a historical repetition of the story lines.

Although I encourage readers to begin any series with the first story, Gauthier's writing style allows the reader to begin with any book in the series and not feel as if they are missing some key elements to the story lines from previous works. Tom Gauthier is able to catch his readers up on pertinent facts from prior stories without rehashing the entire story.

Dr. Gauthier is able to paint an historically accurate story for his readers without subjecting them to what could be a tedious academic experience. In short, his writings are what made reading so enjoyable for so many people in the first place; just quality stories that captivate the reader and make them want to find out what is going to happen next.

LTC Peter Clark, USA (RET)

LTC Clark Served as Information Operations Planner, Special Operations Command Central and as Assistant Chief of Staff G-7, III Armor Corps.

INTRODUCTION

KOREA

World War II ended with the unconditional surrender of Japan to the Allies. Fighting ceased—except for the Soviets who continued with their planned invasion of Manchuria. They decimated the Japanese army while conquering Manchukuo, Inner Mongolia, southern Sakhalin, the Kuril Islands, and northern Korea, stopping at the 38th parallel in Korea as the designated demarcation between Soviet and American responsibility areas. Only then did they join the Allies in accepting Japans surrender.

After World War II the American intelligence services were badly fragmented, and at the onset of hostilities in 1950 on the Korean Peninsula this became a crippling issue.

Adding to the problem was the efficient infiltration of Communist agents and spies into nearly all facets of the American government. Senator Joe McCarthy's crusade on Communism served to allow Soviet plants to simply hunker down and hide in plain sight until needed, or as opportunities arose.

In 1949 Kim Il Sung, the autocratic leader of the Democratic Peoples' Republic of Korea—North Korea—traveled to Moscow and convinced Joseph Stalin that he could conquer the government of South Korea. The withdrawal of most U.S. forces from South Korea in June 1949 left the southern government defended only by a weak and inexperienced South Korean army. Kim Il Sung's army by contrast had been armed with Soviet WWII era equipment and had a cadre of veterans who had extensive experience fighting as anti-Japanese guerrillas.

Initially Joseph Stalin rejected Kim Il Sung's requests. But the final Communist victory in China and the early development of Soviet nuclear weapons made him re-consider Kim's proposal. Now Stalin agreed, convinced that the United States would not dare to get involved and seeing his chance to push the "cold war" without Russia directly confronting America.

Finally, in early1950 after Mao Tse-tung approved sending Red Chinese troops and other support to Kim Il Sung, Stalin approved an invasion of the South. But he limited Soviet support to advisors and military instructors to train Korean units.

The attack on the South, when it came, was totally unanticipated by American intelligence. America's strategy of containment against the Soviets and Communist China essentially ignored small states like North Korea—to their peril.

THE UNITED NATIONS—SPYING IN PLAIN SIGHT

The Korean Conflict was conducted under a United Nations umbrella—but the United States had full command authority. The "umbrella" of the United Nations provided a source of information to Stalin that is hard to believe as tolerated—or understood—by President Truman.

Soviet Lieutenant General Alexandre Vasiliev was Stalin's representative on the United Nations Military Staff Committee. All plans and action reports for Korea came through this group, eventually finding their way to Stalin. This is the same Alexandre Vasiliev who took a "leave of absence" from his duties in New York to assume de-facto command of all North Korean and Communist Chinese troop movements across the 38th Parallel. During the Korean conflict, Lieutenant General Vasiliev purportedly received military information of troop movements of UN forces in Korea directly from his superior, Soviet General

Zinchenko, who was Under-Secretary of the Security Council of the United Nations in New York.

ALL battle plans were approved by him *ahead of time*.

ATOMIC BOMBS IN KOREA

Little known and frightening history—the United States nearly started an atomic war in Korea. In 1950 the Joint Chiefs of Staff issued orders for the retaliatory atomic bombing of Chinese Manchurian military bases if their armies crossed into Korea or if the Peoples' Republic of China bombers attacked Korea from there.

President Truman ordered the transfer of nine nuclear bombs to the USAF 9th Bomb Group, the designated carrier of such weapons. Truman then signed an order to use the atomic weapons against Chinese and Korean targets.

When imminent defeat seemed a possibility to him, the military commander, General Douglas MacArthur, considered using the Atomic bomb. Actually, MacArthur's plan was to use numerous bombs. The United States held a stockpile of nearly three hundred atomic bombs and, though only President Truman could order them used, MacArthur insisted he should have the sole right to use fifty of them as he saw fit. His plan was to drop between thirty and fifty atomic bombs in a string across the neck of Manchuria that would spread a belt of radioactive cobalt from the Sea of Japan to the Yellow Sea. He predicted that there would be no invasion of Korea from the North for at least sixty years— and that the Soviets would be intimidated and do nothing. A very faulty prediction, indeed.

Even though President Truman publicly announced the United States was considering using the Atomic weapon against North Korea, General MacArthur was criticized for actually planning the same thing. The state of affairs was rapidly going from bad to disastrous. When he requested that the Pentagon grant him a field commander's discretion to employ nuclear weapons as necessary, the request was denied, and for the first time the idea of "relieving" MacArthur was on the table in Washington.

Still, the United States government moved closer to atomic warfare in Korea when the Peoples' Republic of China deployed new armies to the Korean frontier. Orders went out to crews at Kadena Air Force Base in Okinawa to assemble atomic bombs for Korean warfare—lacking only the essential nuclear cores.

With atomic weapons already on Okinawa, the stage was set to proceed with the actual detonation of numerous nuclear bombs. All ranking military and government officials, including President Truman agreed to the plan.

Everything was ready— just waiting for the *word*.

PROLOGUE

OKINAWA, JAPAN

Three Japanese fishing boats slipped into the harbor near Kadena in Okinawa. Two of them were pole-and-line tuna fisherman, the likes of which had become more and more common by the 1950's. The third was much larger and rigged for drag net fishing, looking much like a mother ship.

No one paid any attention as they slipped up to an unused pier, and fewer noted those who climbed over the rail of the large vessel, sea bags in hand, and moved in pairs toward a darkened warehouse about one hundred yards away. As they approached the shadow darkened side away from the road that separated the waterfront for the American Airbase, a door opened and they silently slipped inside.

"Do you have everything you need for this mission," said the man who had opened the door for them.

One of the crew stepped to the front and answered, "We have. Where are we to set up our base?"

"Follow me." The six men, a medley of Korean and mixed-blood Chinese-Koreans, shouldered their gear and followed to a dimly lit stairway that led to the second level. Once there they found all in readiness for them. The leader said, "We will unload the trucks after dark." Back on the fishing boat the rest of the "fishermen" appeared to go about their usual duties, giving the impression of a routine port of call for a boat that has been at sea. But below deck the work was far from routine.

6

Across the road from the waterfront and well beyond the perimeter security fence, American Air Force crews were busy tending to a flight line of Boeing B-29 bombers. Training missions had been ordered for the flight crews that sent them flying routes out from Okinawa, over North Korea and return, carrying dummy or conventional bombs.

Security on the base was not extraordinary. America had won the war and there were no more enemies lurking in the Pacific. It seems America has the same tendency after every conflict: relax, down size and believe the peace has been won "in our time."

The darkened windows of the upstairs floor of the warehouse did their job of giving the place a placid, vacant look. But the coverings were designed so that the team from the fishing boat could observe their target without being seen. Across the road and beyond the fence U.S. Air Force ground crews and technicians were busy in and around the WWII era hangers, since converted to a new use.

The U.S. Joint Chiefs of Staff had issued orders to deploy atomic weapons on Manchuria if the Chinese or North Korean armies crossed that border into Korea. President Truman, who held sole control of nuclear weapons, ordered nine nuclear capsules to be assigned to the Air Force's Ninth Bomb Group and stationed in Okinawa—on Kadena Air Base. The hangers were now ground zero for the components of MacArthur's new weapons, authorized by President Truman and flown in from the United States. Crews assembled atomic bombs, stopping short of inserting nuclear cores. The cores would complete the mission, inserted into the bombs near the time for actual detonation. A string of nuclear bombs along the North Korean border with China—turning it into a no-man's-land and halting any Chinese intervention—had all official approvals in place.

It was now just a tedious wait for "the word" from Truman.

Nearby, the "fishermen" also waited *for the word of their own.*

Characters

Americans

Amos Mead	*Attorney, Marine veteran of OSS/CIA*
Brigit Mead	*Psychologist, former OSS intelligence*
analyst	
Harmon Wetmore	*CIA Deputy Director, Operations*
The Director	*CIA Director*
Eli Jorgen	*Force Three Russia*
"John"	*Captured CIA Aircrew*
LCDR Ed Wilson	*CO of NAVCOMMSTA Rincon*

Chinese

Gui Suen	*Force Three China*
Yang Kuisong	*Communist Chinese General*
General Su Yu	*Communist Chinese General*
Mao Tse-tung	*Leader of Communist Chinese*
George Huang	*Chinese/American scientist*

Koreans

Kim Il-sung	*Leader of North Korea*
Park-Liu	*Team Leader, Soviet Embassy security*

Russians

Lt. Gen. Vladimir Suslov	*KGB*
Col. Gen. Arkady Lermantov	*KGB*
Col. Gen. Terenti Shtykov	*Russian Ambassador to North*
Korea	
Ivan Ivanovitch Glebov	*Force Three Russia*
Nikita Khrushchev	*Communist Party Chairman,*
Moscow	

CHAPTER ONE

Associated Press Dispatch, Jan 1950—Truman's Secretary of State Dean Acheson confirms Korea and Taiwan are outside American Far East security cordon.

Jilin Province, Manchuria—April 1950

The bright crystalline light of the full moon failed to penetrate the deeper woods as Harmon Wetmore groped his way through the trees, oak branches clawing at his flight suit, moving away from the direction of the noise of the excited Chinese. A deadfall grabbed his foot and sent him headlong into the tangle of dense undergrowth, sending a sharp pain through his lower back. Briefly he thought of how bad that injury might be, but the sense of panic he was squelching overrode it. In seeming slow motion he scrambled back to a low crouching run, suddenly breaking into the silvery light, stepping into a small rushing stream.

He stopped, dropped to a knee and peered up and down the streambed's opening to the sky. Leaning back into the underbrush, he listened, letting his breathing slow. Nothing. No sound but the usual night rustles and calls of the woods—the sharp chic-chic of reed-warblers and the scurry of rodents sounding far too loud to his adrenaline pumped ears. He concentrated hard to slow his breathing, and gather his thoughts …

Only moments before Harmon Wetmore was flying in a CIA aircraft from a base in Sokcho, South Korea. This veteran of combat in WWII—and earlier—showed more wear than his mid-forties age should have. His 5' 9" frame carried a stout, muscular body scarred from combat. His hair grey and brush-cut, his eyes clear and steely blue-grey, Wetmore was a formidable adversary. He maintained his condition as "battle ready"— he liked to say.

But now he is in a place he should not have been, flying a mission he should not be on, pushing the envelope of his job description to unthinkable places. But he had a very personal reason for being here.

A reason connected to his past—and now to his future.

The weather calm, the skies cobalt blue and the snow-speckled fall foliage on the hillsides grows distant as the plane climbs toward the north. Harmon Wetmore takes note of these details as a mental tool to stave off succumbing to complete exhaustion.

The flight from Washington, D.C. to Seoul, Korea, and on to the tiny airstrip at Sokcho, nearly twenty hours long, had Wetmore badly in need of a change of clothes—and some real sleep.

Instead he found himself volunteering to replace an injured crewman on the very mission he had come to observe. With no time to train a replacement, Wetmore pulled rank on the station chief and got on board the mission aircraft—an action that he increasingly is coming to regret.

Harmon Wetmore, Deputy Director for Operations, CIA (Central Intelligence Agency) had been in this part of the world before. As a "China Sailor" he fought alongside the Chinese Nationalist forces against the Japanese before they attacked Pearl Harbor in 1941. Initially recruited by U.S. Naval Intelligence, he moved on to serve with the OSS (Office of Strategic Services—predecessor to the CIA).

But both of these assignments were cover for an ongoing and highly secret mission known to only a very few people.

Wetmore spoke two Chinese dialects fluently and as the Second World War progressed he was once more sent to Southeast Asia as an OSS agent along with Major Amos Mead, USMC, on a special assignment for the president of the United States. This assignment nearly claimed his life and ended his active military career in a hospital. Though he'd grown to respect the Chinese, from his hospital bed he swore he'd stay away from China until *they learn to quit making war among themselves.*

The airplane carrying him to Manchuria had seen better days. His gaze went up to the monorail that extended beyond the open rear doors of the C-119 "Flying Boxcar." The doors, called *clamshells*, which usually enclosed the rear of the cargo bay, had been removed and a cable run from a winch bolted to the aft deck to a pulley on the end of the overhead monorail, ending with a large weighted hook. The other CIA aircraft crewman was trained to use this new aerial pick-up system and had provided Wetmore with a quick and all too brief lesson.

Wetmore sat on a canvas troop seat that ran the length of the cargo area, his back to the left side of the plane, near the open edge, securely buckled into a five-point harness. The other crewman, a former U.S. Air Force loadmaster, showed total ease in this environment as he walked to the edge of the open space, running his arm around the loading jack for support, and watched the world move by below them. Both men wore the requisite parachutes. Wetmore shouted over the cacophony of engines, slipstream, and rattling rivets, "Have we crossed into the north yet?"

"Coming up on it," the crewman responded. "Then another hour until we make it into Manchuria."

Wetmore just nodded and turned his gaze back out to the passing scene of the rugged Manchurian mountains, his eyes growing heavy, his gray bristled chin finally nodding onto his chest, succumbing to his body's demand for sleep.

This all began when Harmon Wetmore made the hurried trip to Korea when word came that a CIA team of five ethnic Chinese that parachuted into the Jilin region of Manchuria in July had made contact with a dissident general from the Red Chinese PLA (Peoples' Liberation Army). The team requested air exfiltration— first for the courier sent in to verify the contact and who possessed the documents to prove the general's identification and operational documents, and then the general himself. An earlier message, secretly encoded and routed to him through Naval Intelligence sources, had triggered his eagerness to be where he was.

The CIA trained on the unique method of picking up agents, but this mission is the first attempt at a real operation. The technique involves flying the aircraft in low and slow while reeling out the cable rigged in back and hooking a line elevated between two poles on the ground. The line between the poles is connected to a harness worn by the OSS agent. Once the picked-up subject is airborne, the line is winched into the aircraft.

For this flight the two pilots had received special training from Civil Air Transport Company (CAT)—the CIA's not so secret air operation. The two winch operators also trained with the crew for their part of the operation. But with the last minute injury to one of them, Wetmore insisted on filling the slot—over the objection of the station chief.

Now the C-119 transport plane lumbered along on its two Pratt & Whitney R-4360 engines at a cruise speed of two-hundred miles per hour, making the flight just over three hours. The plane lurched and Wetmore's head snapped up with a start, the thick backlit grey mist swirling into the cargo compartment further disorienting his already sleep-foggy mind. The other crewman laughed. "We just flew into some cumulous … a little bumpy for a while. But I'm glad you're back with me, sir. Let's run through this rig's operations once more—won't be that long 'til we go live."

Wetmore popped the central release of his five-point seat belt with the heel of his hand and stood unsteadily, stretching his back. Before he moved toward the crewman and the retrieval rig in the open door he tightened the straps on his parachute harness, causing him to shuffle-walk with a stoop. He knew the alternative of leaving it loose, and what would be the painful consequence if he had to jump out. The plane lurched again then emerged from the cloud into the clear evening sky. As Wetmore watched the rising, nearly full moon, he knew that visibility for the air snatch would be good.

They ran through the procedure one more time then sat down to await the pilot's signal. The crewman opened a survival kit that had been shoved under the troop seat, withdrawing a .32 caliber pistol and noting that it was not loaded. He mouthed toward Wetmore, "No ammunition."

Wetmore smiled, patted his shoulder holster containing his trusty 1911 Colt .45 and mouthed back, "Loaded."

They flew on into the gathering night, the passing landscape taking on ethereal qualities in the moonlight. The crewman held a hand to his headset, listening to the pilot's verbal alert that the target was close. He reached out and tapped Wetmore on the knee, shouting over the din of engines and wind, "Show time, sir!"

Moving to the aft edge of the open fuselage the two men moved a parachute-rigged bundle of supplies and equipment needed for the aerial pickup into position for drop. The crewman clipped the static cord that would open the chute to a D-ring near the edge. Keeping a good grasp on the loading jacks for support they peered down at the silvery landscape. As they reached the designated area the pilot called the crewman on the intercom, "Recognition signal from the ground checks out … drop the load." The crewman put a shoulder to the bundle and pushed it over the edge. The parachute deployed, taking on a ghostly appearance as it drifted toward the small group of men on the ground that were now in view of Wetmore and the crewman.

Something caught Wetmore's eye—the strange, seemingly out of place mounds of earth on each side of the drop zone. He didn't know why they bothered him, but his years of surviving on instinct had the hair on his neck raised. He strained to see them as they faded into the gloom. *What's wrong with me? Too tired? But this doesn't feel right.*

The pilot flew the aircraft away from the area to allow the ground team time to set up the poles and the cross line for the "snatch." Orbiting the location the aircraft came back over about

13

thirty minutes later and received a *ready* signal. The pilot dropped down and flew a dry run over the pickup point, serving as a way to both orient the flight crew and alert the man being exfiltrated that the next pass would be for him. As they passed a couple of hundred feet above the target, Wetmore saw five people on the moonlit landscape below, one of them in the pickup harness, facing the path of the aircraft. The man raised a hand and waved at Wetmore and the crewman.

This time Wetmore concentrated on the mounds. They were not right, not natural—but why he couldn't figure out. His mouth was dry, his lips sticking together. He continued to peer at them as they climbed into another orbit.

On the final pass the C-119 came in low at tree-top level for the pickup, flying just over its stall speed. Wetmore felt the rush of adrenalin clearing his head as he braced for the unfamiliar action. Seldom—maybe never—did he feel *not in complete command* of a situation. This time *he* was the rookie. As he peered down, the scene began to change before his eyes. The world seemed to go into slow motion as he finally realized what was about to happen.

Suddenly, the mounds erupted. White tarps camouflaging two antiaircraft guns on the snow-flecked terrain flew off. Blinding gunfire flashed into the night, arcing death toward him. Straddling the plane's flight path, they raked a murderous crossfire into the defenseless aircraft. A crowd of men emerged from the woods, firing AK-47s at the lumbering plane.

Wetmore went to his knees, trying to be as small as possible as bullets stitched the forward cargo space, splinters from the plywood deck flying with the errant red hot lead up through the plane's overhead. The holes traced their way forward to flight deck, tracers igniting the fuel that leaked from the wing. The nose of the sinking aircraft came up as the pilot tried to miss the trees ahead—and an imminent crash.

The plane's speed fell below stalling and it mushed into a grinding controlled crash in the clearing beyond the trees, the twin booms of the C-119 snapping off and dropping the tail to the ground.

Wetmore and the crewman were secured to the plane with safety lines to keep them from falling out during the winching operation. As the plane impacted the ground in a grinding cacophony of screeching metal and blinding dirt and debris they both slid along the wooden floor to the end of the tethers, partially cushioned by their heavy winter flight suits.

The crewman's tether broke sending him on into the bulkhead aft of the nose wheel-well and knocking him out. Wetmore, groggy from the impact but with adrenalin coursing through his body, released his tether and got to the crewman just as he woke. With the same thought, they both rushed to the ladder going up to the flight deck, yelling for the flight crew. The flight deck above them burned fiercely and the smell of burning flesh reeking through the hellish heat forcing the pair back. The Chinese gunfire had targeted the flight deck and Wetmore was sure the crew had died in their seats.

Clearing his head with the need to survive, he realized they had to get out quickly before the Chinese covered the ground between the ambush site and where they had hit the ground beyond the trees. Wetmore pointed at the flames and yelled, "We can't help them!"

He grabbed the arm of the crewman who was backing away from the horror in a trancelike state, yelling again, "Come on! We need to get clear before those bastards get here."

Both men jumped the few feet out the open rear cargo bay to the ground and stumbled to their feet, turning to head toward the trees to the left of their downed plane. Wetmore ducked under the wrecked tail boom, scraping his head and feeling a sharp pang in his lower back. They heard the Chinese soldiers whooping and hollering, randomly firing wild rounds from their AK-47's as they came crashing through the woods along the gouged earth end-of-flight path of the wrecked plane.

Wetmore hit the edge of the woods and kept his pace as quickly as he could to move deeper into the shadows as he fended off branches with his forearms, adrenaline drowning out any pain for the moment.

Behind him, the other crewman turned his head at the sound of their pursuers and missed ducking under the tail boom, taking a nasty crack on the head and dropping to the ground. Reflexively he bounded to his feet, but as he reached the tree-line a Chinese AK-47 opened up with its distinctive report. Dirt flew all around him and tree branches were clipped off in front of the American. He slid to a stop, raised his hands, and awaited the inevitable.

Far above the crash scene, watching the unfolding action from a well camouflaged observation point dug into a nearby hill, a man noted the location of the Americans through his binoculars.

His heart pounding from the exertion more than fear, Wetmore noted the smell of rotting wet leaves at the stream's edge—pungent, but not unpleasant. His thoughts raced as he assessed his situation. By now he knew that his crewmate was not behind him. Between panting breaths he struggles to clear his thoughts. *What was his name? John? Or was that the alias?* He could only hope that John's fate was capture, and not worse. *Damnation, I swear these people are always fighting about something. Said I'd never come back ... and here I frigging am again. Okay ... high ground—* He peered across the gurgling water, just making out the terrain rising beyond—*so here we go.* Gingerly picking his way across the stream and up the bank Wetmore moved as quietly as he could, seeking higher ground. The slope was not too steep, but rocky with sparse underbrush that he used as handholds for the climb. Snow clung to the shadow edge of rocks and brush. About a hundred yards up the slope it leveled out onto a narrow bench. Wetmore rolled onto it, swung himself around on his belly and looked over the edge to his back-trail for any pursuit. Apparently the Communist Chinese soldiers were satisfied that their one captive was all there was, as he saw no one seeking him.

Lying there in the night-cooling earth Wetmore let the adrenalin drain out of his aching body, his breathing slowing, the realization of his utter exhaustion coming fully aware. Still prone he crossed his arms under his face and let his eyes close, his body relax.

In an instant he tensed … from … what … and just as he became aware of a slight sound nearby he felt the cold, hard barrel of a gun rest against his neck. He felt himself go numb at the realization of what was about to happen. A rough whisper delivered through clenched teeth accompanied the cold shock of the deadly gun barrel, "Добрый вечер, господин американский. Добро пожаловать в Манчжурию (Good evening, American. Welcome to Manchuria)."

As he felt his own 1911 Colt .45 being slipped from its shoulder holster, Harmon Wetmore knew that he'd reached the end of any ability to resist. In a haze of mixed feelings, it took him a moment to register the words.

The words he heard were *Russian*.

CHAPTER TWO

AP June 1950—Intelligence reports indicate North Korean Army strength estimated at 135,000, with seven assault divisions and 150 Russian T34 tanks.

CIA Headquarters, Arlington, Virginia

The Director slumped in his large leather chair, his back to the desk, facing the window that looked over the freshly planted landscape of the new CIA facility, his telephone pressed to his ear, his other hand slowly rubbing his forehead. Finally he asked the caller, "You're sure? It's confirmed? And you're sure he was on the flight?"

The voice on the other end of the international call replied, "Yes, sir, we're sure. When the mission flight went overdue we sent another plane up there to search. They spotted the wreckage near the pick-up point. It looked burned out, no sign of anyone around. They could be inside it, or—"

"Keep me posted." The Director turned around and replaced the phone. Slamming a closed fist onto his desk, he said to the empty room, "Damn you Wetmore! If you're dead ... if you're alive *I'll* kill you!" He looked up to see Sarah, his longtime secretary, standing in the doorway, her fist tightly balled and pressed to her mouth, her brow furrowed, fearing the news she suspected. The CIA Director looked at her for a moment, choking back his feelings, and then quietly said, "Get the President on the phone, please."

Sarah made the call to the White House and left an urgent message for President Truman's chief-of-staff, John Steelman, to pass on to his boss. Now they would wait for a return call. It took only ten minutes.

The Director sat upright, the phone to his ear, his voice level and steady, "Mr. President, it was an ambush. There was no Chinese general ... an ambush ... it brought down the plane. Also, sir, Harmon Wetmore was aboard that flight. No sir, I don't know why or how, but I will find out very soon."

Listening intently to the caring but measured words of the President, the Director finally replied, "Yes sir, the search flight reported sighting the burned out wreck. No sir, I don't yet know the fate of the crew—or Wetmore. Yes, sir, you'll be the first to know. Thank you, Mr. President."

He replaced the warm receiver and leaned forward, his elbows on the desk, his face in his hands, rubbing futilely at the tension he felt. *Secret mission, secret Wetmore ... keeping it secret ... finding out where those guys are ... damn!*

Santa Barbara, California, USA

The subdued gold-lettered sign on the street entrance to the historic old Carrillo Adobe landmark read *Law Offices of MEAD & SOKOL*. Built in 1825, the romantic history of this Santa Barbara landmark, including its being a wedding gift to the granddaughter of the first *Commandante* of the Royal Presidio of Santa Barbara from her husband, intrigued the ex-Marine, now a lawyer who settled there after the war. The telephone on Amos Mead's desk rang.

Dr. Brigit O'Hare Mead stepped across the narrow hallway from her office to answer her husband's call, "Law Offices—well, hello, Director. This is Brigit. No, sir, he's at the court house, but may I take a message? I understand ... your private number ... just as soon as he comes in. ... Oh, yes sir, thanks for asking. The little guy's doing fine. Spittin' image of his daddy."

She hung up the telephone, keeping her hand resting on the black receiver, thinking about the *unspoken* message the Director of the CIA had just left—the message of tension, distress, distraction.

A practicing psychologist, Dr. Brigit Mead's professional mind was hard at work. *There's more to the story. Amos will either be excited about whatever this is, or ...*

Yanji Airfield, Jilin Provence, Manchuria

The site of the aerial pick up and the ambush of the American CIA plane is on the northern slope of the Changbai Mountains that form the border between Korea and China on the eastern peninsula. It is known to the Russians as *Vostochno-Manchzhurskie gory* (the Manchu-Korean mountain range) and it separates China from Korea and the Russian *Primorsky Krai* (Maritime Provence). Vladivostok is the administrative center of the province.

Wetmore first heard the word *Vladivostok* while being marched to the small observation post from where his captors observed the crash of his CIA mission aircraft. He noted that the outpost, though small, was well equipped and obviously used by a military unit. After a flurry of radio-telephone communications by his captors—in Russian and mentioning *Vladivostok*—he was marched over a concealed trail to a small clearing where a Russian BTR 40 Armored Personnel Carrier sat parked in the shade of a dense grove of Larch trees. His captors had allowed him to wash away the congealed blood on his face from the scrape in his head, but he did not reveal to them the pain in his back. *I need to retain some sense of control* the old warrior thought. After a jarring two hour ride, broken only by a stop to refill the fuel tanks from cans carried on board, and the invitation for Wetmore to join the crew in relieving themselves against a tree, the Russian vehicle arrived at a remote edge of the airport near Yanji, parking among other Russian equipment.

Totally exhausted, his back knotting up, the pain dull and throbbing, he had been able to sleep fitfully most of the trip. He felt somewhat alert as he was escorted to a corrugated steel shack, the small building apparently served as air operations, and turned over to a military officer—obviously *KGB* (The Committee for State Security of the USSR).

His hands bound behind him, Wetmore squirmed in the straight-back wooden chair. The KGB officer stood in front of him, hands on hips, staring into his face. Finally he spoke, first in Russian then in English, "Вы говорите по-русски? Do you speak Russian?" Wetmore stared back, his still fogged mind assessing his options—which he found to be few to none. Slowly he moved his head side to side his head, *no*.

In perfect English the KGB officer continued, "You wear a flying suit, but you have no unit patches on it. Your aircraft is an American model, also with no tail number or markings. My people tell me you carry no identification. Tell me, please, your name."

The other three CIA crewmen on the flight had been issued false identity papers, and had well-rehearsed stories. But Wetmore's knee-jerk decision to replace the injured crewman had left no time for him to get any papers, and the station chief had insisted he leave his official ID papers behind—which now provided him his only way to control some semblance of a cover. Wetmore knew he'd screwed up badly by not preparing a cover story or name.

His tired mental state, and hurried decisions about the mission, came back to haunt him. His thoughts raced, *might as well use my own name ... couldn't keep anything else straight now ... good chance this guy won't recognize it anyway ... at least not yet.* Slowly he said, "Wetmore, Harmon Wetmore."

The KGB officer continued to stare unblinkingly into his eyes. "American. What is your unit?"

Wetmore stared back, answering slowly, "I have no unit. I work for the air service. Just do my job."

"Mr. Wetmore, you look to me to be somewhat old for this line of work. Tell me why we find you on this airplane?" The American waited a full measured beat, and then answered, "Everybody needs a job … just doing my job." The Russian let out a guttural laugh that melted into a hacking cough. He put out his hand to a soldier standing guard and was immediately given a cigarette. The soldier struck a match and lit it. After a deep draw, now drifting out through his nose and tobacco yellowed teeth, the officer said, "I had hoped you would have some American cigarettes, but you carry nothing in your pockets."

"'Cuz I don't smoke," Wetmore tossed back to him.

The officer laughed again, this time keeping it quieter. "Empty pockets are a sure sign you are something more than you say you are. I'll waste no more time with you, Mr. *Wetmore*—if that's your real name. You will enjoy your flight to Moscow. And I'm sure your memory will improve under the quiet questions of the First Chief Directorate. Possibly, my American friend, you may be able to provide answers directly to General Yevgeny Petrovich Pitovranov himself!"

Wetmore knew the name—the Chief of the KGB. The officer turned toward the door and began to leave the hut. Wetmore said, "May I have some water?"

The KGB officer stopped. Turning to face him he said, "Your airplane is landing now. There will be water on board. Have a good flight." The guard reached for Wetmore's bound hands, lifted him to his feet and began to push him toward the door—and the sound of the aircraft pulling up on the tarmac in front of the shack. A door opened in the fuselage just aft of the right wing and a ladder-type stair was dropped to the ground and secured into position. The guard began to push Wetmore toward the plane just as the KGB officer stepped over to him and held up his hand. He produced a knife that Wetmore recognized as an NR-43 combat issue from World War Two. The knife was thrust forward and for an instant Wetmore stiffened—but the blade slipped into the bindings and his hands dropped free. The officer turned and walked away without a word, and Wetmore proceeded to the ladder and climbed stiffly into the aircraft and the arms of another guard.

There were no more than a dozen people on the plane, most in uniform. None paid any particular attention to the new arrival beyond a casual glance. The guard hustled him up the aisle to the front row of seats. Shortly, and without ceremony, the door in the *Ilyushin* IL-12 Russian transport closed and the twin engines coughed to life. They taxied out to an empty runway and immediately began the take-off roll, lurching into a clear sky and banking through a climbing turn toward Vladivostok, Russia. Wetmore shivered, finally realizing he was cold and ill prepared.

CIA Headquarters, Arlington, Virginia, USA

The CIA Director picked up the telephone on the first ring, already informed by Sarah, his personal secretary, that Mead was on the line. "Hello, Amos. Thank you for returning my call."

Amos Mead replied, "Always happy to be of service, sir. To what do I owe your interest? Is Mr. Wetmore in some kind of secret trouble again?" Mead was knowingly a bit flippant with his remark, recalling the way his last CIA association had ended. The Director delivered the answer flat and emotionless, "As a matter of fact, Amos—yes."

The tone caught Mead's attention and he continued to listen, knowing more would come. It did.

"Amos, Harmon's missing in China."

"What?" Amos blurted out. "When in hell did he go to China? Why? The last time we talked—"

The Director interrupted, "Not here on the phone. I've spoken with the President and we agree that the situation calls for your unique position … and your wife's—"

"Brigit?" Wha—"

The Director interrupted Mead's stuttered words again, "I'm coming out there, Amos. When I get there you'll have your answers. You already suspect that I will ask you … and we hope you'll come back in. I'll call when my schedule is firm."

Santa Barbara, California

The phone clicked to silence in Mead's ear. Brigit watched the puzzled look on his face. She waited for him to tell her what was going on. Mead held the warm phone in both hands, staring down at his desk. Slowly he set it on the cradle and looked up at Brigit. "Harm's missing in China. The Director is coming here to talk about it … and me … and you."

Brigit spoke, "He wouldn't tell you on the telephone? Bad sign, Honey. Bad sign."

During WWII Amos Mead served with the OSS—first in an innocuous assignment in London, tracking German Nazi spies by radio intercepts and field reports. When one of his discoveries turned out to be a dangerous threat to the security of a vital new American secret technology Mead's world changed from passive to active spy chaser. He got his man, but only after a harrowing experience on the oil slicked waters of the South Pacific.

His second OSS assignment was with Harmon Wetmore in the China-Burma India Theater of operations and nearly cost him his life—but it also added Brigit O'Hare to his life. After the war and his return to law practice, the CIA and old contacts pressed him back into service as a Nazi hunter. It made sense then. The CIA could not operate on US soil by law. Mead was not officially CIA—so he got the nod.

With the mystery now involving China, Mead knew that Nazi's would not be involved. But just what the CIA wanted with him again—with his friend and war-fighting buddy missing—and with the Director breaking all protocol and coming to him?

I can only wait.

Amos Mead rose extra early the next day. He sat at the small kitchen table with his first cup of coffee and the morning edition

24

of the Santa Barbara News Press. He looked up as Brigit shuffled into the kitchen in her powder blue housecoat and "bunny" slippers. She kissed Amos on the head as she bee-lined for the coffee pot.

Amos said, "Sorry I woke you—but good morning to you."

Pouring her favorite china mug to the brim Brigit said, "You didn't wake me. Too big a day for us to sleep in. Leaving the news about Harm just hanging there …it's not fair!"

The Director's flight was expected mid-day—and the answers to burning questions for the Meads.

Amos stood up and finished his mug of coffee. "I'm going to get cleaned up." He sounded calm, but inside he churned with the knowledge that the way the CIA was handling what the Director reported can only mean the worst trouble. Brigit nodded a reply as she picked up the paper, compartmentalizing similar feelings. She was a psychologist—and one with war experience that had seen Amos and Harmon in deadly circumstances while she could only listen in to the action. This morning revived those feelings.

On his way to the shower, Amos peeked in on little Nathan. The baby was fast asleep, his little diapered butt sticking up in the air. Amos smiled, thinking about how fast the tyke was growing. He started the shower and took a moment to look at himself in the small mirror over the sink. Mead was 5'10" tall and still kept most of his Marine Corp shape, though not quite as "high and tight" in some spots. He glanced at the pronounced scars the went from his shoulder and across his back—the souvenirs of the bomb fragments and marble shards that finished his war and nearly finished him so few years before. He stepped into the shower and the hot water played on his back in a soothing stream.

No more Marine Corps, no more OSS—but maybe more CIA, he thought. *Couple more hours and we'll know.*

CHAPTER THREE

Aboard a Russian *Ilyushin* IL-12, en-route to Vladivostok

Harmon Wetmore stared out of the small square window into the star-speckled night. The guard sitting in the next seat glanced at him with his nose wrinkled in a universal message that the smell was not pleasant. After many hours without water to bathe or clothes to change, Wetmore was well aware of his condition—and it felt no better than he smelled. *Your problem, buddy*, he thought as he turned away.

A few minutes later a uniformed officer walked back to Wetmore's row and motioned the guard to move out of his seat—which he did without hesitation. The officer sat down. Without looking at Wetmore he said, "Добрый вечер. Длинный рейс уже, да?"

"I don't speak Russian," Wetmore replied, only glancing at his new seatmate.

"I am sorry, Mr. Wetmore. What I said was, 'Good evening. Long flight already, yes?'"

Wetmore shrugged and turned back to the window saying, "Yah, long flight, yes." Then thinking, *Длинный рейс уже, да? I blew the ID and the name ... but I'll keep my Russian as my little secret.* His subdued smile reflecting in the night-blackened window, Harmon Wetmore was feeling more ready for what may come, beginning to feel like he was getting back in the game. The Russian said, "I have arranged for some clothing and a bath for you at Vladivostok. We will also have some food … and maybe some vodka. Вы ведь не против?"

Wetmore answered, "Clean clothes, a bath, food … and what?" *Damn right 'it's all right with me,' asshole. But I ain't tellin' you I comprende your lingo.*

With a laugh the Russian said, "I'm sorry, my friend … What I said was, 'is that all right with you?'"

"Oh yah, sure, fine." He closed his eyes and slouched against the side of the plane, first feigning sleep, and then slipping into its welcome arms. A loud *BANG* assaulted the dozing passengers.

The *Ilyushin* aircraft lurched to one side, swayed back the other way then settled on course. Like everybody else, Wetmore was now wide awake, starring out the window at the brilliant flames roaring back from the vents on the Shvetsov Ash-82 radial engine.

He looked back at the Russian officer who was staring past Wetmore at the fiery sight. "Это не хорошо," the Russian said, showing little emotion—except in his eyes.

Wetmore understood. *You're right there my Ruskie friend, it is definitely not good.*

He was familiar with this Russian aircraft, known as *Coach* in western military parlance. He knew she had experienced problems with vibrations during testing and, more important to him now, that she has poor engine-out performance.

The fire seemed to get worse, obviously not responding to any extinguishers, if any had actually been deployed. He settled back in his seat trying to calm rising concern, knowing from early reports that the *Ilyushin*—at least early models—used magnesium in struts near the engines. He'd read reports of uncontrolled engine fires damaging wing structures and bringing down at least two of these birds that he knew of. *What's with me and airplanes?* Wetmore thought. *Bailing out in Burma … crashing in Manchuria … and know this?*

The PA speaker from the cockpit blared, "Оставайтесь на местах... Посадка во Владивостоке. (Remain in your seats … we are landing in Vladivostok)."

Wetmore stared at the roaring fire.
And in a damn hurry I'm hoping!

Santa Barbara Municipal Airport, California

The sleek Aero Commander 520 rolled to a stop next to the Spanish-style terminal so familiar to visitors to Santa Barbara. But it was the first visit for the man who exited the sleek, high-wing, twin-engine transport plane.

Amos Mead, standing on the tarmac, extended his hand. Consciously subduing his churning thoughts, fears—and stomach, he said, "Welcome to our little bit of paradise, Director. I trust you had a good flight."

The Director of the CIA took his hand and shook it warmly. "A couple of good flights actually. I must say I'm impressed with this new Aero Commander." He gestured over his shoulder at the airplane, then looked past Mead and added, "Would this be the lovely Dr. Mead?"

Dr. Brigit O'Hare Mead, PhD. smiled broadly and said, "And this would be the handsome Director?"

"Irreverent as ever, eh Brigit—"

"Guilty as charged, sir. Welcome …" Brigit couldn't contain her anxious concern for their friend any longer. "And Harm? He's—"

"In due time, my dear." The Director gestured to his bag already set on the outdoor covered luggage rack. "In due time."

Amos Mead picked up the bag and asked, "Are you traveling alone? I thought maybe you—"

The Director quickly responded, "Traveling alone … against the rules. But the detail will remain unobtrusive, though always there."

"Enough said, sir." Mead led the trio on the walk through the Spanish style arches and beyond where his '38 Hudson Terraplane sat parked at the curb. He glanced around, but couldn't identify their "tail.' *Just how it's supposed to work*, he thought.

28

The drive down Hwy 101 into the city proper took about twenty minutes, most of it in silence, the Director gazing out the window at the unfamiliar landscape. The window was rolled down and he noted the soft, dry floral note of the soft warm passing breeze and the profusion of flowers lining the route, topped by majestic palm trees. "You're right, Amos. This does look like a little bit of paradise. A far cry from the Capitol."

At the Law Offices of Mead and Sokol, Amos and Brigit Mead and the CIA Director sat around Mead's desk. The Director, looking as tired as he felt, began to speak slowly, "Frankly, I'm not sure where to start. But I have a feeling it should be with Harmon."

Neither Mead nor Brigit spoke, but the look on their faces grew tense and apprehensive.

The Director continued, "First, we don't know where, much less *how* he is. The aircraft he was on was ambushed by the Red Chinese and shot down. We've made low over-flights of the burned-out wreckage and can see no survivors … or bodies."

Mead spoke, "Red Chinese? Just where was he?"

"Manchuria, Amos, Jilin Province just above the North Korean border—"

Brigit interrupted, "What the hell was he doing there? … sir."

The Director looked from Brigit to Mead. "He was observing a mission—A mission that *he wasn't supposed* to be involved in." He paused, rubbed his chin in a thoughtful gesture and continued, "Let me back up and explain more. It's important that you know. About four months ago we air dropped a four man team into Manchuria from our forward operating base at Sokcho in northeast South Korea. We haven't heard a word from them since. They were Chinese operatives trained by the CIA. Then a second team, also ethnic Chinese, parachuted in two months ago. There were also four of them. They too dropped in near Jilin."

Mead felt the pause in the Director's story and interjected a question, "Have you heard from them … had contact with them?"

The Director, visibly a little more relaxed, answered, "Yes, we have. They established radio contact with the station. They were even resupplied once by air. Then we dropped the courier to join up with the team—the guy they were going in to extract on this flight."

Mead asked, "Extract? Is there an airfield?"

"No airfield, Amos" the Director responded. "They extract people by flying low and slow overhead and snagging a trapeze type wire attached to the man on the ground. He's winched into the plane— at least that was the plan."

Mead revealed no reaction, good or bad, to the conversation. He just listened, harboring a deep, but unclear feeling about how this operation was working out. Always fearing for his friend, Harmon Wetmore, he wanted to focus on learning all he could about the mission—and his involvement in it. *I will be in the middle of this—the Director isn't here on a lark.* Then he reflected, "This looks a lot like our ops in the last war—the OSS operations in Europe."

The Director nodded and replied, "That was the plan in Europe, Amos. Back then we parachute in and link up with guerrilla forces, collect intelligence, maybe even a little sabotage where you find the opportunity—"

Mead cut him off, "And how's that working out, Director?" Quickly adding, "And why was Harmon on the damn plane?" "Not working very well, Amos. Not this time. And Harm? He was on the plane because a regular crewman got hurt and Harm jumped in—"

"To get closer to the action, I'm sure ..." Mead's voice trailed off as he looked down to the floor. His personal concerns were beginning to bubble up.

The Director nodded with a slight smile, well aware of the blood-brother relationship of Mead and Wetmore, as he continued, "At first Harmon thought they were sending people in to pick up a Chinese general who had defected from Mao's army. That was the reason he went to Korea himself. But he was quickly told that they were going in to extract someone—but it was not the general. Not yet. First they were picking up the courier that jumped in a month ago. He's carrying operational documents and official credentials for the big guy … the Chinese general. When they could validate what's in the documents, then they go back for him. At least that was the plan."

Brigit spoke, "The CIA has done this kind of thing before, Director?"

His brow furrowed with the frustration of having too few answers, he said, "Since you asked, Brigit. No. We've never done an aerial extraction."

Mead spoke, "How is the whole insertion concept working, Director?"

"Not that great, Amos. That OSS model you mentioned … It assumes a cooperative captive population waiting for us with open arms—"

"And?" Mead pressed the point.

"And, well, that's not China. We're pretty much on our own in there … All we've really got is *Force Three*."

CHAPTER FOUR

Vladivostok, Russia, USSR

The crew of a well-used war surplus fire truck watched the Ilyushin IL-12 dive steeply toward the runway, its landing gear deployed, flames trailing the wing. They fully expected a deadly crash, but at the last second the airplane leveled off and settled hard to the runway. Almost immediately the landing gear beneath the burning wing collapsed, outboard of the engine the wing broke away and the aircraft began a flaming pirouette down the runway, coming to a stop near the top of a dirt berm that covered an old ammunition dump.

Before the trailing fire truck arrived with its wailing siren, the door of the plane dropped open and passengers, including Wetmore and his KGB keeper emerged at a run, putting as much distance between them and the burning plane as unsteady legs could provide, finally diving over the edge of the next berm in the row and landing in a muddy heap in a shallow, water-filled depression.

The Russian stood and looked at Wetmore. Laughing, in his best English he said, "Now you will need clothing and a bath, my American friend ... and the food, and some vodka. And I will join you." His hands trembled even as his words were delivered with a nonchalant air.

Wetmore nodded and climbed to his feet. Guards with AK-47s already stood at his side.

The KGB agent showed his credentials to the fire truck driver who immediately stiffened and followed the order to radio the tower for a staff car to come to the crash site. In about ten minutes the car pulled up and Wetmore was ushered into the backseat with the KGB agent. One of the armed guards climbed in front. After a short drive the men were delivered to the officers' quarters on the Soviet base.

The KGB officer spoke with the Air Force officer who emerged to meet the car. Wetmore could not hear well enough to understand the conversation. Any concerns he had were by now overshadowed by hunger—and the deep desire to take a hot shower. The KGB officer turned to Wetmore and said, "Follow the guard, Harmon Wetmore. He will take you to quarters where you will clean up and receive suitable clothing to replace what you've been living in. When you've finished we shall enjoy a hot meal."

Wetmore nodded and gestured to the guard to lead the way. The KGB officer laughed at the gesture. "I see you have not lost your spirit, Mr. Wetmore. Perhaps you will also be ready to talk with me soon."

Harmon Wetmore smiled and turned to his guard without a word. They went into the building.

The KGB officer turned to his Air Force host. "Please take me to a telephone that I may place a call to Moscow. Also, we will need hot food. It has been an eventful day and I believe we are all a bit more shaken than men can let on in the presence of other men."

The Air Force officer laughed and said, "Пройдемте со мной, сэр. У нас есть все, что вам нужно. Я удивлен, сотрудника нашего уважаемого КГБ может признаться в какой-то слабости. (Follow me, sir. We have all you need. I'm surprised an officer of our distinguished KGB would admit to any weakness.)"

The KGB officer responded without a smile, "На этом пока остановимся. Сначала телефон (We'll leave it at that. First the telephone.)"

Lubyanka Square, Moscow, Russia, USSR
Headquarters of the First Chief Directorate—the KGB

Lieutenant General Vladimir Paulovich Suslov slid out of the rear seat of his chauffeured ZiS-111 (*Zavod Imeni Stalina*) limousine and glanced up at the large building with its yellow brick façade, noting the time on the clock perched under a cupola centered on the uppermost band of the façade. Looking down to watch his footing on the cracked sidewalk, he strode the four paces and entered through the large carved door, instantly enveloped in the blast of warm air that fought vainly against the Moscow winter. The door closed behind him as he slipped his heavy wool uniform greatcoat from his shoulders, draped it over his arm, and moved down the wide main corridor, his shoes clicking a cadence on the elegant parquet floor, echoing against the pale green walls of the KGB headquarters. The *Lubyanka*.

Colonel General Arkady Alexandrovitch Lermantov called to his visitor when he first caught sight of him at the outer door, "Vladimir Paulovich you are late!"

Vladimir Paulovich Suslov walked directly up to the general's desk and saluted smartly, saying, "I did not know you cared so much about me, Arkady Alexandrovitch. That makes me feel warm all over."

"Ha! You have never been warm all over, Vladimir Paulovich. You are as cold as a Siberian winter. That is your strong suite—and why I keep you around. Now, where is your guest? What news do you have for me of your American captive?"

Lieutenant General Vladimir Paulovich Suslov first hung his greatcoat next to his host's on a wall hook and then took a seat across from him. "And I do have news for you, Arkady Alexandrovitch. I received a telephone call this morning from my agent in Vladivostok. The one who is bringing us our guest. The first leg of their journey ended in near disaster—their aircraft had to crash land, but they are safe and proceeding here."

The Colonel General interjected, "It is a long flight to Moscow. When do you expect them?"

"Sir, it will be longer yet. They are now traveling by train—"

Colonel General Lermantov leaned forward and interrupted his guest, "By train? We had hoped to find what he knows before we have to meet with our Chinese visitors."

"I understand, Arkady Alexandrovitch. But the practical fact is that it will take time to interview this one. My agent who travels with him informs me that he is very clever—more than a simple CIA aircrew man. He believes that the time together on the train will be fruitful—"

Once again interrupting, Lermantov asked, "Do you know exactly who you have captured?"

"No, sir. Not exactly. But we have a strong suspicion—"

"And your suspicion, Vladimir Paulovich?"

Suslov looked around, even though he knew they were quite alone, then turned toward Lermantov.

Soviet Air Force Base, Vladivostok, Russia, USSR

Harmon Wetmore luxuriated in the nearly hot water shower. He let it run on his back for what little relief it provided his *old knotted frame*. Drying off, he inspected the neatly folded clothes laid out for him. Happy to be rid of the tattered and stinking flight suit, he didn't care much what they were. Though slightly large, the linen *tolstovka* shirt and the black wool trousers were an adequate fit. Last in the pile lay a brown military trench coat with all insignia removed. The guard nodded his approval, pointing to his nose to indicate he preferred the new smell of his prisoner. So did Wetmore.

Directed by his escort, he entered the small dining room and took the chair offered by his KGB keeper. Soon a server appeared with steaming bowls of *rassolnik*, a soup of long Russian tradition. Wetmore's first spoonful caused him to pause as he got used to the taste of the soup base of pickled cucumbers. But it was only a pause as he dug in to the rich mixture of barley and beef kidneys—and the cucumbers. Looking up from his own bowl and reaching for a slab of the dark peasant bread on the table, the KGB officer asked, "This is good to your taste, Wetmorevich?"

Wetmore only nodded and continued his attack on the first food he'd had in too long a time. Shortly the server placed a bottle of vodka and two shot glasses on the table. The officer poured and pushed a glass toward Wetmore who raised it in salute and tossed it back.

The KGB keeper laughed. "You must know, my friend Wetmorevich … the *rassolnik* is traditional for hangover … so do not be shy with the vodka. This is Russia."

The meal finished and the warm glow of the liberal vodka shots beginning to settle in, the two men rose, donned overcoats against the cold, and walked from the building to a waiting automobile.

Wetmore figured another ride on a Russian airplane was in store and he was puzzled when they drove through the perimeter gate and left the airfield.

The KGB officer in the front seat offered no explanation.

Beijing, Communist China

Mao Tse-tung, Chairman of the Chinese Communist Party and hero of the *Long March* that culminated in the defeat of the Nationalist Kuomintang Chinese, left Beijing by train on the long journey to Moscow.

The war had been over for only a short while and Mao was fearful of being away from his capital, fearful of attacks by National dissidents still roaming the countryside. The newest steam engine commandeered by Mao, named the *Jiefang* (liberation), pulled the short military style train toward the Russian Soviet capital. Mao traveled in an armored car and had sentries posted every hundred yards along the railroad tracks.

It had traveled nearly four hundred miles when the train pulled into Shenyang, the largest city in northeast China. Mao had ordered the stop and disembarked with his entourage to check for posters of him. He was angered to discover that not only were there few posters with the face of Mao, but there were many more, a great many more, of Stalin.

After Soviet and Chinese Nationalists occupied Shenyang, the city fell to Mao's communist forces in October 1948. Today Mao was suspect of the strategic city's allegiances in these times of turmoil.

He soon learned that the Stalin posters were the work of Chinese Army Marshal Gao Gang. Mao was convinced that Gao was a pro-Soviet communist and this display only fueled his anger, and he ordered that a railway car in his train carrying gifts for Stalin from Gao be uncoupled from the train.

The train then resumed its mission to Moscow.

Mukden, Manchuria, Communist China

The young, CIA air crewman, survivor of the Jilin ambush and crash, had been in solitary confinement since his capture by the Communist Chinese army and transport to the Manchurian city of Mukden. His initial interrogation had been harsh but not physical, sometimes lasting many hours, and he had revealed only his name, pleading ignorant to the purpose of his mission—which was mostly true.

Sleep deprivation was part of the game. Prohibited from sleeping during the day, the Chinese often hauled him off for a midnight interrogation after just a half hour sleep. He did manage one deception when he was asked what happened to the other crewman seen in the back of the plane from the ground. "As I told you before," he said slowly, his head on his chest, eyes barely open, "that man had gone forward to the cockpit just before the crash. He and everybody else died in the fire."

At least I can give Wetmore a head start, he thought.

His cell, a concrete box, was cold, mildew damp and smelling of its former occupants. Stripped of his flight suit and given the ubiquitous padded jacket and pants of the Chinese army, he was surprised it fit his lanky frame. The Chinese had told him that no one knew he was alive—and that no one would ever know until they decided to announce the fact—if they ever decided to do so.

But he knew that he was not alone in the prison.

He also knew that the others were receiving much harsher treatment than he, hearing the beatings and the begging for mercy—in English.

One day, though he couldn't really tell day from night, he heard a group march past his cell. The cadence sounded to him like military. They stopped a few paces past him. He heard an order given—in Russian. He did not understand Russian any more than he did Chinese, but he made out the name Angus Ward. The speech changed to heavily accented English and he soon found out who his jail-mate was—the consul general of the United States.

My God, if that's the American consul general ... I'm toast.

CHAPTER FIVE

Santa Barbara, California

Brigit leaned toward the Director and said, "Okay, sir. I'll bite. What is a *Force Three*?

The Director smiled coyly, then looked over at Mead and asked, "May I have a drink of water?"

"Of course." Mead rose and turned toward the hall, then stopped and turned back. "Late enough for something stronger, Director?"

The Director nodded. Mead returned with three short glasses of whiskey and a tumbler of water on a tray, saying, "A little something we have for medicinal purposes."

After first a sip, then a longer drink from the glass, the Director turned to Brigit—who was on the edge of yelling at both the men for ignoring the important question—and continued, "*Force Three*, Brigit, is a code name for an operation that has its antecedents in the American response to the communist takeover of China last year. Under some new U.S. policies, questionable at best, and foolish at worst, the CIA was tasked with taking steps to exploit the potential for a Chinese "third column" by trying to link-up CIA trained Chinese agents with alleged dissident generals on the mainland. I told you that was what put Harmon in his situation." He paused, thinking about that last point. He cleared his throat and continued, "We tagged the operation *Force Three*. The operation name has roots in an earlier one that I'll tell you more about later. The people recruited for the operation are anticommunist, but they are totally separate from the Nationalists Kuomintang—who have pretty much lost their legitimacy on the mainland."

Brigit spoke, "Are those the same people that Harm thought he was meeting when he was ambushed?"

The Director nodded *yes* as he took another drink of his whiskey, then shook his head *no* when Mead pointed at the glass. He rubbed his eyes, sat back in the chair, and continued, "Brigit, I know this is boring stuff—but you both need the background to understand what Harmon Wetmore tumbled headlong into. You see, this *Force Three* got new emphasis when we pretty much determined that the Communist Chinese would intervene in the Korean War. Our intent was to divert Chinese resources from the war in Korea by promoting domestic guerrilla operations. Those teams of Chinese agents I mentioned, inserted through airdrops, were to link up with local guerrilla forces, collect intelligence, and possibly engage in sabotage—even psychological warfare."

Mead spoke, "As I said before, just like our OSS experience in Europe during World War II—which also assumed a cooperative captive population. If I hear you right, a situation that doesn't prevail in China."

"You heard me right, Amos. It's a crash and burn situation—pun intended. And we still don't know what has happened to Harmon Wetmore—even whether or not he has survived."

Brigit stood and said, "What are you doing to find out ... to find him? Has there been any contact at all?" She was beginning to show her anxiety, and some impatience. "And why, if I may ask, are you sitting here ... with us ... instead of?" She caught herself, slowly shaking her head, a hand held up in a sort of apology for the heart-felt outburst.

The Director rubbed his forehead and squinted his eyes, reflecting his own growing weariness after the long trip from Washington. "I'm sorry, Brigit. I should have explained that first. We *have* developed a contact—but not with Harmon." He paused and put his hand out to Brigit slowly adding, "The contact involves you, Brigit, but I'm not ready to talk about it until I get more specific information that I expect to receive tomorrow."

Brigit smiled, her tone softened, "Okay. I'm sorry I pushed there. But, as the doctor in the room, Director, I am prescribing a night's sleep before we finish this—and we *will* finish this ... sir."

The Director set his glass on the edge of Mead's desk and stood, stretching his back. "Must follow the doctor's orders ... where am I staying?

The Upham Hotel, Santa Barbara, California

The next morning the Director rose early, dressed and took a stroll around the verdant gardens of the hotel. Flowers, exotic to his eye, flourished among shrubs proudly flashing their own colors, all beneath trees gnarled with age and softly moss bedecked. The experience was new for the east coast born and bred Director of the CIA and he let himself relax as he took in the earthy smells of the rich soil blended with the heady aromas of roses and honeysuckle. The chirping and flitting birds and lack of a background of traffic noise were not lost on his enjoying the rare moment of peace in an otherwise chaotic life. Reluctantly he returned to his room and reviewed material for his meeting. He ordered breakfast to be delivered.

At the exact hour designated, there was a knock on his door, opened by a security officer to admit Amos and Brigit Mead. The trio sat around a table in the Director's hotel room set with a full American breakfast. Though the small talk was somewhat forced as the Meads held back their anxious need for some action to find Wetmore, the comfort of the room and the beautiful surroundings of the hotel's grounds predominated most of the meal.

Finally, the Director of the CIA moved on to business. "Brigit, your doctor's orders were spot on. I'm in much better shape to take you deeper into the weeds today."

"And we're ready to hear you out, sir," Brigit said, topping her cup of coffee. Mead did the same, saying, "Director, it's strange to me that Harm got himself this deep into an operation that wasn't his. I worked with him enough to know he's not the type to just rush in to something blindly. But since he did—and you are here on a mission—what do you have for *me* to do?"

The Director stood and walked to the glass doors that opened to the garden. After a moment he turned and said, "Soon enough, Amos. Yesterday I said that the Chinese *Force Three* Operation was named after an earlier one. Actually, that original *Force Three* still exists—in a form. And its story is also Harmon Wetmore's story, so best I begin with that. It'll play on what we need to get started on—and that *we* includes you too, Brigit."

The Meads sat with full interest in what was to come. They had worked with Harmon Wetmore since 1943. First in solving the *Orion's Eye* espionage case and then through the deadly trek through Southeast Asia, and most recently the tragic murders and death of Nazi spy—turned post-war CIA operator—Otto Hauptman. Silently Mead was struggling with memories of Wetmore's strange behaviors that bothered him at the time of that tragic death—though he couldn't pin down what exactly they meant. He dropped the thought and stayed in the present.

The Director continued, "Before World War II all of the American intelligence was conducted on a scrambled, ad-hoc basis by practically every executive department in government. The State Department competed with the Treasury, and they with the Army and Navy—not to mention the War Department. There was no overall direction, no overall control or coordination. You two I'm sure had a sense of that in your work during the war."

Amos and Brigit nodded knowingly without taking eyes off the Director as he continued, "President Roosevelt was concerned about these deficiencies as the European war and the Sino-Japanese conflicts crept toward our shores. So, in 1938, he established a secret unit reporting only to him—and known only to the Vice President and a tight personal staff."

Mead asked, "Excuse me, sir, but was that legal?"

"Legal or not," the Director continued, "he did it ... and it was known as *Force Three*." Pausing to refresh his coffee, he continued in a professorial tone. "A simple concept, it called for three pairs of field operators—two each in Europe, the Soviet Union and China. One of each team was a native, the other an American. They coordinated, but operated apart for security reasons. The native was to penetrate as far into the military structure as possible. Call him a mole."

Brigit Mead raised her hand and spoke, "Director, I'm detecting something here. Harmon often talked of his China adventures before the War. You're telling us that Harm is *Force Three China*, right?"

The Director's demeanor eased and he laughed. "Amos, do you know how this lady of yours earned her reputation while you were traipsing around Vietnam and points east?" He turned to Brigit. "Yes, my dear, you're right. Harmon Wetmore had developed his reputation fighting alongside the Chinese against the Japanese. In late 1937 he evaded capture by the Japanese at the battle of the Marco Polo Bridge. Survivors of Wetmore's China-sailor detail made it the one hundred seventy-five miles northeast to Peiping and reported in to the American Legation. Wetmore's detailed after-action report and his intelligence analysis impressed the brass so much that he was assigned to ONI (Office of Naval Intelligence), ending up on Admiral Layton's staff in Pearl Harbor after we got into the war. Then President Roosevelt's *Force Three* people tagged him as half the China team."

Mead spoke, "So Harmon went back to China?"

"No, Amos. Here's how the set-up worked. As I said, one member of each team was a native—recruited from partisans in their country. Over in China, Harm's original partner was the Chinese Nationalist Colonel who led the defense of the Marco Polo Bridge, Harm fighting at his side. His name was Ji Xingwen, but it turned out that he was too well known to the communists and finally decided to escape with the Nationalist forces to Formosa."

Brigit said, "So this plot thickens. Assuming that Harm stayed active in China how did he get things back together when Mao and his boys were about to win?"

The Director walked to a seat near where she sat. "We can thank Ji Xingwen for that. One of his lieutenants volunteered to stay behind to join the communist forces. Changes of allegiance were common in this time of turmoil—"

Mead interrupted, "Where is he now, Director?"

"Fortunately for us he worked his way up in the, as they call it now, Peoples' Liberation Army and is proving to be of great value as a listening post." The CIA Director stood and moved to the nearby desk where his attaché case rested. He peered inside and retrieved a paper. Glancing at it for a moment he turned to the Meads and said, "What I'm going to share with you is highly classified. Knowledge of its existence by anyone outside *Force Three* could cost people their lives ... and everything we've worked for." He stepped to Amos Mead and handed him the document, adding, "This was the last of a list of communications that Harmon received from his Chinese partner. This one triggered his flight to Korea. He was sure that more would be forthcoming with the pick-up operation of a defecting Chi-com general officer. I have omitted the cover with coded addresses and routing. No *need to know* just yet." He turned and sat down, indicating they should read it now. Brigit rose and stepped behind Amos's chair. They began to read what appeared to be a transcription of a conversation among Communist Chinese generals—exactly what it was.

DATED: *December 1949 - Beijing:*
SUBJECT: *Discussion of situation in Korea and Formosa invasion.*
PRESENT: *Mao Tse-tung, Chu The, Peng Tehuai, Su Yu, Nie Rongzhen, Deng Xiaoping, Ho Lung and Staff*
TRANSLATION:

Gen. Peng: Our army is not ready to invade Formosa. They will need modern weapons and transport.

Gen. Su Yu (Commander of the Taiwan invasion army): Also the American Navy is in the way. The last American ground troops have left Korea. They have only a token force left there. If Kim Il-sung gets his way and invades the south we must wait until they conclude any war and the American Navy is withdrawn from the Formosan Straits.

Gen. Tai Li (Deputy to Su Yu): My experience with the American Navy taught me to never turn your back on them.

Gen. Nie: The North Korean Army is bogged down and the tide is about to turn against it. I'm very concerned about the excessive loss rate of the North Korean Army. It is more than 40%

Gen. Su Yu: What, General Nie, is China supposed to do about it?

Zhu Te (The PLA Supreme Commander): The Revolutionary Committee has spent a great deal of time discussing the possibility—and I emphasize the tentative nature of our talks. The Committee feels, after giving the matter lengthy consideration that we should urgently prepare contingency plans to back up the Korean People's Army if the situation on the Korean battlefront deteriorates. There seems little likelihood of this happening, but I need not remind you of the need for planning for any and every contingency.

*Gen. Ho Lung: Is there any chance of the Americans using the **atomic bomb?***

Mead looked up from the document and said, "Atomic bomb—they're talking about an atomic bomb? Is that a factor now?"

The Director said, "Read on, Amos. Then we'll talk about all of it …" Mead nodded and looked down at the sheet in his hand.

Gen. Nie: *It is not likely because Stalin has the bomb, too. But, will Stalin help?*

*(Note: Another general asked: If the PLA (*Chinese Peoples' Liberation Army*) is not up to invading Taiwan now, how can it fight the Americans in Korea? There was much debate, but the generals agreed that China must be prepared to help Kim Il Sung.)*

Gen Peng: *There is every indication that this bridgehead will be eliminated within the next two weeks. If it is not, then the possibility of protracted war in Korea cannot be ruled out. Look carefully at the geography. The Korean peninsula is long and narrow. Remember the enemy, MacArthur the— what's the word?—the 'island-hopper.'*

The peninsula lends itself to amphibious operations, though this will require a lot of daring. Our Korean comrades discount the possibility, but remember whoever makes the first move wins. Remember also that a long and narrow landmass imposes its peculiar limitations on our field armies. In past campaigns we have habitually traded space for time when confronting a better-equipped opponent. Korea has no such space. It could turn out to be a straitjacket. A peninsula presents unusual supply difficulties.

This occurred to me when I reviewed the American situation in Pusan. The American's problems are considerably eased because distances within the Pusan perimeter are short. Although it is true that the enemy is forced to transport men and materiel great distances by sea. Those supply lines are inviolate. They cannot be cut.

Our Korean comrades, on the other hand, are operating a long way from their supply bases. This is becoming a dreadful disadvantage. American air attacks on those supply lines are causing serious losses. The basic problem of Korea, for either side, is that the farther you advance the slimmer your supplies are likely to become.

China will become involved in hostilities in Korea only if the integrity of their Democratic People's Republic is directly threatened. There is no likelihood of any such disaster at present. Still, comrades, it is our business to cover every contingency, so let us assume that some incredible turn of fortune enables the American imperialists to launch a full-scale invasion north of the 38th parallel.

The Chinese response, in my opinion, should be on a limited scale, sufficient to warn the aggressors. If that fails, we should attack with the full weight of the People's Liberation Army."

Mead finished reading. Brigit took the document from him and also completed reading it. She spoke first, "Director, if this is accurate, and not a plant, is our military aware of these plans … or thoughts … or whatever?"

"Trust me," the Director replied. "It's authentic. Its content was included in a CIA assessment for the President."

Mead said, "They talked of our atomic bombs—and the Russians bombs. As I asked …is that a factor?"

The Director said, "It's a factor, Amos. A large and troubling factor—"

Brigit spoke, mainly to herself, "And Harmon is in China … in the middle of this … and a prisoner of these people."

Mead added, "We can only hope he's a prisoner—and not worse."

"Agreed," the Director said. "Okay, Amos, about the atomic bomb. I'm waiting for word as we speak about developments."

Brigit idly ran her finger down the document and stopped at one entry. "Amos, this just registered on me—did you see this name?" She tilted the sheet toward him with her finger laid on *Gen. Tai Li.*

Mead said, "I did. Are we sure it's him?"

Brigit said, "Look at his reference to the Navy—it's him, alright."

The Director listened to the exchange. After Brigit's remark he said, "You know one of these?"

Brigit turned the sheet toward him. "This one, Director. *Tai Li.* He's the son-of-a-bitch who nearly got Amos killed in Hanoi. He was the head of Chiang Kai-shek's Intelligence unit and worked closely with the U.S. Navy—but in reality he was really a murdering bandit. Amos and Lt. Essington saved Ho Chi Minh from one of his assassins too. Last we knew he was arrested by the Nationalist Chinese."

The Director said, "I recall the incident, Brigit, but I'd forgotten any names. During Chiang Kai-shek's hurried evacuation of his government from China to Formosa a lot of his people switched sides. This guy could well have escaped custody—"

Brigit interrupted, anger in her voice, "He's one to watch!"

CHAPTER SIX

Russia, the Trans-Siberia Railway.

Another flight coming up … or?

Harmon Wetmore had his answer.

For four days now the special military train forged its way west along the Trans-Siberia Railway, with another week and a half before arriving in Moscow. The train sat in the station at Ulan Ude, a city of one hundred twenty-five thousand people—and closed to foreigners. But that didn't matter to Wetmore. He wasn't getting off the train.

He marveled at the wild scenery since leaving Vladivostok. Just sixty-five miles back along the track from Ulan Ude the train had skirted the southwestern edge of the enormous Lake Bakail, passing over two-hundred bridges and through thirty-three tunnels.

The train pulled out of Ulan Ede but only progressed one mile before being shunted off onto a siding. Idly wondering about the diversion, Wetmore peered out the barred window of his small compartment at the mainline tracks. In a moment the reason became clear. Out of the corner of his eye he saw the engine of a speeding steam engine bearing down on them. The nose of the sleek black machine sported a huge red star with bright yellow edges and a figure in the middle which he could read as *8* and *1*. Wetmore's knowledge of Chinese history filled in the blanks: 8 1 symbolized Aug 1, 1927, and the birth of the Red Army.

As the apparent newly painted six car train sped by, Wetmore's KGB keeper idly commented, "We've been expecting him."

Wetmore said, "Him?"

"Mao Tse-tung … visiting President Stalin … hat in hand."

Wetmore stared down the track. *Oh boy ... we're getting' deeper and deeper, old man. Wonder when the rough stuff starts.*

The Upham Hotel, Santa Barbara, California

Brigit handed the document back to the Director, saying, "This *Force Three* … the war is long over in Europe. What became of the two assigned there?"

Putting the document back in his briefcase, the Director paused a moment before answering. But first Mead said, "There's a lot going on with the Communists in Europe. Is *Force Three* still in play?

The Director spoke, "The native agent's name was Hans Haeften—"

Brigit interjected, "Was?"

"Yes … *Was*. Haeften had successfully worked his way up to a senior position in the *Waffen SS*. He also kept close ties with the *Wehrmacht*. This was very dangerous for him as the two had very different roles in Hitler's world. Unfortunately after Operation Valkyrie failed—"

"Operation Valkyrie," Brigit jumped in again. "Wasn't that the assassination plot to kill Hitler?"

The Director smiled. "I'm waiting for a phone call that will move us along with Wetmore's situation, Brigit. So, in the meantime I guess a little history lesson is in order here. It's true that Operation Valkyrie *is* the title most associated with the attempted assassination of Hitler in July 1944. But you see, ironically it was *actually* a plan approved by Hitler. It was to be put into operation if Allied bombing or some kind of uprising made communication between the Nazi High Command and Hitler himself untenable. Operation Valkyrie called for command to be passed to the Home Army, and the conspirators planned to use it to remove Hitler's three major bastions of his power base: the SS, Gestapo and SD."

Brigit stayed in the conversation. "A palace coup in the classic sense?"

"You could say that. And it held the deadly results often told of in tales of a palace coup. One of the conspirators was a soldier, General Fromm—who just happened to be in command of the Home Army. The death of Hitler would be enough to trigger Valkyrie, as quite clearly there would have been no communication between Hitler and Berlin. The fact is, besides Hitler only the commander of the Home Army could put Operation Valkyrie into effect—General Fromm."

Mead finally spoke, "As I recall a guy named Stauffenberg was the one who pulled off the bomb plot. Was he *Wehrmacht* or SS?"

"You're right, Amos," the Director said. "Colonel Claus von Stauffenberg—and he was *Wehrmacht*—acted with a few others including General Olbricht, Colonel Mertz and Lieutenant Haeften."

Mead quickly said, "*Our* Haeften?"

"The very same ... *Force Three* at its finest. After the bomb exploded at the Wolf's Lair the four of them went to Berlin. But for a few hours after they arrived nobody would act—including Fromm—because there was no confirmation of Hitler's demise."

Mead said, "I remember now ... Hitler got on the radio and pronounced the rumor of his death as exaggerated—or was that Mark Twain?"

The Director laughed, "Both, I'm afraid. But it was bad news for the plotters. Fromm ordered them arrested and after a short and phony court martial all four were shot by firing squad."

Brigit said, "So an unhappy ending. But I'm glad we know the final ending for Herr Hitler. So, Director, was Haeften replaced?"

"No, there was no time left and our OSS was very effective—so *Force Three Europe* faded away."

"Director ..." Brigit spoke, then paused. "I'm seeing a picture here. One of the two *Force Three Europe* agents died. As you've already told us, only the President and the close principals know of *Force Three* … yet you know all about it. Are we sitting here talking to the other half of *Force Three Europe*, sir?"

The Director turned to Amos Mead. "Amos, do you have any doubts about why we want this lady on the case? And, yes, Brigit. I'm also *Force Three*."

Lubyanka Square, Moscow, Russia, USSR

Suslov looked around, naturally suspicious of speaking anywhere in the KGB's inner sanctum—even though he knew they were quite alone and the office was constantly "debugged." He turned toward Lermantov and said, "My suspicion, Arkady Alexandro'ch, is that we have a very high member of the American CIA in our custody … very high, indeed."

Arkady Lermantov, looking puzzled, asked, "And on what do you base this suspicion?"

"I know the name he has given. I know it from the last war. If I am correct and it is the same man he will be very valuable to us. We can only wait and see."

Lermantov pushed for more. "Valuable? What value?"

Suslov answered quietly, "He may be a direct line to the President of the United States, my friend. A direct line."

Arkady Lermantov sat back and thought for a moment. "If you are correct, this could fit nicely into our plan."

The Upham Hotel, Santa Barbara, California

Mead laughed at the Director's remark about Brigit. "Director, you don't have to convince me about my lady's mental prowess. She kept my backside out of the fire more than once—and solved our assassin case in Germany. But, sir, how, specifically, is she in this one?"

Brigit cut in, "Gentlemen, I'm sitting right here. Speak to me please."

"Whoops," Mead added. "Sorry." It was the Director's turn to laugh. "Okay, it is time to get into action in this search for Harm. You both needed the background information to put you on track with the rest of us. Doctor … eh, Brigit, you made many valuable contacts in China during the war. Frankly, we've made some progress in re-establishing one or two of them to search for Harm."

"What about our *Force Three* contact?" Brigit asked.

The Director said, "His name is Gui Suen, Brigit. But we are very afraid of compromising him if we all of a sudden start trying to contact him out of our usual channels."

Brigit said, "That makes sense, Director. So what have you got for me?"

The Director paused thoughtfully and then turned to one of his security detail and said, "Go out front and let me know when the car from Rincon Station arrives." The CIA agent nodded and left the room. The Director, rubbing his chin in thought, turned to Brigit to answer her concern, "Brigit, think back to the war and your work at Pearl Harbor. Do you remember *Operation Ichigo*?"

Brigit rose from her chair, walked to the window that overlooked the hotel's garden and thought about the question for a moment. Finally she turned and spoke slowly, "*Ichigo* … that was when Amos was still missing … Yes. The Japanese shifted units from Mongolia and threatened to take the rail line from Peiping."

Brigit began to speak more rapidly as she pieced together her memories, "I got wind of it from a contact in Huangshi. The report at first was ten or fifteen divisions—and nobody in Naval Intel would believe me. At first, that is."

The Director smiled. "That's it exactly, Brigit. And the Japanese clobbered the Chinese in Honan Province and started—"

Brigit picked up the narrative, "—to move south toward the Burma Road."

Mead sat in amazement as Brigit and the Director poured out the story of his wife's amazing intelligence interpretation abilities in the war. *So this is Glinda,"* he thought. Then he spoke, "Okay, this is the work of the *Glinda* I've been told about?"

This time the Director laughed out loud. "Good catch, Amos. After Tai Li's arrest, Brigit got involved in solving some coded stuff from the Japanese that was sent to Kuomintang spies ... she even did some stuff for Mao Tse-tung. Amos, she's a famous lady among the cloak and dagger set—on both sides of the pond. And yes, she had her own coded identity—*Glinda*."

"I'm still listening for my role here," Brigit said. There was a tinge of impatience in her tone. The Director continued, "Do you also remember Yang Kuisong?"

Without hesitation Brigit said, "Yes, I do. He was the Chinese commander directly in the way ... the first in danger ... of the Japanese offensive—"

"And you warned him, allowing him to pull back his group to fight another day."

Brigit added, "And there was a Pai Hai-feng. Yang's number two I recall. What are you telling me, Director?"

"That after the defeat of the Kuomintang by Mao many of Chaing's officers took the pragmatic choice of going over to the new Communist army—Pai and Yang included. We've been able to contact both of them using *Glinda* as the contact. They're wary—as would be expected—but waiting to talk further. *Glinda* still has credibility with those she saved."

Brigit said, "And you want me to—"

"Exactly, Brigit. We're set up and ready."

The telephone rang once and the Director picked it up.

"Okay, we're on our way."

CHAPTER SEVEN

Mukden, Manchuria, Communist China

The CIA air crewman who survived the crash of his CIA mission plane, the crash that set Harmon Wetmore in a totally different direction, shivered in the concrete box that was his cell. The smell of mildew damp and so many of its former occupants had faded to him—assimilated into his world. His Chinese army-issue padded jacket and trousers provided little relief. His interrogations are now few, as he has no more to tell them. He heard nothing more from or about Angus Ward. What he couldn't know was the international turmoil his prison-mate's presence in Mukden Prison was causing.

Before the crewman's capture and imprisonment, the American government had ordered the U.S. consulate closed and ordered Consul General Angus Ward and his staff to evacuate Mukden. But Ward delayed too long and the Chinese charged that the American consulate served as a center of espionage activity and Ward was arrested. The crisis deepened. President Truman retaliated by asking American allies to withhold recognition of Mao's newly established government.

In response, the People's Liberation Army accused Ward of inciting a riot outside the consulate. Angus Ward was brought to trial. Now he languished in a cell near the young CIA flyer in the dank, cold prison.

When word of the consul general's situation and the PLA actions reached the U.S., the American public's anger verged on explosive. The President could not afford to show weakness in the face of the Chinese Communist challenge and he met with his military advisors to discuss the feasibility of a rescue operation. But it was not to be. Still naively looking for opportunities to reach accommodation with the new China regime, the U.S. backed off the threat. Instead they sent a message to Mao that the US would not recognize the new Chinese government until all of the Americans at Mukden Prison were released. Saving face, Mao had Ward and his staff charged with the inciting-to-riot and ordered them deported.

The CIA airman listened once more to military cadence as soldiers marched into the cellblock. An iron door creaked open, shuffling and mumbles came next, and the iron door slammed shut. The marching resumed—but this time the orders the airman heard were in Chinese. Then silence.

Rincon Beach, near Santa Barbara, California

Amos and Brigit Mead followed the Director down the floral carpeted hall of the hotel to the front lobby where they were met by two of the protective detail that accompanied the Director. The agents held the front door open for the group, pointing at the pair of gray sedans parked in the portico, marked U.S. Navy. As they moved toward the cars Amos asked Brigit about their baby son Nathan. Brigit said, "Amy Sokol has him, Amos. It's all covered. I had a suspicion we'd be delayed." The Navy drivers had the sedan doors open and stood at attention. The Director got into the front car, directing the Mead's to the rear seat. The two CIA agents climbed into the second car. The two cars eased out of the hotel grounds and headed toward Hwy 101, turning south for the ten minute drive down the coast to a popular surfing beach, the Rincon. A few minutes later the small convoy turned off Hwy 101, their backs to the Pacific Ocean, and proceeded up a graded gravel road that wound through one of the steep eroded cliff-lined canyons across from the ocean beach. Passing through a low security gate marked 'No Entry Federal Property' the cars reached the top and turned onto an oiled road, allowing the following billows of dust to dissipate in the onshore breeze. Dead ahead, past the sentry-manned main gate, they saw the group of buildings festooned with antennae of varying heights and complexity. The Director looked over his shoulder at the Meads and said, "Welcome to NAVCOMMSTA Rincon."

The two cars pulled up in front of the building marked 'Headquarters.' The trailing car quickly disgorged its security detail. The Director and the Meads exited the lead car and were met by the base commander who introduced himself as Lt. Commander Edward Wilson.

"Thanks for handling the details, Commander," the Director said. Let me introduce our party. This is former Marine Corps Major and OSS agent Amos Mead." Mead shook the commander's hand and stepped back as Brigit moved forward. The Director continued, "And this is former US Army Major, Doctor Brigit Mead—also former OSS and reputed to be an exceptional intelligence analyst." Brigit smiled and took the commander's hand.

"Welcome to all of you," the commander said, nodding toward the security detail also. "I heard from Pearl Harbor shortly after you called me, Director. You folks don't waste any time."

"None to waste, Commander," the Director said, moving toward the door. The group was escorted into the facility, down a long central hallway and into a room that buzzed, literally buzzed, with radios. Sailors with headsets monitored their stations on three sides of the room. The fourth side had a conference-type table with chairs and a blackboard. Mr. Wilson invited everyone to take a seat. "First, welcome officially to Navy Communication Station Rincon—lovingly known as NAVCOMMSTA in Navy lingo. The Director has asked me to tell you about some of what you see here. Our mission is to provide communication with US Navy ships as well as friendly ships and airplanes operating in the Eastern Pacific."

Mead raised his hand and asked, "Does that reach the Eastern Pacific mainland—China maybe?"

Lt. Commander Wilson replied with a wry smile, "Not officially, Mr. Mead. You were—are— a Marine, sir, so you'll understand that military techies with toys just won't leave well-enough alone." Mead nodded, his thoughts going briefly back to Sgt. MacIntire and his unofficial technical contribution to their survival during the trek across Burma—though Manny didn't survive.

Lt. Commander Wilson walked over to the nearest station. "We use single-sideband in both clear and encrypted voice modes." He pointed to the next station and added, "And we've also got ciphered radio-teletype modes for Fleet Broadcast."

Brigit took her turn at a question, "Are you the only such facility doing this work, Commander?"

"No, ma'am. Originally this activity was centered in San Francisco. But when the threat of nuclear strikes from the Soviets took hold the Navy decided to get out of Dodge—the prime targets—and disperse down the coast. We've got sister operations near San Diego at Chollas Heights and out at Pearl Harbor in Hawaii."

The Director stood and motioned to the others. "Let's get on with our mission today. Hopefully Harmon Wetmore is awaiting our call."

"This way, folks." Wilson led the way out of the room to a smaller one next door. "My briefing said that Dr. Mead will be transmitting in the clear. The signal will be intercepted in Hawaii and contact relayed to certain sites in China. Hawaii will encrypt as requested by the Chinese."

Brigit took the chair indicated by Wilson as the Navy radio operator slid to one side to assist and handed her a headset with microphone. Lt. Commander Wilson added, "We didn't know if you speak any Chinese dialects—or if your friends speak English—so we have simultaneous-translation services standing by in Hawaii."

The Director moved behind Brigit. "Okay, make your call much like you used to do at Pearl. Pearl Harbor is already monitoring the channels we are using into mainland China."

Brigit nodded and turned her head to smile at Amos Mead.

"Your show, Brigit," the Director said as he stepped back and took a seat nearby.

Dr. Brigit Mead took a deep breath and keyed her microphone as memories flooded back to 1944 and a similarly hard chair in an office in Pearl Harbor, Territory of Hawaii. She remembered that Yang Kuisong's code name was *shandian yun*—lightning cloud.

"Calling *shandian yun*, calling *shandian yun*. This is *Glinda*, repeat, *Glinda*, in the clear. Over."

Brigit looked down at the ledge in front of her, intent on the tiny sounds coming from the headset. Once more she broadcasted, "*Shandian yun*, this is *Glinda* calling in the clear."

The crackling static in her ears increased, then a voice, "*Glinda*, this is Pearl Harbor. We have a reply and are translating for you—*Shandian yun* requests that you provide the countersign confirmation code. But he asked that it not be the last one you used, but the one from the first contact you made with him at the beginning of *Operation Ichigo*. Over."

"Roger your request, Pearl Harbor," Brigit replied. She sat back in her chair staring at the Navy gray ceiling … thinking. Quickly she straightened up and leaned into her microphone, "*Glinda* calling *shandian yun*. Countersign *Gung Ho*. Repeat, countersign is *Gung Ho*. Over."

After an interminable moment Brigit heard her reply—not from Pearl Harbor, but in broken, but understandable English, "*Glinda*, this is *shandian yun*. I verify *Gung Ho*. It has been a long time, my friend, and many changes in circumstance, as I'm sure you know. Over."

"Indeed it has, my friend. I'm glad we are able to make this contact and I know how much risk you may be taking to talk with me. Over."

A muffled laugh came over the warming headset. "Some risk, *Glinda*. But there is risk in everything. I would not be here without a great respect for *Glinda* and her help. Over.

Brigit smiled and keyed her microphone, "Your Confucius told us that 'without feelings of respect, what is there to distinguish men from beasts?' I share this respect and also am here because of it, *shandian yun*. Now, may I ask for your help with a personal problem? Over."

Amos Mead leaned over to the Director and whispered, "She is a pro at working the culture and style angle. I would have just jumped in and asked my question—and blown it!"

Brigit smiled and glanced over to her observers as she heard her Chinese contacts flowery invitation to proceed with her request.

"Thank you, *shandian yun,* I have lost a friend somewhere in your country. He was on an airplane that crashed in Jilin Province of Manchuria. Many died in the crash but we believe he and possibly others survived and are in the custody of the PLA. Since I believe that the PLA does not have many American prisoners, possibly one or two would be known. I cannot ask you to intercede. That is too great a request. All that I am asking is that you confirm for me that he is in custody. Over."

The Director and Mead slid to the front edge of their seats, straining for a wisp of what may be coming. Brigit keyed her microphone, "I must apologize, *Shandian yun*. I do not wish to disclose his mission or his name at this time. I do not wish to burden you with the knowledge, and place you in some jeopardy. I can say he is not military. He is an older man, gray hair, short cut, about 1.8 meters tall. If I can learn whether you have him or others in custody we can talk further if you wish. Thank you for allowing *Glinda* to make this request. Over."

A long moment later, after listening with focused attention, "Thank you *Shandian yun. Glinda* Out."

There was only silence as Brigit sat back in her chair and slowly removed the headset, setting it on the radio's ledge. She sat for a moment, then seemed to sigh as she turned to face the others. The Director broke the silence, "Brigit, that was all we could have expected—and more."

Mead stood and stepped to Brigit, taking her hand. "Honey, if I had understood half of what you taught us at Pearl before the China mission … you make me very proud."

"Thanks, both of you. But it's the next message that will prove this pudding."

The Director turned to Lt. Commander Wilson and said, "Please get me hooked up with the White House switchboard—I'll take it from there." Wilson nodded and reached for the proper telephone. In a brief moment he handed it to the Director, who nodded and spoke into the phone giving a code word, then punching in more numbers. He glanced at Mead and Brigit as he waited. "Yes, Mr. President. It went better than we could have hoped, sir. At least for now. It's up to the Chinese what happens next. Yes, sir, we are waiting. Dr. Mead? Yes, sir. She performed perfectly—as we knew she would. Yes, sir, I will. I'll be back as soon as we have more." He listened a moment then set the phone back in its Navy type cradle. "Brigit, President Truman sends his thanks and best wishes."

Brigit smiled and lowered her head. It wasn't over yet.

Military Headquarters, Dongchen District, Beijing, China

Shaojiang (Major General) Yang Kuisong turned to the small group of his staff listening to one side of the radio transmission with the Americans. He spoke, "It is best we not speak of this just yet beyond this room. Mao and all senior staff are on their way to Moscow and no one here needs know."

Kuisong's Aide said, "May we know what the Americans wanted of you?" Kuisong (known to U.S. Naval Intelligence as code name *shandian yun*—lightning cloud) responded, "They asked if we know the location of one of their intelligence officers who seems to have gone missing in Manchuria."

61

The Aide asked, "Does this have anything to do with the mission of General Su Yu?"

Kuisong said, "For now, I say to all of you, I will think about our next action. You know nothing of General Su Yu's mission. Again, this is for no one else to know of these proceedings. Please leave me." As the heavy door clicked shut, the old warrior peered out his window at the ancient city.

Who could be so important as to cause them to contact me? But important to be sure and tomorrow I will inquire.

CHAPTER EIGHT

Russia, USSR, Trans-Siberia Railway
Mao's Special Military Train

The sleek black machine clacked on into the night, sporting a huge red star with bright yellow edges and the figures 8 and 1.

The newly painted Red Army six-car train sped along well ahead of Wetmore's Russian Army train, gaining distance with each mile. Mao's private car was in the middle, well protected by armed troops ahead of and behind him. In the last car, used to cook for and feed the train, two men sat alone. One, a tall Chinese gentleman in civilian clothes spoke, "Are you ready to deliver the information?"

The other, General Su Yu, wearing the four starred epaulets of his rank and the badges of the Order of Independence, Order of Liberation, and Order of the Peoples' Liberation Army on his tunic, nodded as he answered, "Ready? Yes I am ready. But I still ponder the wisdom of it." The two men stood and straightened already impeccable clothing, then left the kitchen car and its din of food preparation activity. They moved forward along the rocking train to rejoin their peers. It is a few short days until they reach Moscow—and the answer to their nagging doubts.

The Trans-Siberia Railway, Russia, USSR

The lightly loaded military transport train from Vladivostok to Moscow that carried the KGB's prisoner, Harmon Wetmore, pulled into the yard at Kirov. It was announced that there would be delay—its length unknown.

The tiny room that was Wetmore's cell during the long journey was completely dark now. Its one small window had been securely blocked a few days before, just after Mao's train had passed them by. A brief knock on the door preceded the blinding light of its opening. Wetmore blinked and held his arm up to shield the shock and try to see his visitor. The KGB officer who had been his companion since shortly after his capture stood in the doorway. Speaking English the officer said, "It is time to talk, Mr. Wetmore. It is time to be serious and help me to help you."

Wetmore grunted and lay back on his narrow cot with no other response. The KGB officer stepped back and let one of the two guards pass him, aimed straight at Wetmore. He grabbed his arm and pulled him to his feet with a grip of steel. Wetmore tried to pull away but to no avail as the fingers dug into already sore flesh.

KGB said, "I said it is time to talk, my friend. There was no question there, no option for you. This can be easy or very difficult. Of this only do you have a choice."

Harmon Wetmore said, "What more can I tell you. You know my name. I have no unit or rank, and I sure as hell don't have any deep dark secrets to share."

The officer motioned for the guard to allow Wetmore to sit back on the cot while he took the one chair in the small space. The guard stepped to the door and closed it, remaining inside.

Beginning softly, the officer said, "We know you were on a mission to pick up someone from Manchuria. We saw the crash of your aircraft—and we saw you escape. So you are an aircrew member. Your aircraft was unmarked, as is your uniform. The only unmarked aircraft and uniforms are clandestine operatives—criminal or intelligence. Your bearing is military, down to your hair style. But you are also an old man. Old men usually lead such ventures, and leaders know the plans. So, Mr. Wetmore, please fill in what I've missed."

Wetmore had time to think about where this might be going. He answered, "You've pretty much covered it, Mr. Russian. But I ain't no leader. I confess to being old, but I ain't no leader. If being old means being smart, I weren't no genius flying with a crew that can't see an ambush."

Harmon played as close to the rube underling character as he thought would sit with this guy. A quick and unexpected slap across his face told him it wasn't very effective. He slowly raised his hand to check for blood at his mouth and said, "Hey, you got no call to do that. I told you what I know and you know the rest."

"Mr. Wetmore, there is only one conclusion for me. CIA. You are not dumb enough to fly into an ambush. But you weren't in charge of the operation of the airplane. You were in charge of the mission though. Why you flew the operation you must tell me. That parts fits with the dumb act."

Wetmore rubbed his chin. He looked up at the KGB officer and said, "You've got all I know—and all you know. What else can I say?"

"I think I've learned what I need from you for now." The KGB officer motioned the guard to depart. As the officer stepped through the door he turned and said, "Mr. Wetmore, we saw all you did and how you've acted with us. We have respect for a warrior. Sadly, the people who will take you in Moscow have no such respect."

The door closed and the darkness enveloped the sudden tiredness that flooded over Harmon Wetmore, Deputy Director Operations, CIA, the United States of America.

The KGB officer stepped down from the train and entered a building near the track. Through the window he could be seen picking up a telephone—if anybody cared to look.

The surrounding city had a long history. In 1180 it was a fort called Khlynov situated just west of the Ural Mountains. In 1489 it was drawn into the Grand Duchy of Moscow. Its cathedral, an imposing wooden structure of five onion shaped domes has survived since 1689. By the end of the nineteenth century it had become an important waypoint on the Trans-Siberian railway. In December 1934 it was renamed for a Soviet Leader who was assassinated there: Sergey Kirov.

The KGB officer paused under the carved wooden sign *Kirov* and walked back to the train. His mission done for now.

Rublevca, Moscow, Russia, USSR

Mao Tse-tung paced the floor of the dacha like a caged tiger. Officially it was a *gosdacha*, larger and more opulent than the common dacha, owned by the state and used by very high government officials and the occasional special visitor. Located in a suburb of Moscow called Rublevca, it now served in Mao's mind as a prison and an insult to his power and position in the Communist world.

Nearly two weeks before, Mao Tse-tung's private train had pulled slowly toward the Kursky Railway station in Moscow. Mao remained seated regally in his chair, but strained to peer down the platform to see what a grand greeting awaited him. Finally, already appearing too eager, he sat back and told one of his staff to report what he saw. The officer peered out the window just as the train lurched, banging his head painfully against the glass. Mao froze in his chair, grasping the arms. The officer recovered as the train moved onto a small siding short of Kursky Station. Fearful to do other than what he'd been ordered to do he reported, "I see only a small party, Comrade Chairman. Perhaps the main celebration will be at the Kremlin."

"Perhaps," Mao said, smoothing his tunic and trying to reestablish his cool demeanor. He added, mostly to himself, "But we expected to have a reception and ceremony here."

Gaudily uniformed Chinese Army officers opened the door and set out the steps to Mao's private armored railcar. Mao had ordered a sumptuous luncheon buffet for the Russian notables who he expected would be greeting him. Anxious staff scurried to reestablish order on the table after the unexpected jarring. Mao was anxious to begin his first meeting with his Communist peers since defeating the Nationalist in China.

The small group of Soviet official greeters was led by two senior politburo members, Vyacheslav Molotov and Nicolai Bulganin. Stalin was not on the platform, nor any of his immediate staff or military generals. Mao seethed, but regained his composure and ordered his staff to invite the party aboard. He remained seated until they had climbed the steps and now faced him. With a broad grin and an extended hand he rose, stepped toward them and said, "Comrades, please share a celebratory drink with me."

Molotov's face remained a blank slate as he said, "We must decline, sir. Protocol does not allow us to accept." In quick succession the Russians also refused to sit and share food—or to accompany Mao to the accommodations scheduled for the Chinese visitors.

Mao Tse-tung's disappointment and growing anger showed on his now stern face as the Russians turned to leave the car. He had fully expected to be welcomed as the victorious leader of a great revolution who had delivered one of the world's greatest and oldest nations into the Communist orbit. Instead his greeters treated him more like the visiting head of the Bulgarian Communist Party—of little consequence.

Now it was evident that no major festivities were scheduled to welcome him to Moscow and Mao was painfully growing aware of his place in Stalin's universe—the "little brother" to the real Communists of the Soviet Union. His anger grew.

The office door of the head of the Moscow Communist Party opened as an aide to Nikita Khrushchev entered the room.

"Comrade Khrushchev, there is someone named 'Matsadoon' in Moscow to meet with—"

"Who?" Khrushchev interrupted.

"You know, sir—the Chinaman."

67

This short conversation described best how the Russians saw Mao and treated him—the Chinaman.

There was a reception held for the Chinese Communist visitors, but it was at the Metropole Hotel—the usual location for entertaining minor visiting dignitaries. Politboro members and minor functionaries provided the minimal protocols for Mao. The Main Hall of the Kremlin, the venue for Communist VIP receptions remained dark. Things got no better after the first reception. Mao's requests to meet with high level people were briskly brushed aside by his Russian contact, Kovalev, with the explanation that no one else could meet with him until Stalin had met with him. When Mao first arrived in Moscow, he announced that China looked forward to a partnership with Russia, but he emphasized as well that he wanted to be treated as an equal. Instead he is being taught a lesson each day. Stalin is taking his time.

For two weeks Mao is completely isolated, waiting for Stalin to arrange meetings, his frustration growing to a point that his own staff feared to be in his presence. As he paced the floor of the *gosdacha's* main room he shouted at the walls, "I am as much a captive as your guest." Convinced that Stalin had bugged the house he lashed out to the walls, "I am here to do more than eat and shit!"

Kovalev arrived for his daily visit to the *gosdacha* and was escorted into the room in the middle of this tirade. Mao narrowed his scowl at the Russian. "Do you hear me, Kovalev? Eat and shit is all I do now—and I do not like Russian food!" He raised his hand and pointed out the window. "Bad, bad!"

Remaining calm, and secretly enjoying Mao's discomfort, Kovalev said, "What do you mean 'bad, bad,' comrade?"

Mao fumed. "I am rightfully angry at the Kremlin and your officials. They have no right to treat a peer and hero of the Chinese revolution in this manner—"

Kovalev cut him off, "You, sir, have no right to criticize Premier Stalin. I must go now and report your comments." At that remark, Mao Tse-tung stormed out of the room. Kovalev stood smiling and accepted his hat and coat from the butler.

CHAPTER NINE

Lubyanka Square, Moscow, Russia

Wetmore had been in his cell in the KGB's Lubyanka Prison for over a week now. As he was escorted off the military train that brought him to Moscow he glimpsed the Chinese train parked on a spur off the main line. The snow on its roof and the tracks around it spoke of its arrival some days earlier. He had been hustled along to a parked Russian Zim, the limousine style sedan, luxurious by Soviet standards, used by government officials. As he slid into the darkened recess of the tinted window enclosed rear seat, Wetmore confirmed for himself that his captors were highly placed and that he was in for a long and dangerous game. *What's next*, he thought.

He met the cold reality in his Lubyanka Prison cell—the home of the KGB.

The Kremlin, Moscow, Russia

Kim Il Sung, the autocratic leader of the Democratic Peoples' Republic of Korea—North Korea—sat across from Joseph Stalin, Chairman of the Soviet Union.

Kim had secretly flown to Moscow to convince Stalin that he could conquer the government of South Korea. He had emphasized the fact that the withdrawal of most of the U.S. forces from South Korea in June 1949 had left the southern government defended only by a weak and inexperienced South Korean army. His own army by contrast was armed with Soviet WWII era equipment and had a cadre of veterans who had experience fighting as anti-Japanese guerrillas. Kim Il Sung was ready to take over the Korean peninsula—but he knew he needed the strong backing of Stalin and Mao.

His secret visit with Stalin was the reason that Mao Tse-tung was being held at bay. Stalin wanted Kim's views before listening to Mao. Kim was sent home with only the assurance that he would be informed soon about his wishes. He also had to agree to an annual shipment of refined lead from Korea—a commodity in short supply in the Soviet Union. He'd agreed to twenty-five thousand tons per year. He was not happy, but it was enough for now. As Kim departed for the airport, Mao Tse-tung was summoned, finally, to the Kremlin.

Stalin rose to greet the Chinese leader, extending his hand but exhibiting no warmth toward his guest. He gestured toward a pair of chairs arranged so that their interpreters could be both heard and seen. Stalin opened the conversation before Mao could make his wishes known, catching him off guard with the subjects. Stalin looked at Mao and said, "Why did you not seize Shanghai? Why did you wait so long before entering the city? The people suffered."

Mao listened to the translation and slowly replied, "Why should we? If I'd chosen to capture the city, I'd have six million inhabitants to feed!"

Stalin already feared that this man favored peasants like himself over workers in the cities. His fear was now founded in Mao's comments and he was appalled by this proof that the workers had been purposely left to suffer.

Getting back to the agenda, Mao made his requests. But he got very little of the economic and military aid he sought in this first meeting. To make matters worse, Stalin also required some Chinese territorial concessions as part of the deal. And Stalin got confirmation on one item he wanted: China would come to the aid of North Korea if necessary.

Mao's trip to Moscow was a disaster for him on every level. Seething over how he'd been treated, he vowed to have a long memory about it. The lack of Russian generosity defied all his expectations, staggering the Chinese delegation. Mao was keenly aware of the scale of his triumph at home and what it meant to history. His treatment by Stalin and the Soviet hierarchy was a humiliation that he had been forced to accept without complaint or recourse.

At this point Mao engrained his abiding hatred of the Soviets. As he entered the limousine for the ride back to his quarters he exclaimed to an aide, "They do not realize that this was like taking meat from the mouth of a tiger!"

With Mao's commitment to send troops and other support to Kim firmly in hand, Stalin had a message sent to Pyongyang, North Korea, giving his support and approval of an invasion of South Korea.

It contained, however, conditions and restrictions: The Soviets support is limited to advisors to help in planning, and military instructors to train some North Korean units. Stalin made it clear that the Soviet Union would not participate in direct confrontation with the United States over Korea. He would not send ground troops even if Kim had a major military crisis.

Moscow, Russia, USSR

General Su Yu sat at a table at the rear of a small, seedy shop on *Kursfogo Vokzala Place* that passed for a restaurant. It was just steps from Kursky Station and the Chinese Military train. Slight of build with sad eyes, his face reflected the hardships endured as Mao pursued his revolution. His greatcoat covered the four starred epaulets of his rank.

Next to him a tall Chinese gentleman in civilian clothes prepared to take his seat, obviously nervous, eyeing the front entrance and surveying the room with flitting eyes. Across from the two Chinese with his back to the door sat Russian Colonel

General Terenti Shtykov. Looking well fed, short with thinning hair, if he was nervous it didn't show.

Su Yu spoke first, "This is our first meeting face to face. I am not comfortable with it, but since we are only taking advantage of the proximity we find ourselves in there is little chance of anyone anticipating it—"

Colonel General Shtykov interrupted Su Yu, "I agree, and there is little chance anyone, the KGB or someone else, will find interest in this. We have been together with our individual missions and are traveling accordingly, so this sharing a small meal appears quite ordinary. Do not worry. But now I have very little time. I am to meet Kim's flight back to Pyongyang shortly. What have you to report?"

General Su Yu still looked around furtively, then said, "I have confirmed from eyes we have in place in Japan that the American General MacArthur is planning to use small atomic bombs in the north of Korea to block Chinese intervention and ensure his success—which has been very small so far. So our plan is even more important now."

Su Yu looked to the civilian at the table, who nodded without expression, then turned back to Shtykov and said, "We are ready. Everything is in place. With your agreement we can execute."

Shtykov said, "I received word of Stalin's decision. The action against the South is growing. Proceed with the plan. By the time the package gets to Jeju Island we will be ready to transport it to the final planned location under cover of the confusion of the military action."

The Chinese civilian spoke, "My people are ready. It took a great effort by a few people—we desired to keep its knowledge close. The team you provided is in place and well trained. The special equipment is on board the also specially equipped vessel and should by now be in port and awaiting word. I shall send that word to them. With our success we shall be able to take all of Korea regardless of the American forces. The threat of *our* atomic bomb will be of great power."

72

Colonel General Terenti Shtykov rose from his seat. "It is done then." He turned without another word and strode out of the building and toward a waiting car.

The Soviet general had been head of the Soviet military mission in Seoul in 1946. He was now the first Soviet ambassador to the Democratic People's Republic of Korea, the DPRK. He believed that a carefully planned and well supplied blitzkrieg-type attack by the North Korean armies would produce a communist takeover of the entire Korean Peninsula. He was not a traitor to the USSR, but he had developed a great belief in the future of the DPRK.

He also had begun to amass a fortune of well hidden assets that would secure his future, and he held no moral doubt about the operation they planned and now set in motion. If successful, an invasion would increase both Soviet influence and power of communism in the world, and this was good for Shtykov. Losing the war for control of the Korean peninsula would end his dream. He knew that Stalin would not wield his new found atomic weapons and that Mao was long away from having one. He believed that the United States must be countered in their use of atomic power in this war so he joined the small group who shared his dreams and acted upon them.

A telephone call went out from the seedy restaurant, its message wending its way to a fishing pier in Okinawa. That task completed, the two Chinese walked briskly to the train that would take them back to Beijing to await the results. The food on the table cooled, untouched.

Navy Communication Station, Rincon, California

Brigit was back at the communication station after getting word of an impending incoming contact from China. The Director and Mead took chairs out of the way of the technicians who worked on linking Hawaii and China with their station. The technician signaled to her with one finger up then pointed at her.

Brigit spoke, "*Shandian yun*, this is *Glinda*. We are calling in the clear."

On the other end of the line *Shaojiang* (Major General) Yang Kuisong said, "Greetings, *Glinda*. I shall get right to the message as we have not much time. We located a survivor of your crashed spy plane in Mukden Prison. He is being brought here to Beijing, but I have no control, no authority, over his situation—"

Brigit cut in, "Just one, *Shaojiang*? There is only *one*?"

Kuisong said, "Only one in our custody, *Glinda*.

Brigit asked, "How is he? What is his condition?"

"My people said he is not hurt," the General answered. "He is a young and strong man, not much more than *qīngshàonián*."

Brigit gasped, her head drooped. "A teenager, *Shaojiang*, your prisoner is a teenager?

"That is what was reported to me. I detect that this is not to your liking, *Glinda*?"

Brigit recovered, realizing this was not the place to reveal more. "No, *Shaojiang*, any survivor is a joy to us. I hope we can find mutual interest in his release at some point."

"That is beyond my control, *Glinda*. I must go now."

The connection clicked in Brigit's ear, then an American voice said, "That's it, ma'am. China's gone off line."

Brigit said, "Thank you," and set her receiver down slowly on the ledge in front of her.

No one in the room spoke, all watching her intently. She raised her eyes and looked at the assembled group, then said, "There is a survivor, Director. But it is not Harmon Wetmore."

The Director said, "We can identify the survivor by simple elimination as we know the one remaining crewman."

Mead stood and walked over to Brigit, placing a gentle hand on her shoulder. "So the search begins." With his hand resting on Brigit's shoulder he spoke to the Director. "Is this all we've got, sir? We're just going to sit around and deduce stuff by elimination while Harmon is either scrambling for cover somewhere or sitting in a cell—or worse? Come on, Director, there has to be—"

74

Brigit cut him off, "Amos! We're all frustrated. The Director most of all, I'm sure—"

The Director cut in, "And the President, all the CIA staff … damn, Amos, we know we've got to find out more."

Mead said, "Sorry, sir. Just welled up … Harm and I have been through a lot together … I've got to help."

The Director escorted the Mead's back to his car and the caravan of security vehicles returned to Santa Barbara.

Dr. Brigit Mead was instructed to be ready to return to NAVCOMMSTA—Navy Communication Station Rincon——if another attempt is made to reach her by her Chinese contact.

Amos Mead was told that he will be in play when—and if— Wetmore is located, but that role would be determined by circumstances.

The Director headed for the airport and the long flight back to Washington, D.C.

Amos Mead stayed deep in thought. Questions, old questions, lazing around in his head—not yet taking any real shape.

CHAPTER TEN

AP June 1950—North Korea launched full-fledged offensive across 38th parallel. Seoul captured. President Syngman Rhee and his government forced to flee south.

Kadena Air Force Base, Okinawa, Japan

The darkened windows of the upstairs floor of the warehouse proved to be a perfect tool for the team to observe the activities and routines of the U.S. Air Force ground crews and technicians working on the B-52 bombers, and those working in and around the WWII era hangers. They also took note of the security routines near the planes and around the perimeter fences.

They had unloaded their special vehicles from the fishing boat—special because of the need to handle the weight and size of their target. Now after a few days of watching and waiting, boredom is the enemy. But the leader spent the time having each member of the team recite his role when the time comes for action.

As he once again watched an Air Force security jeep pass by in the inside of the fence on its hourly patrol, the leader noted, "I find it odd. The Americans are so sure of their safe surroundings that security is no more than routine—even with their new weapons."

The team leader is a Korean of Chinese mixed blood named Park-Liu. He and his five team-mates had been selected as part of the fifty man protection force for the Soviet embassy in Pyongyang, North Korea. Then Park-Liu and his team were further recruited by Colonel General Terenti Shtykov, the Soviet Ambassador to North Korea, and specially trained by the Soviet *Spetsnaz* (Special Forces) for a secret mission—the one that they were now deep into on the island of Okinawa.

One of the team spoke, "They won that war. They have no fear of an Army or a Navy to attack—only local common thieves. We will provide them a surprise."

The special phone the leader had been provided, silent since their arrival, chirped, startling the men who now looked at their leader. He picked up the receiver and delivered a code word, then listened.

The message to proceed received, the leader of the group said, "It is time. We go as soon as it gets dusk. Recheck everything."

With the waning light the six man team shouldered their gear and proceeded to the dimly lit stairway that led down to the first level of their hiding place. Two vehicles sat on the oil stained concrete floor. One marked with a Red Cross, and both with U.S. Air Force designators. They looked like the trucks the Americans used to haul ammunition—and provide ambulance duty. But inside they were rigged for another mission. The Red Cross "ambulance" was larger than the original, higher and a bit longer—though at the speed of their planned mission it should pass muster long enough.

The leader gathered them around him. "If we fail—small chance—we drive away from the boats in the other direction. We will not reveal the boats' role. Understood?" Heads nodded as he continued, "We have good information ... eyes on the ground. It is a good thing the American's like their toilets cleaned and their grass neatly mowed—and do not do it themselves."

Back on the fishing boats the rest of the crews still appeared to go about their usual duties, but below deck on the largest boat the work was complete, and far from routine. The booms that swung out from the side of the fishing boats to handle nets looked normal to the casual eye. But on close inspection they were well camouflaged reinforced steel and rigged for much heavier loads than a fish net.

The doors of the darkened warehouse on the side away from the airbase opened and the two trucks emerged, their occupants dressed in USAF fatigue uniforms, caps pulled low on the forehead. The Red Cross marked truck with four of the men drove as far as the edge of the building and stopped out of the light from the base perimeter. The other truck, with the leader driving and one other man in the back, proceeded across the road, its target a little used service gate in the fence.

The truck looked right, the uniforms were right, and the subdued lighting at this point in the fence drew no notice as the man in the back of the rig jumped out and approached the gate. He quickly cut the chain free and swung open the gate, returning to his place in the truck. The leader turned and peered back into the bed of the truck and whispered, "Is all in order? Everything ready?"

His partner, sitting among an array of explosive ordinance he had prepared answered in the positive. The truck pulled onto the edge of the tarmac and proceeded around the perimeter fence until it was even with the soaring tail of their target. Then it turned and with increasing speed drove directly toward the nearest American B-52 bomber. The man in the rear opened the canvas flap he had rigged that would allow him to do his work. The giant bomber was bathed in the brightness of the mechanics' work lights so the truck seemed to loom from the darkness.

At first no notice was taken of the truck, then as it continued to approach at an unsafe speed for on-field vehicles airmen began to watch, and then draw away from its seeming aim point. The truck swerved beneath the tail of the behemoth aircraft, the driver marveling at the actual size of the plane. Forty-three feet above them the tail soared skyward. As the truck reached the tail and lined up with the aircraft the first explosive charge was thrown from the back of the truck.

Crewmen scattered in all directions, and outlying sentries were finally reaching the plane at a run—and directly into fire from the truck. The first rounds returned by the lead sentry's M-1 Garand rifle bounced harmlessly off the armored sides of the attacker.

One after another fire bombs landed beneath the plane, under the landing gears and out toward the wings. The plane's bomb bays were open and engine cowls and inspection plates removed. Most of the charges contained white phosphorous and stuck to every surface it touched. Fire was everywhere, mayhem ruled, men ran for their lives.

Just as quickly as it appeared, the truck sped across the tarmac toward the dark fence, its mission complete. Security forces and fire trucks already converged on the blazing aircraft. Another truck, marked with a Red Cross, entered the field through the open gate and approached the scene, seeming to be part of the response. As it neared the lighted area it turned and proceeded to the hangar containing their target—an atomic bomb.

The truck quickly backed up to the open end of the building and extended an I-beam from the rear with lifting points that extended over the bomb. As it slid from its transport dolly, the six-thousand pound, three foot diameter Mark VIIII bomb squeezed nicely into the truck—as planned. The few American airmen who had remained behind were gunned down with silenced SKS Carbines. Quickly the attackers secured the bomb and then located the small packaged nuclear core that would arm the bomb and placed it into the truck. All secure, they climbed aboard and headed toward the blazing B-52, neatly mingling with the incoming real emergency vehicles. At the right time they turned and headed toward the base hospital displaying flashing red lights and acting like the others en route with wounded. Passing the hospital they excited the main gate, surprising the sentries left there but not engaging them, and disappeared into the darkness.

Approaching the blackened warehouse where they'd begun the mission they drove around to the pier side and entered a canvas shelter that had been erected next to the fishing boat. The booms from the boat reached out and penetrated the open side of the shelter, right above the door of the truck. Soon the bomb and its nuclear core were transferred to the boom and swung into the hold of the boat, resting on the specially built cradle.

Four of the six men carried their gear and quietly boarded the fishing boat. The other two drove the trucks in the darkness to a predetermined spot on the long breakwater. With a weight on the accelerator pedal each truck made a final plunge into the sea. Back at the boats the canvas shelter was struck and stowed on board, the task completed as the two drivers walked into the dim working lights.

Across the road they could see the glow of their night's work against the cloudy sky—interspersed with bright bursts of delayed fuse grenades scattered under the plane. The mingled sounds of the explosions, the fire's roar and vehicles circulating to search for them filled the air. They looked at each other, smiled and quickened their steps to the boat—and safety. Just as dawn was piercing the eastern sky, three fishing boats sailed in loose formation from the harbor on their regular trip to sea.

On Kadena Air Base the message "Broken Arrow" was transmitted to higher authorities—*nuclear incident not involving a detonation.*

The White House, Washington, DC

Reacting to the attack on an American aircraft in Okinawa, the President of the United States assembled key members of his cabinet and defense advisors. Secretary of Defense Johnson opened the comments, "Mr. President, the *Broken Arrow* alert involves a missing atomic bomb—and an attack on, and destruction of, a B-52 on the ground at Kadena. The attack was swift and focused, confined to the one area on the airfield containing the plane and the nearby bomb storage. Reports are that there was nothing identifiable about the assailants—in fact they seemed to be dressed in American uniforms and driving USAF marked vehicles … two of them."

"We found the trucks in deep water off the end of a fishing boat dock. We can only suspect that they left by sea—but how … with the bomb? … We are trying to figure out. That's all we know at the moment. We have assets on the ground investigating—"

Secretary of State Acheson chimed in, "Sir, as far as we know the initial broadcast alert spoke only of *Broken Arrow*. News agencies who are reporting on it provided the definition as 'a nuclear incident not involving a detonation,' which is true and accurate. There has been no mention of the fact that the bomb was stolen. Sir, I believe we should keep it that way. No information about the missing bomb. We don't need foreign governments speculating—"

FBI Director Hoover interrupted, "I agree with the Secretary, Mr. President. It is a crime scene. And with war threatening to grow on the Korean peninsula we don't need to acknowledge—we should not acknowledge—that an A-bomb is in the hands of unknown parties."

The President said, "Gentlemen, it is my opinion that we cannot, indeed, should not, attempt to recapture the bomb at this time. The CIA is working to locate it, but we know little of the skills or intentions of the thieves. Are they foreign government or entrepreneurs? I want you all to prosecute the actions in Korea, stay aware of anything your people find out about the bomb—but leave the sleuthing to CIA for now. Agreed?"

Everyone nodded assent and mumbled things in support. The President listened and then directed a question to General of the Army, Omar Bradley, his chairman of the Joint Chiefs of Staff, "General, where are we at Kadena? How secure is the situation?"

"Mr. President," General Bradley replied, "It is on full lock-down with all personnel even remotely connected to the event assembled in a secure situation."

The President stood up at his desk. "That's what I wanted to hear. Gentlemen proceed with your duties, and this event is now a black hole for information. We have a war to face now. Thank you and good day." The group rose and moved toward the door.

"Omar, please stay a moment," The President said. General Bradley returned to his seat.

"Omar, I want to talk to you about General MacArthur. We have some decisions to make soon."

Lubyanka Square, Moscow, Russia, USSR—the KGB

General Suslov turned toward General Lermantov and said, "My suspicion, Arkady Alexandr'ch, is that we have a very high member of the American CIA in our custody ... very high, indeed."

Arkady Lermantov said, "You've told me that. When will we know?"

Suslov answered quietly, "In a moment, my friend. He is being brought up now. We will meet our American prisoner."

Lermantov said, "Who knows that he is in our custody?"

Suslov said, "Only the officer who escorted him, and those who have seen him along the way."

Harmon Wetmore stood stiffly as his jailor pushed the large key into the old lock, turned it and opened the door that squealed with rusty age. Wordlessly the jailor gestured for him to follow. As Wetmore shuffled out of the cell two uniformed guards stepped in behind him. His legs had seen little use in recent weeks and he was slow climbing the many stairs that took them into the core of the formidable building. The guards did not hurry him. Finally they stopped at a door and Wetmore was ushered into a small stark room, one table and two chairs sat in the middle. There was no window, but one wall held a large mirror. Wetmore knew it was two-way—and he knew why. The guards pointed to one of the chairs, then backed out of the room, closing the heavy door with a loud metallic click.

After a few, long moments the door opened and a man of medium build, obvious military bearing, and wearing a civilian suit of clothes entered. Without looking at Wetmore he stepped to the other chair and sat down. Wetmore followed his every move, passively thinking about how he would handle what was to come. He'd been on the receiving end of similar rooms before.

Finally his visitor looked up and made eye contact. He said, "Welcome to our little home, Mr. Wetmore." His English held only a hint of his Russian first language. "I hope your treatment has not been too harsh. I know you've had a long journey to be with us." He looked down and paused, then added, "Your journey was from a place that you should not have been, Mr. Wetmore. I should like to learn more about that."

Harmon Wetmore kept his face expressionless, but kept his eyes locked onto his visitor's eyes, thinking, *I've been playin' this story one way up to now—need to keep it up.* The interrogator, General Vladimir Suslov, sans uniform or introduction, said, "You, Mr. Wetmore, are CIA, American, correct?"

Wetmore leaned forward, his elbows on the table, and answered, "American, for sure. CIA, not for sure. Your fellow in the train told me the airplane was a CIA craft. Don't mean nothin' to me. My paycheck says Civil Air Transport—"

General Suslov laughed. "So you do not know who you really work for?"

Wetmore said, "Don't much care who I work for … long as I got work. Those boys paid good so I signed up. Did what I was told. Course I didn't figure on gettin' myself killed in no plane crash. Bad move on my part, I'm thinkin'."

Harmon Wetmore had given his real name to his original captors. Partly because of slow thinking, but mostly because he had no other story prepared—a lapse for a professional like him. He knew they would connect him to the CIA and his real job at some point, especially here in Moscow with the real KGB pros. But he also knew that if his boss in D.C. was doing his job—the job of covering up the fact that he was even among the missing—then the KGB would not be able to prove anything. He had no photographs on record, nothing public. Thus his role of the 'good old boy just gettin' along' was born.

Suslov stared at him. "You are somewhat old for flying CIA missions, Mr. Wetmore."

Harmon sat back, absently looking at his fingers, and said, "Yah, I'm feelin' it in the old bones too. But my regular job is just workin' around them airplanes—not flyin' in 'em. The kid who was supposed to be there fell out of the plane and broke his damn arm. I just filled in for that one time. Dumb move, eh?"

"I would agree with 'dumb move'," Suslov said. "But I think it's time you tell us your real job, Harmon Wetmore."

"That's it, sir. My job's—that is, it was—to keep those old birds flyin'."

Suslov leaned back in his chair. "Come now. We know that Harmon Wetmore has a very important position in the CIA. And that Harmon Wetmore is about your age. Now, can there be two men of your age and your name in the CIA?"

Harmon sat back, mimicking Suslov's sitting position. "Well, sir. My uncle's name was Harmon and his pappy before him. I've got a cousin Harmon, though I ain't seen him in years. So maybe this other Harmon Wetmore you say is in the CIA is a shirtsleeve relative? I'm sorry. I am who I am. I may be too old for you, but old guys need to eat too—and these CIA boys put good money in my bank back home so maybe I could keep on eatin' when I get *really* old."

Suslov stood and smiled at Wetmore. "That would be a very large coincidence, Mr. Wetmore. Would it not? He turned and opened the door, gesturing the guards to take over and return Wetmore to his cell.

Lieutenant General Vladimir Suslov motioned toward the one-way glass mirror and a moment later Colonel General Arkady Lermantov entered the small interrogation room. Suslov said, "He is either a simple fool or an incredibly skilled agent. What did you see?"

Lermantov replied, "I am beginning to doubt that we have an intelligence coup with this one. Maybe he is just what he says he is."

Suslov sat down and stretched his back. "Have we any word on surveillance in America? Is CIA's Harmon Wetmore missing?"

"Sadly we have only long distance observation," Lermantov responded. "We are not staffed to handle things this close to the CIA. So far they report normalcy in the comings and goings of a person who appears to be Wetmore. One thing keeps me wondering though—we have not heard routine communications related to Wetmore. But, as you said, it is either a cleaver ruse—or what it is what the fool says it is."

Suslov said, "I see nothing to be gained by such a ruse. Do you Arkady?"

"I do not, sir. I do not. Do we send him to the holding camp at Arkhangelskoye until there is more to know?"

Suslov slowly shook his head, deep in thought. "I think not, Arkady. Time may work for us yet. Let him spend some time with Dr. Olav. We will soon see how deep this story goes."

CHAPTER ELEVEN

Washington, DC

Word was waiting for the CIA Director about the *Broken Arrow* incident at Kadena Air Force Base. The President had called out all "the dogs"—elements of General MacArthur's Intelligence and Security units, FBI, CIA, and Air Force were converging on the base. It was very hard for any of them to admit that no advance warning—even suspicion—of such an attack was detected. Also, they had no idea which foreign power—and it must be only a nation state that could accomplish this—would attempt such an audacious act, and succeed.

The Director met with the President in his role of *Force Three* and brought him up to date on Wetmore and the Meads—as little as there was to report. The President was pleased with Dr. Brigit Mead's role in gaining information from China—something no other overt part of the American government could do now. He was not pleased that Wetmore was ruled out as the prisoner that the Chinese held. The President said, "I'm counting on your people. With this situation building in Korea everybody is scrambling to get back on a war footing."

As they were winding up the meeting there was a knock on the Oval Office door. The Vice President stepped into the room, aware that this was a *Force Three* session, he being part of the inner circle, and said, "Mr. President, we have just received a communication from China—from *Force Three*."

The President motioned him into the Oval Office and said, "Sit down. What channel did it come in on?"

Taking a seat next to the Director on the sofa across from the President's desk, The Vice President responded, "Sir, it is from Gui Suen and came in on Wetmore's secure link. He reports that during his return trip from Russia with Mao he learned of the plot by General Su Yu to steal an atomic bomb from somewhere in General MacArthur's command. He also reports that the plot appears to include Russian Colonel General Terenti Shtykov."

The Director spoke up, "Shtykov! He's the Russian, excuse me *Soviet* ambassador to North Korea. In fact, we believe he's calling the shots on this invasion of the South."

The President said, "Well it's more than we knew before—but we've still got to sort this out. Are Stalin and Mao involved? Why? Stalin has a bomb. Is it a 'palace coup' by these two lower level officials? But Russian and Chinese together?"

"Ask Suen for all the detail he can find. And bring me some actionable plans on this! Oh, and confirm if Suen knows of Wetmore's situation—maybe he can find something without endangering himself. On second thought, he may not know because he came in on normal *Force Three* channels. But we still must ask."

"Right away, sir," the Vice President said. He and the CIA Director rose and left the President to his private thoughts. *Are the ambush on Wetmore and the stolen a-bomb linked? Is it China trying to flex new muscles? Or planning to blackmail the UN on Korea? This is more a detective novel than national security.*

Looks like Force Three rises again.

CIA Headquarters, Arlington, Virginia

The Director called a meeting of the department heads closest to the challenge of sorting out the new information. They were assembling in his office when his intercom rang. "What is it Sarah? Line One? Thanks." He picked up his phone and pushed the button.

"Hello, Dr. Mead. Certainly I have a moment for you … yes, yes, there are photographs of the crash site ... I don't know if there are wide-angle shots."

He listened as Brigit explained her thoughts. Wide-angle photos of the crash area could reveal Wetmore's egress route, possibly Wetmore himself if studied in tight detail. "I'll get people on this, Brigit. Thank you. No more word from China? Okay, we'll talk soon." He hung up wondering if he should have shared the recent information he had—but thought better of it for now.

The Director turned to Wetmore's Number Two and asked him to have the analyst who had worked on the photo evidence from the crash to contact him. It was done, and a few minutes later Sarah interrupted the meeting with a gesture to the Director. "Someone here you asked to see, sir," she said.

The Director excused himself and stepped into the outer office to meet a very nervous young analyst, not at all used to being in these premises. "Sir, I have the pictures you asked about. What can I tell you?"

"Do you have wide-angle photos of the scene?"

"Yes, sir. There are three as I remember."

"Have they been thoroughly examined?"

The analyst hesitated. "Sir, I believe we concentrated on the wreckage—trying to get body counts and such. No, sir. The wide-angle shots got no special notice that I'm aware of."

The Director said, "I will meet you in the lab in thirty minutes to examine those pictures in detail."

"Yes, sir!" The analyst turned on his heel and rushed out to retrieve the prize and prepare the equipment.

Santa Barbara, California

"How'd he take your thoughts?" Amos asked Brigit.

"He's going to look at them. I'm sorry, Honey, but I'm just not able to sit around while we don't know where Harm is. At least another look is something …"

Mead said, "Hey, it's a good idea. I'm with you in this helpless—no, this useless feeling. At least you're talking with old friends in China. I'm twiddling my thumbs—"

Brigit cut him off, "Lot of help my friends were."

"They were, Brigit. You know that eliminating some things can lead to adding things—"

"Ha!" Brigit laughed. "Now you're a philosopher."

They both laughed—a nervous, frustrated laugh to fill the void they felt.

Amos Mead was struggling with his thoughts. He wanted desperately to help his friend, Harmon Wetmore, but he now wanted more. From the beginning, 1943 in Los Angeles, Harmon Wetmore had been a mystery. *The guy seemed to be able to get anything, or anyone, that he needed for a mission. When we kidded him about it he just smiled ...*

But Mead's need for answers went further. Now that he found out about *Force Three*, a lot of the "power and influence" is explained. What is still not explained is Wetmore's behavior during their world-wide chase for the killer of the Nazi war criminals. *At first I credited it to Harm's quirky sense of humor—but then began to think it strange. Especially in Wewelsberg Castle ... the last showdown with Hauptman ... He went blank, like he was just watching a show. Strange.*

Mead decided right there that he would dive into the search for his friend. He would find him and ask him all he wanted to know. The Director made sense—CIA couldn't work in the U.S. and *Force Three* was fragmented by country.

Only he—Amos Mead—could cross all the lines and work with the power of the Presidency behind him.

CIA Headquarters, Arlington, Virginia

The Director completed his meeting with each member of his team carrying away a charge to move the mysteries forward. He walked into the CIA photo lab exactly thirty minutes from his meeting with the analyst, who stood holding the three prints awaiting his instructions. The Director reached out his hand and took the photos, looking at each one and noting nothing that could be useful to him. He said, "Son, can you put these on one of your machines here and make them bigger—more details?"

"Yes, sir." The analyst took the photos and placed them under a lens. An enlarged image appeared on a screen above it. In a moment he had sharpened the detail and focus.

"Okay, lets starting looking from the wreckage out," said the Director, thinking of what Brigit had suggested to look for. He added, seemingly to himself, "From the disturbed ground behind and to the right of the plane I'm thinking if someone escaped the crash they'd be moving to the left, into those woods ..."

Over the next few minutes they were not able to detect anyone, or any route through the wooded area. The Director sat back, rubbing his tired eyes when the analyst spoke up, "Sir, take a look at this. Here at the very outer edge of the frame. I totally missed it 'til I unraveled the shadows ..."

The Director swiveled his chair back to the eyepiece and blinked to clear his vision. He saw the analyst's finger circling a dark point at the edge of what he'd uncovered.

"Holy God!" The Director shouted. "Thanks, son."

He rose and rushed back to his office. "Sarah, please get Dr. Mead on the phone."

Moscow, Russia, USSR

Eli Jorgen, the assistant to the Minister Counselor for Commercial Affairs of the America Embassy, reached his usual turn-around point on his morning run—Red Square. A keen student of all things Russian, Jorgen had discovered that the name *Red Square* was not a link to communism as everyone thinks. He found that the name emerged because the Russian word *krasnaya* can mean either *red* or *beautiful* and that the original application was *beautiful* and applied to Saint Basil's Cathedral—gradually being also applied to the square in the 17th century. Jorgen enjoyed his reputation as a fountain of local trivia for the embassy staff.

Jorgen had enlisted in the Army from his hometown of Thief River Falls in Minnesota. He finished his college studies during his first enlistment and applied for a commission. The Army discovered his talent for languages and wearing a freshly minted gold bar on his shoulder he was sent to the language school at Monterey to learn Russian. Upon graduation his next assignment was to the 525th Military Intelligence Group at Fort Meade, Maryland. He was noticed by people with high connections and after thorough vetting by the FBI he was recruited to serve in a small, select, and top secret unit—*Force Three*. First promoted two grades to captain, his identity shifted to a civilian in the diplomatic corps—with a ticket to fly to Moscow.

His morning run covered one mile to the square and the Kremlin, and one mile back to the embassy—Spaso House, the residence of American ambassadors in Moscow since the USSR and the US established formal relations in 1933.

Located at No. 10 Spasopeskovskaya Square it is not far from the Garden Ring Road (*Sadovoye Kol'tso*) and the ancient Moscow region of Arbat. The location greatly facilitated Eli Jorgen's second identity—secret to all but a close knit group around the President of the United State, *Force Three Russia*.

Contact with his Russian *Force Three* counterpart had been routine for a long time, mostly minor background intelligence. But today he spotted a mark that had not been used before. A mark that read *urgent*. This was basic field craft—the innocuous "mark" like a chalk line on a power pole or such. He noted the signal with only a sideward glance, as he was fully aware of his usual tail of three KGB operatives that pretended to be casual folks, much to his comedic pleasure. Sometimes he would stop and tie a shoe, or turn up a side street, then return just to provide them with a startled moment of indecision.

Today he would begin his contact routine as soon as he got to his office, his curiosity high, wondering if it involved Korea or the Broken Arrow incident—or what.

Now he waited for the message to arrive. *Urgent?*

Santa Barbara, California

Brigit picked up the ringing telephone. "This is Dr. Mead, may I help—yes, Director." She listened as he passed on what the wide-angle photographs had revealed. The CIA Director had called the President first, setting their world in motion. Now the Meads will know what comes next. "Russian?" Brigit exclaimed. "So we are going on the assumption that Harmon fell into Russian hands?"

"Yes," the Director responded, "when we got deep enough into those shadows on the edge of the picture we made out the straight lines of some kind of bunker and the tail end of a vehicle ... like a staff jeep type. The analyst enhanced the *CCCP* and numbers painted on it."

The Director went on to explain the Russian presence in Manchuria—left over from the final agreements of WWII. It was not surprising to find them, at least after the analyst made the discovery. Now it all made sense. "With no body evident in the wreckage, no captive of the Chinese—Russia is what's left," he said. "Brigit, I'm asking Amos to get back here as soon as he can."

Brigit said, "Russia? Looks like he needs to bring some warm clothing." The phone clicked off. Brigit sat for a moment as the message sank in. "Amos!"

Mead readied his gear for a hurried trip to Washington—and beyond. At least he was finally getting into the action. He would leave the next day. Today he held his small family close, with no clue when he could do it again.

That night Amos Mead was restless as he tried to find a comfortable position for sleep. Finally he drifted into a fitful slumber.

Pain. Pain. My foot is twisted painfully beneath me.

Now I can only watch ... Otto Hauptmann takes a step forward to the edge of the Black Sun symbol emblazoned in the floor—its golden core reflected in the lights. He is dressed in the uniform of Reichsführer Heinrich Himmler, complete with the round eyeglasses and the Death's Head symbol on the cap glinting silver in the light.

He grips a Luger P-08, his hand hanging at his side.

Slowly he raises the pistol, bending his arm at the elbow.

I cringe, a cold chill running up my back.

Stay calm, stay quiet ... my thoughts raced, but I'm frozen in fascination of the specter in front of me.

I look at Wetmore and Devorah—they seem strangely relaxed--I mouth the words, "I want to keep him talking"

Devorah nods in an off-hand way. Her eyes are giving me a confusing message of indifference. Wetmore stands leaning back against the wall behind the pillar that had deflected the first shot.

I feel like somehow outside of a secret that everyone else is privy to.

Otto Hauptmann finally speaks, "I have one last act to perform to complete the cleansing."

Slowly ... he's putting the pistol back into the leather holster at his hip, leaving the flap unlatched. I watch him reach behind and withdraw a dagger—an SS ceremonial dagger.

Its polished blade flashes in the light. I recognize it as the same kind of dagger that killed the Nazi in Brazil. The dagger that started the bloody journey of revenge.

Strangely I feel no fear.

Again I look over at my two companions.

Devorah meets my glance, but again with no emotion in her eyes. Wetmore is looking down at his feet, still leaning easily against the marble wall, acting as if he's bored.

Bored? What the hell's the matter with these two? Am I the only—?

93

Suddenly against my own fear, my own good judgment, I rush forward. Hauptman's hand moves in a flash and retrieves the Lugar. My heart jumps into his throat, but he doesn't break stride.

... my leg drives forward—not in my control. My arms flail, trying to catch any balance as my foot slides on the thick, freshly wet black painted cross. Now the pain comes! The sliding foot drives forward, my other foot twisting painfully beneath me ... I crash heavily onto my back on the marble floor.

Hauptmann's next move caught my eye. My God ... no—!

Otto Hauptmann, is striding toward me ... he stops at a point opposite the edge of the Black Sun, the Lugar in his hand ... pointed down at me.

Helpless.

I take a deep breath and slowly release it, almost resigned to my fate. What's happening?

A strange calm comes over Hauptmann. He slowly lowers the pistol to his side, then still more slowly kneels to lay it on the cold marble floor.

I can't move. Why?

His eyes burn into mine. But they show no hint of evil.

He stands again, ramrod straight, legs slightly apart in a stiff military pose. Without hesitation, with his left hand he unbuttons his tunic from just below the Iron Cross around his neck to his leather belt and pulls it back to reveal his bare chest.

His right hand with the dagger ... it's pointed at his chest.

I hear his loud cadenced voice saying, "I now complete my mission!"

My God ... What? ... He drove the weapon to its hilt into his chest, aimed into his heart.

His eyes are wide, but no sound comes from his lips, the ornate hilt is throbbing in the middle of a widening dark stain on the tunic.

Why can't I move?

Where is Harmon? Why is he just standing aside?

Where is the Jewess—the woman—just standing too.

Wait, her face ... it's Brigit. Brigit!
I can't move.
Nobody cares ...Hauptmann's dead. I watched him die.
The Jewess—no it is Brigit speaking to me, "Amos, there's one more thing before we let this die. There's somebody else besides Hauptmann. I'm positive there is someone else calling the shots. Somebody—"
Who, Brigit? Who? I can only think. I cannot move.
Something is tugging at my arm ...

"Amos, honey—wake up. You're having a nightmare. Amos."
He opened his eyes with a shocked look—staring into Brigit's worried look. "Wha—oh. Sorry. It, it was real ... back in Germany. Harm acting strange ..."
Brigit just sat on the edge of the bed quietly rubbing his shoulders.
"Brig, this whole thing is confused. Harm's a prisoner—in China? No—maybe Russia? An a-bomb is stolen—Chinese, Russian? Are they connected—Harm and the bomb?"
"Honey, you'll not find answers tonight," Brigit said in her most soothing voice. "I'm going to get you some milk—then you're assignment is to sleep. You've got a long boring day tomorrow on an airplane to confuse yourself."

95

CHAPTER TWELVE

Moscow, Russia, USSR

Eli Jorgen did not have long to wait as Mr. Chin knocked and entered his office carrying a piece of stained and rumpled paper. He did not speak, but simply handed the material to Jorgen, bowed slightly and retreated, closing the office door.

Mr. Chin was the last leg of a carefully organized chain of handoffs that provided Jorgen contact with his Russian counterpart, Ivan Ivanovitch Glebov, who served as special assistant to Nikita Sergeyevich Khrushchev, the head of the Communist Party in Moscow.

Jorgen and Glebov did not officially know each other, although they attended occasional official functions at the Kremlin. Glebov was recruited by Jorgen's predecessor. Though his personal beliefs were very nationalistic, he had suffered greatly under Stalin's purges of the party and military. His father General Yev Kamenev and his two brothers, Army Captain Yu Kamenov and Air Force Lieutenant A.L. Kamenov were executed on sham charges. He spent time in a labor camp but was released to go to school. He excelled in his studies and gradually gained his own credentials with the party—and Khrushchev.

With the guidance of the CIA Chief of Station the new *Force Three* communication process was set up. Khrushchev was working on changing the structure of the collective farms around Moscow and the activity gave the intelligence team a natural pass-through base in the form of a Moscow vegetable and meat distributor. Khrushchev had established a kitchen to serve his office and that of the aging President Stalin. Glebov arranged for the best quality produce and meats to be delivered on a regular basis to the kitchen, where he supervised the unloading and passed on the quality. When a wooden crate of produce was unloaded a message was slipped under the stained paper lining the box and a simple mark affixed to the end. The wooden crates were returned to the distributor and used again. Refilled with produce, the marked crate joined a load delivered to a small, seedy shop on Pl. Kursfogo Vokzala that passed for a restaurant. Located near the Kursky Train Station, the small restaurant was actually quite popular with the locals.

As the crates were unloaded and returned to the delivery service a small soiled bit of paper was slipped into the apron pocket of the proprietor, a slight, graying Chinese lady who is married to the Russian owner of the shop. Neither Glebov nor Jorgen knew any of the individual connections in this chain—except Mr. Chin.

In spite of constant harassment by Soviet security services, Mr. Chin and his brother Tang had worked at the American Embassy for years and had been vetted to a fault as to their loyalties. They had come to the Soviet Union years before with their sister and had married Russians, but could not leave the country because they could not secure exit visas for their families.

Eli Jergen opened the paper to see what he expected, an encoded message hand-written on the soiled surface. It consisted of lines of numbers.

He reached for a certain book that rested among his collection of Russian literature. The book was Mikhail Lermontov's *A Hero of Our Time* written in 1840 and later translated. He opened it to the middle and retrieved a sheet that held the key to the *straddling code* currently in use and began the tedious task of transcribing the numbers into letters—and a message.

Lubyanka Prison is holding a male American prisoner, ID unknown. Seen in interrogation by KGB. Trying to ID but access limited. Advise.

Santa Barbara, California

Brigit saw Amos off at the airport with little ceremony or tears. This was getting too routine for them and she vowed to change that upon his safe return. Mead's first stop was D.C. for documents, a new identity and cover complete with a little training, then on to Moscow to meet with Eli Jorgen and no idea what to look for.

Brigit returned home to Islay St. She sat at the kitchen table with a mug of stale coffee thinking. Finally she picked up the phone and called Amy Sokol.

"Can you take Nathan for the day, Amy?" She asked, knowing the answer. Next she called the special number she had for Navy Communication Station Rincon and asked for Lt. Commander Wilson.

"Commander Wilson," Brigit said, "I need to come down and contact China as we did before. Can that be arranged?"

Lt. Commander Wilson said, "Absolutely, Dr. Mead. I'll have a car meet you at the lower gate."

Brigit hung up and went in to change her clothes, and don her cryptic Naval Intelligence ID. She went out to the Terraplane and drove south, mentally rehearsing her message for *Shandian yun.*

After the short drive she pulled in to the lower gate of the Rincon facility. A gray U.S. Navy jeep was parked nearby, its driver dozing at the wheel. As her wheels ground onto the gravel at the road's edge behind the jeep the young sailor sat up with a start and leaped from his seat. Brigit got out smiling and walked around the jeep without an invitation. The sailor trotted over to open the gate, returned and drove them through, again dismounting to close the gate.

"Glad you were on duty," Brigit said to the driver, who was also the radio operator who had led here through the process the first two times here.

"Me too, Ma'am. Your radio work is impressive," he replied, thinking *and you're sure not hard to look at.* "We've already got

Hawaii working on the China connection. Should be up by the time we get there."

Brigit smiled and said, "I'm always impressed with the Navy's work."

The driver just smiled broadly.

Within a few minutes they were sitting at the console with Lt. Commander Wilson perched just behind them. In her headset Brigit heard, "Connection secure, Rincon. It's all yours." Brigit keyed her microphone, "*Shandian yun,* this is *Glinda.* Thank you for responding to my call."

"You are welcome, *Glinda*—though we must not make these contacts too regularly."

"Understood, *Shandian.* My first call was a request for your help in locating my friend who may be a guest there. I know you cannot add information or take any action. But I would like to add that knowing if he is dead or alive is desired also."

General Yang Kuisong—*Shandian*—replied, "I shall report when I have information, *Glinda.*" Quickly he added, "The young prisoner has not arrived yet—"

Brigit interrupted the general. She was keeping strict control of the pace and tone of the conversation, but she kept her tone soft and feminine, "Thank you, sir. I have one other thought to share. *Sun Tzu* spoke of moral law. He saw his principle of harmony to be not unlike the *Tao* of *Lao Tzu* ... at least in its moral aspect. I do not intend to be too philosophical in my thinking, but I believe the principles of harmony may bring you and me an opportunity."

Shandian said, "I am listening, *Glinda.* Your thoughts intrigue me. Please continue."

Brigit smiled, then spoke, "At present there is a wall between our countries—a wall that is high and sturdy and built on misunderstandings and poor knowledge. It came to me that you and I have created a small hole through that wall. It is too small to threaten anyone—but large enough to speak through and share thoughts and views. We do not have to brag of our small piece of daylight and sound ... but I pray that we will keep it open. It is strange for me to cite *Sun Tzu*, the man of the *Art of War*, for my peaceful overture. But it seemed to be appropriate in trying to make my feelings clear. Is there a chance, *Shandian*, to accomplish it?"

"More than a chance," Yang Kuisong responded, speaking softly. "Consider it done on my end."

Brigit said, "Thank you, sir. This is all I have—hoping for information about my friend. I look forward to our next call. *Glinda* out."

The radio operator, Lt. Commander Wilson and Brigit sat quietly for a moment, letting the tensions ease. The radio operator finally spoke, "Smooth, Ma'am. You are absolutely smooth."

Wilson added, "Your work is impressive. There is no question why you are valued by our Intel folks."

Brigit smiled and took a deep breath, releasing it slowly. "Thank you. Now, mister, may we head down the hill? I've got a baby boy waiting for dinner."

The sailor took the approving nod from his commander and said, "Aye, aye, Ma'am." His broad smile remained as he held the door and trotted to the jeep.

Later in the day she telephoned the Director of the CIA and told him what she'd done and explained her reasoning. There was no resistance from the Director. He said, "Brigit, it will take a moment for me to absorb that. You're way ahead of me—but it feels like the right direction."

Military Headquarters, Dongchen District, Beijing, China

General Yang Kuisong sat back in his chair, pondering the many possible meanings or implications of *Glinda's* call—and offer. After a moment he called in his Aide. "Bring the American prisoner to me, please."

The young American CIA flyer had endured the trip from his prison to Beijing, wondering what would come next. At least there was no torture or interrogation during the train trip. By contrast, it was almost pleasurable—though he knew it would not last. He had held to his story, truthful about the mission but not so about his falsely documented identification. Now he sat in what he determined to be a small military prison because of the guards. It was low tension and he was alone—until a small guard mount, marching crisply, approached his cell. The senior person opened the cell and motioned to him. *"Nǐ huì gēn wǒ lái,"* (You will follow me) he said.

The American stood and shrugged as he stepped toward the cell door, following orders as he could only assume they were. They marched to an adjoining building within the compound, entered and proceeded down a stark hallway, stopping at a door being held open by the Aide to General Yang Kuisong. The leader of the detail saluted and stepped back against the opposite wall as security. The American, "John," entered the small room and stood at attention in front of the Chinese general officer seated at the far end of a table. "Please, sit," General Kuisong said, almost gently, as he pulled out a chair.

"John" sat down, still at attention.

It didn't take long for Kuisong to decide that the young flier had no working knowledge past what he's told them. They already knew of the flights, they had captured the Chinese agents and had broken up the plan to cause dissent among the people. He also knew that release of his captive would not be soon—nor word sent to the Americans. Not yet.

CIA airman "John" returned to his cell.

CHAPTER THIRTEEN

AP July 1950—North Korean 6th Army drove unnoticed down the West Coast, capturing Chonju and outflanking the U.S. Eighth Army. Eighth Army is withdrawing to prepared positions. Infantry with attached Marine Brigades arrive at Pusan in time to reinforce U.S. and ROK troops falling further back. Pusan Perimeter defense established along the Naktong River.

Jeju Island, Korea

Just after nautical twilight, with navigation via the sea's horizon now impossible, the small fleet of fishing boats hove-to in the shelter of the hook of land that jutted out below the village of Seongsan. A volcanic crater loomed over the scene, its caves providing the final resting place for the cargo on one of the boats. A tall Chinese gentleman stood on the concrete quay defining the small harbor. He stood out among the group with him, shorter, sturdy and looking of men used to work. The gentle lapping of the sea against the barrier and the smell of seaweed mixing on the breeze from the open sea belied the stark scientific—and horrific—mission under way.

On a gesture from the Chinese man one of the group held up a small light and blinked a pre-determined number of times, aiming it at the fishermen. A single light blinked back and a moment later the sound of the diesel engines drifted to the quay. The Chinese gentleman waved another signal to the darkened vehicle that sat back in the shadows. Immediately it moved slowly toward the group.

The boat edged into the quay and the team on the deck of the largest boat recognized the same silhouette as one of the trucks they had left submerged in Okinawa. It was indeed the twin of their truck, built especially for the task at hand. The fishing boat's captain stepped ashore with the team and the Chinese man asked, "You had a pleasant trip, I presume."

"Yes, sir," the captain replied. "There are many American ships about. Some came close and exchanged waves with us friendly fishermen just trying to feed our families. It looked from their courses that Pusan is a main destination."

"Correct," The Chinese man said. "We have enjoyed much success. They are pushed into a perimeter around Pusan."

The captain shook his grizzled head. "I will assume that is good news to you. It means little to us who wins what. We are happy to help you with this mission—the pay is good. But at the end we must fish—and survive."

The tall Chinese man just smiled and turned to watch the men. Within half an hour of quiet work the bomb rested in the truck's dolly and was moving toward the volcano, the tall Chinese man in the truck's cab.

His name is George Huang, the son of an American mother and a Han Chinese father. They were Protestant missionaries who returned to the United States before the war when George was in his late teens. George excelled in school, especially mathematics and science, and earned a scholarship to MIT, graduating with a PhD in Physics—specializing in nuclear physics. He returned to China to study his roots in Han history and became entangled with the Communist movement. He met General Su Yu at a meeting and the two soon understood that they shared a concern about where the Mao movement would lead.

The fishing boat's captain had one more mission—to sail to Inchon, Korea, and to return the party of raiders to their duties in Pyongyang.

George Huang stayed on Jeju and awaited the progress of events beyond his control.

Moscow, Russia, USSR

Amos Mead deplaned at Moscow's Domodedovo Airport after a mind-numbing flight from Washington, D.C. to London and on to Moscow. Eli Jorgen, assistant to the Minister Counselor for Commercial Affairs of the America Embassy, met him in customs and assisted with his progress through the red-tape. Speaking fluent Russian helped. Neither man relied on any diplomatic status.

As they exited the terminal a black Yukon with tinted windows pulled up to the curb. Jorgen said, "Pretty hard to miss the embassy ride, Amos. We'll get you to the hotel and give you a chance to catch up before the work starts."

"Fine with me," Amos Mead said, noting that Jorgen was the same height and about the same weight as he—but younger. His blond hair was longish and tended to fall over one eye. Mead's crew cut precluded that problem and even if his hair was grown out, aging thinning rendered it moot. He was having some difficulty concentrating on much of anything now, just ready for a shower and long sleep.

The Yukon pulled up to the Metropol Hotel after the twenty-three mile drive from the airport. The hotel was opposite the Bolshoi Theater and a few minutes' walk from Red Square and the Kremlin. Perfect for his purposes.

Jorgen handed Mead his card. "Here's my number. We'll pick you up tomorrow at ten and get on with our business."

Mead looked at the card. "Thanks, ten it is." He was not yet aware of it, but Jorgen knew that every word was being recorded. Mead allowed the doorman to take his one bag and followed him to the desk.

A few minutes later he was sound asleep.

The listeners heard only the deep breathing of an exhausted man.

KGB Prison: Lubyanka Square, Moscow, Russia, USSR

Harmon Wetmore sat in his cell, a shiver going through his body as he once again felt the temperature in this part of his prison.

Not as warm as that interrogation room, he thought. *I should have stretched that session out a while longer. Can't tell what's coming. Wonder if that pompous Ruskie bought my academy award performance?*

The building where Wetmore sits has a long history, even before the KGB. Built on Lubyanka Square in 1898 it was originally the grand headquarters of the Russian insurance company, *Rossiya*. In grand neo-baroque style it is noted for its parquetry and pale green walls that survive today. Following the Bolshevik Revolution the building was seized by the new government and turned into the headquarters of the secret police— the *Cheka*. The basement storage areas were turned into cells. Soon there was a joke circulating that the building on Lubyanka Square was "the tallest in Moscow—because you could see Siberia from the basement."

Although the Soviet secret police changed its name many times, its headquarters remained in this building—as did the prison where the Deputy Director of the Central Intelligence Agency of the United States sat shivering in the damp cold of his cell. But the worse had not yet come. He heard the footsteps descending the concrete steps and proceeding down the cellblock. Wetmore had seen no other prisoners up to now and he wondered if they were coming for him once more. *So soon?* The familiar jailor and two guards stopped in front of his cell, this time with a companion, a short, gray haired, bespectacled dwarf of a man with a sallow complexion and sunken eyes that looked like dark holes in his head in the subdued light of the cell. The cell door was unlocked and the gnome came in and stood in front of Wetmore. "Good afternoon, Mr. American. I am Doctor Sigmund Olav and for some reason you have earned my services." He gestured to the two guards who moved in and grabbed Wetmore's arms, dragging him to his feet then pinning his arms high behind his back.

So now it starts, Wetmore thought, trying not to grimace at the pain in his shoulders.

Dr. Olav stood toe to toe with his prisoner, looking up into his face, his putrid breath nearly causing Wetmore to choke as he said, "Вы понимаете, что мне от вас нужно?"

Wetmore understood *'do you understand what I need from you'* but his expression stayed blank. He was feigning fear—but only barely feigning as the reality of the intent of this gnome sunk in. The doctor repeated himself, this time in accented English. Wetmore opened his eyes wide and shook his head violently, now grimacing from the increasing pain. Again the gnome nodded at the two guards. They released their hold on his arms and immediately stripped Wetmore's grimy jacket from his shoulders. Before he could feel relief from the pain Wetmore felt his arms once again wrenched back, but this time tied by a thong produced by one of the guards. He was lifted until he could barely touch the floor and the thong was tied to a rusty iron ring fastened to the spalling concrete wall of the cell. He steeled himself to the pain and worked his thoughts down deep in his mind. But he was quickly reminded that, *I'm way too far past my prime for this ... we'll see—*

"Mr. Wetmore," the gnome said with a thick accent. "Do you know of the *Psikhuskas* in my country?"

Wetmore moved his head from side to side without trying to look up. The answer was *no*, and a truthful answer for him.

The gnome continued, "The *Psikhuskas* are mental hospitals, some where I work. We really do not care of your mind's condition when you come to us—but we see that there is not much left when, if, you leave. People like you who defy the state tend to disappear in the *Psikhuskas*. You can avoid this you know. Have you anything to say to me?"

Wetmore again moved his head from side to side without trying to look up. The answer was still *no*. But now he was weighing his options.

Dr. Olav grunted and made a quick gesture to one of the guards who rushed from the cell and returned dragging a length of rubber hose with a nozzle on the end. Another quick gesture and the second guard ripped Wetmore's trousers loose and dropped them down around his ankles.

Then the water came, a frigid spray that moved from head to toe. Soon water dripped from his hair down past his eyes to the floor. He began to shiver uncontrollably. The already dim lights went out, plunging the cell into inky, cold silence—then the water came again, and again, and again.

Metropol Hotel, Moscow, Russia, USSR

Eli Jorgen, assistant to the Minister Counselor for Commercial Affairs of the America Embassy sat patiently in a side area off the lobby of the fine old hotel admiring the frescoed ceiling and gilded statuary. He marveled that such finery was maintained—indeed, survived—the early Soviet upheavals. Of course he knew the answer was that they needed somewhere to showcase themselves for the western bourgeoisie elite visitors, bringing capital and prestige to the new regime.

He looked up to see a much refreshed Amos Mead approaching and rose to greet him. "Good morning, Mr. Mead. I trust you—"

Mead interrupted his host, "Yes, Eli, I slept well. Now I need strong coffee—and please call me Amos. I also need some good news from you. Is there any more word on the American prisoner? Anyway we can identify him?"

"Mr. Mead—Amos," Eli Jorgen said. "I know well of your concern. We search for a mutual friend. I know you've been briefed. But this is not the place to talk of it. So let us get some breakfast."

Mead started to resist, then realized that everywhere in this country must be considered a listening post for the KGB.

"Lead the way, Eli." Mead also did not resist Eli's ordering traditional *zavtrac*—breakfast—for them, including a bowl of *kasha*, dark bread and cheese, and a boiled egg. Next to the coffee served in a clear glass nestled in an elegant filigree brass holder, Mead most enjoyed the *kasha*—a multi-grain porridge that he promised himself he'd try to duplicate at home. When they had finished with a final refill of the rich coffee, unique to this dining room, especially for western guests, Mead and Jorgen walked out to the front of the hotel. The black Yukon pulled up a moment later and they got in. Jorgen said the driver, "The Kremlin, sergeant."

The non-uniformed U.S. Marine driver who spoke fluent Russian pulled the car into traffic for the short trip. Jorgen turned toward Mead and with a sweeping motion of his hand, said, "I know this rig's clean, Amos. We've got a minute to talk. Your cover is a trade mission, specifically to see about importing Russian tractors. I'm shooting for the top today and have arranged a short meeting with the top Commie in Moscow—Mr. Khrushchev."

Mead spoke up, "Good God, Eli. Can I pull that off?"

Jorgen answered, "Don't worry. This is just a protocol—social type visit. But there is a reason. Though it is not publicized, Stalin is really ill. We think old Nikita is first up to grab his still-warm chair when he kicks off. He's got some brownie points to acquire and we can appear to help. Also, and critical to our search, *Force Three Russia* is close to Khrushchev. We will not have direct contact today, but it's a step in the right direction."

The Yukon stopped in heavy traffic. The driver spoke over his shoulder, "If we were proper Russian royalty we could use that empty lane in the middle—but since we're poor peasant 'mericans it's the creep and crawl lane only."

Eli laughed and said, "You are irreverent, Sarge—but being a Marine I understand—"

Mead cut in, "Hey, I'm a Marine! Cut him some slack!"

All three laughed and Eli said, "Let me give you the Nikita 101 lesson since we've got a minute. This guy honestly believes that it's only a matter of time until Communism buries Capitalism."

Amos said, "No surprise there—"

Eli continued, "Sure, but he's got big plans. Now that the Russians are making tractors instead of tanks, Nikita sees them able to bury the West with superior food production. He fancies himself an agricultural expert—even though he screwed up once already with his Kazakhstan and Siberia great experiment."

Amos asked, "That didn't hit the history book yet—what screw up is that?"

"Well, Amos, he initiated a truly massive program to put vast tracts of virgin lands in Kazakhstan and Siberia under the plow. He "enlisted" thousands of urban *Komsomol* volunteers and shipped them to the fields. These Young Communist League city folks—kind of like Boy Scouts, only political--brought little but their enthusiasm with them to the open steppes. You can figure out how that worked out."

Mead said, "I thought that sort of thing brought permanent residence in a Siberian dacha."

"Usually. But it seems from our sources that Stalin was so paranoid about a coup that he brought Nikita to Moscow, put him in charge of the Communist Party here, and ensconced him in a very visible, and nearby office."

Amos Mead sat back in his seat and said, "I'm getting the picture. I need to do a lot of smiling and listening—and learning the ropes. Just wish there was time … I've got an idea … whoops, no time. Just follow my lead when we get in there."

The Yukon pulled up in a parking area marked только дипломат—diplomat only. A uniformed sentry opened the rear door of the well-marked American diplomatic vehicle and Jorgen and Mead climbed out just as a civilian came through the gate toward them. "Good morning, I trust you found us okay," said Ivan Ivanovitch Glebov, aide to Nikita Khrushchev, in impeccable English. "Please follow me."

Entering a side door where another armed guard stood ramrod straight as they passed by, they proceeded down a long corridor. Mead made note of the fact that there was little or no movement to be seen, unlike typical U.S. government buildings. Finally Glebov stopped at a glass topped door marked НЕ ВХОДИТЬ (Private), opened it and stepped back for Mead and Jorgen to enter. They were in an outer office waiting room, tastefully decorated with an elegant Afghan rug, a tapestry on the wall depicting a revolutionary scene, and leather overstuffed chairs flanking a finally carved oak table sporting a vase of flowers. Glebov said, "Please take a seat, gentlemen." He opened another door to the inner office and closed it behind him. Mead looked around the room and said, "Just your typical peasant décor, eh Eli?"

Eli Jorgen smiled and placed a finger in front of his lips reminding Mead to mind his words in a Soviet space—unless they were for publication to the KGB. A moment later the inner door opened and Glebov announced, "Mr. Khrushchev will see you now."

KGB Prison: Lubyanka Square, Moscow, Russia, USSR

After an hour that seemed a full day, Wetmore decided it was time to move the process forward. He stoically endured the water, using the very depths of his training—though it didn't make the experience any less agonizing. "Okay, okay—p—p—please, please stop the water ... Doctor who-ever-you-are—please ..."

The lights came on, back to their dim yellow, and the next spray of water did not come. Doctor Sigmund Olav—still Wetmore's image of a gnome—stepped into the cell. In his deep Slavic accent he went directly to his business, "Your name?"

"Ha—Ha— Harmon Wetmore. Damn it I'm freezing ..."

Doctor Olav signaled the guard to release the prisoner from the wall shackle and replace his clothes, though their wet state still provided waves of shivers. Wetmore slumped to his knees on the cell floor, his legs had lost feeling. He rubbed his calves with cold numb hands.

"And your nationality?"

"American—" Wetmore continued to rub his legs.

"Your employer?"

"CIA." Now he stopped rubbing and stared at the floor.

The gnome spoke to the guards, "*Privedite yego!*" (Bring him.) Olav had decided it was time to move to the next level of his work and extract everything the generals wanted from this man. A third guard dragged an old Russian army field stretcher into the cell. The other two roughly dragged Wetmore to it and flopped him face down on the rough canvas. It had the coppery smell of death, of human body fluids. He knew that this had not been used to carry live prisoners. Live prisoners seldom left this place.

He tried to minimize any deep breathing. His shivering helped him with it. The guards lifted him and followed the gnome to the stairs where the rear guard lifted the stretcher just high enough so Wetmore did not slide off its gross surface. At the top of the stairs they carried him down a hallway that Wetmore could see was not a cell block. The walls were old, but clean light green tile. They followed the gnome into a room with a large light fixture on the ceiling and a metal table directly beneath it. Glass front metal cabinets lined the walls.

An operating room—or morgue, Wetmore thought as they set the stretcher on the floor and bodily lifted him onto the cold steel table, laying him on his back. The light came on, bathing him in a glare he could not see beyond. His arm was roughly stretched out onto a board that protruded from the table and strapped tightly to it. The voice of the gnome penetrated the blaze, "We will finish our conversation here, Mr. Wetmore. With some things that will make it easy for you to remember—and give you some rest."

He felt the rubber strap tightened around his arm. Wetmore knew what was coming. He had experienced it before—in his CIA Advanced Survival School. He knew to keep his mantra, his story running through his thoughts.

He knew he could beat the gnome. *Maybe, hopefully ...*

A white coated attendant roughly pushed the needle into a vein in his now numb arm. Wetmore could barely make out his features at the edge of the light as he shivered and felt himself slip into the unwelcome arms of Morpheus.

The Soviet truth serum, codename SP-117, analyzed by western sources as sodium thiopental, coursed through his veins. A voice drifted out of the now shimmering halo of light, light that had taken on rainbow hues and waves and swirls to Harmon Wetmore's squinting eyes.

"Your Name?"

"Harmon Wetmore."

"Your Nationality?"

"American."

"Your employer?"

"CIA ... Civil Air Transport."

Doctor Olav wrinkled his brow, missing a beat in his rhythmic interrogation. "Your job?"

"Aircraft mechanic."

"Do you fly missions?"

"Sometimes, when they tell me to."

"Where is your home?"

"San Diego."

"Do you live in Washington?"

"I live in San Diego."

"Your employer?"

"CAT ... CIA ... ABC ..." Wetmore drifted deeper than he wanted to, but the relaxation was the most profound he'd felt in an eternity. "CAT. Civil ... Civil Air Transport ... mechanic."

Unheard by Harmon Wetmore, Doctor Olav told the attendant to remove the intravenous hypodermic, and for the guards to return him to a dry cell. As the attendant complied, Doctor Olav said, quietly to himself, "...loosens the tongue ... has no taste, no smell, no color and no side effects ... except our friend will not remember

112

our visit." The white coated attendant nodded to Olav and finished his task—then quickly disappeared down the hall.

He had another mission to attend to. Doctor Sigmund Olav prepared to make his report to the generals—a report he knew would not please them.

CHAPTER FOURTEEN

AP July 1950—Republic of Korea's capitol, Seoul, falls to North Korean forces. Bridges across the Han River have been destroyed with most of ROK army's best units trapped with their equipment on the northern side. President Truman has committed troops to enforce the United Nations demand.

CIA Headquarters, Arlington, Virginia

The CIA Director, on his personal telephone line to the White House, responded to a question from the President of the United States, "Yes, Mr. President. Mead is in Moscow and is working with *Force Three* to develop more information on the stolen bomb and on Wetmore's whereabouts."

The President said, "Tell me more about his assignment."

"Sir, Mead is traveling under cover of being an attorney for a trade group looking to buy Soviet tractors—"

The President interrupted, "Who the hell wants to buy Soviet tractors? No farmer I ever knew."

"No sir, Mr. President. If he gets an order we'll give him a medal—but the fact is his role is gaining him personal access to Khrushchev—"

Again the President cut in, "Khrushchev? My God, man ... Mead talks to the Russians ... his wife talks to the Chinese. Who the hell needs the Department of State? Rhetorical question, of course."

The Director laughed. "Yes, sir. And once again we see the wisdom of FDR's creating this unorthodox group. During the war they accomplished things—and once more they—"

"Yes, yes—*Force Three* rises once more to go where no attorney general would allow anyone to go. Keep me posted!"

"Yes sir, thank you, yes sir, just as soon as we get anything." The Director of the CIA hung up his telephone, thinking how lucky he's been with the President's patience. Patience was certainly not what he was feeling right now. *Missing: one atomic bomb and one deputy director of the CIA. What's next?*

The Kremlin, Moscow, Russia, USSR

Eli Jorgen and Amos Mead followed Ivan Ivanovitch Glebov into the inner office. Nikita Khrushchev rose from his desk and with a broad smile stepped around it and offered his hand. "Добро пожаловать в Советский Союз." Glebov translated, "Welcome to the Soviet Union." Both men nodded. Mead said, "It is an honor to be able to meet you on such short notice. I realize that we will not bother you with our business, but I did want to recognize your service on another level." Glebov translated once again—a slight look of curiosity on his face as he did. Khrushchev smiled as the translation was completed and said, "What level would that be?"

Mead anticipated the translation and continued, "I am a student of history and a veteran of World War II. In my studies I find that you took the lead to mobilize Soviet troops to fight the Nazis in the Ukraine and at Stalingrad."

Glebov began to translate simultaneously for Mead. "I read that you arrived in Stalingrad for the beginning of that great battle and worked with General Chuikov in planning the city's defense."

Khrushchev now smiled more broadly. "My role was not so large."

Mead continued, "And you stayed in the city for the worst of the fighting—even facing death at more than one point—" This time Mead waited until Glebov had caught up to his dialog. He caught Glebov's nod and went on, "Soviet history told me that you proposed a counterattack. But then you found that Zhukov had already established a plan to break out from your defensive positions and encircle the Germans. The plan was called, I believe, Operation Uranus, and was being kept secret even from Stalin."

Khrushchev said, "It was a great battle—and successful as you know. You are indeed a student of the Great War."

"Yes, sir," Mead continued. "And I found that even before Operation Uranus began you spent much time checking on troop readiness and morale, even interrogating Nazi prisoners. I am impressed, as I said, sir, with your service." As Glebov finished translating the last sentence, Mead rose and said, "Mr. Khrushchev, we have taken enough of your valuable time. With your permission may we retire with Mr. Glebov and conduct some business between us that should be lucrative and productive for us both?"

Nikita Khrushchev once again rose from his desk with a broad smile and shook hands vigorously with his two guests, obviously pleased with Mead's history lesson. He said, and Glebov translated, "Yes indeed. Vladimir will show you to the proper staff of our Minister of Foreign Trade—Anastas Pavelovich Mikoyan. Anastas Pavel'ch would see you personally but he is out of the country at the moment."

Amos Mead, Eli Jorgen and Ivan Ivanovitch Glebov exited the inner office and walked directly to the hallway. Knowing that they were being watched and listened to—and that he had no intention of meeting with Soviet trade weenies just yet—Mead said, "Mr. Glebov, I'm very sorry but I just remembered a very critical call from my clients that I'm expecting at the hotel. This is terribly embarrassing, but can we postpone our meeting with Mikoyan's office?"

"Of course, Mr. Mead," Ivan Ivanovitch Glebov said. "We will reschedule at your convenience. Just contact my office."

Mead noticed the hint of a smile on Glebov's face as they played out their charade. A door opened farther down the hall and an attractive young woman emerged, hesitated for a moment as she looked at the trio, then walked quickly in their direction. "Comrade Glebov, we received an answer to your question," she said as she handed Ivan Ivanovitch Glebov a folded sheet of paper. Glebov opened the note and read it, then folded it again, adding two more folds.

"Thank you, *Annushka*—"

Seeming to blush at the use of a pet name in front of strangers, Glebov's secretary interrupted him, "And Comrade Khrushchev called to request you return to his office."

"Then I must bid farewell to our friends here and ask you to escort them to the west entrance." Glebov turned to Mead and Jorgen and shook hands. Mead felt the object in his hand and deftly palmed it as they stepped away. "We will be in touch soon, Mr. Glebov. Thank you."

As they followed the young lady toward the stairs, Mead chuckled to himself at the thought of a typical female Russian *byurokraty* being over 200 pounds with a stainless steel tooth in front. *This bureaucrat changes my image. Maybe there's hope for the future of Mother Russia.* The uniformed guard at the door snapped to attention as Eli Jorgen, assistant to the Minister Counselor for Commercial Affairs of the America Embassy, and Amos Mead, attorney and pseudo undercover agent for the CIA on loan to *Force Three* for the duration, climbed into their American Yukon, the door held open by an out-of-uniform U.S. Marine who said, "*Gde, gospoda?*"

"Where to, Sergeant?" Eli looked at his watch. "You know that restaurant near Kursky Station? That's where. And practice your Russian on someone else."

"Aye, aye, sir. Chinese cuisine it is."

The black sedan blended smoothly into the late morning traffic where its diplomatic plates still did not allow the driver to use the empty center lane reserved for their host's elite *byurokraty.* In the back seat Mead handed the note he'd received from *Force Three Russia* to Eli.

Подтвердите, что заключенный американец. Его зовут Хармон Уэтмор. Он подтвердил, что он служащий летного экипажа гражданского воздушного транспорта ЦРУ, и был взят в плен в Маньчжурии.

Fluent in Russian, Eli read it aloud, "Confirmed, prisoner is American. His name is Harmon Wetmore. Confirmed that he is aircrew for the CIA's Civil Air Transport and was captured in Manchuria."

Mead sat back in his seat with an audible sigh. *We found you, Harm.*

Back at the Kremlin, Gebov retraced his steps to the office of Nikita Khrushchev. "You wanted to see me, Comrade Khrushchev?"

"Yes. Very interesting man, your visitor. What do you know of him?"

"Mr. Mead?"

Khrushchev nodded.

"He is an attorney representing clients wishing to buy tractors from us."

Khrushchev shook his head. "No, no—before that. He said he was a veteran. What did he do in the war?"

Gebov continued, "Mead was a Major in the U.S. Marine Corps attached to the OSS—"

"So!" Khrushchev interrupted. "He was a spy!"

"Not exactly, sir," Gebov said. "His job was to find German spies who … who were spying in the Soviet Union. He also conducted missions to China and nearby countries for the OSS." Gebov was careful to omit Mead's assignment for the CIA after the war.

"*Хорошо* (okay), he is an interesting man. I would like to speak to him more at some time," Khrushchev said, looking back to the material on his desk.

Gebov knew he was dismissed.

Pl. Kursfogo Vokzala, Moscow, USSR

Mead was surprised when they stopped in front of the small, seedy looking establishment on *Kursfogo Vokzala Place*, but the driver knew exactly where he was and Eli immediately climbed out of the black Yukon. "Park this thing, Sergeant, and join us for lunch," Eli said. He led Mead to the door and into the small establishment that belonged to the sister of his trusted Mr. Chin. Mead knew better than to speak specifically about their morning discovery, but he did say, "So with what we know now, where do we go with—"

"Later, Amos. We have a lot of figuring out left to do."

The husband of Chin's sister was Russian so the cuisine reflected and eclectic assembly of Cantonese and Russian. Eli added, "I recommend the *borscht*, Amos, if you're up for Russian. And the *dim sum* is outstanding."

Chin's sister brought menus for the men, including now the Marine driver. When Eli opened his, he spied the tip of something that didn't quite belong peeking out from behind an insert in the menu. He looked up in time to catch the ladies brief nod. He slid what became three dark photographs of men seated at ... *this very table. Two of the men were Chinese the other ... a Russian general.*

Mead caught his motions but did not look directly at him or ask anything. Eli slipped the three grainy photos into his coat in a single motion unseen by anyone beyond his table.

After eating—Mead did have the borscht saying, "When in Rome …"—the trio returned to Spaso House, the residence of the American ambassador and Embassy.

Spaso House, American Embassy, Moscow, USSR

Mr. Chin was waiting in Eli Jorgen's office when Mead and Jorgen returned. Chin spoke, "I hope it was proper for me to have the photos delivered to you as we did, sir. My sister took the initiative when you surprised her with your visit."

"Not a problem, Mr. Chin. Her tradecraft is fine. Are you familiar with what is in the photographs?" As Eli spoke he spread the three on his desk. Mead moved to the edge of the desk and sat, leaning over for his first look at them.

"I am, sir. The Russian is Colonel General Terenti Shtykov. The shorter Chinese man is General Su Yu. We have not identified the taller Chinese man. They met just before Mao Tse-tung's train left for Beijing some time ago."

"Was anything of their conversation overheard, Mr. Chin?"

Mr. Chin smiled slightly and said, "Of course, sir. As you said, my sister demonstrates fine tradecraft. She was of course suspicious when such disparate men met together in her restaurant. She had never seen them before, but had sources to identify the two military men. Here is what she recorded for you." Chin handed a hand written sheet to Eli. It was not encoded as the restaurant was the last station in his information chain—Mr. Chin making up the last leg directly to him. With Mead looking over his shoulder the men read the entries:

> *Su Yu—We have eyes in place in Japan. General MacArthur is working to use small atomic bombs in the north of Korea to block Chinese intervention. So our plan is even more important now. We are ready. Everything is in place. With your agreement we execute.*

> *Shtykov—I have word of Stalin's decision. The action against the South is growing. Proceed with the plan. By the time the package gets to Jeju Island we will be ready to transport it to the planned location under cover of the confusion of the military action.*

> *Civilian—My people are ready. It took a great effort by a few people—we desired to keep its knowledge close. The team you provided is in place and well*

trained. The special equipment is on board and should by now be in port and awaiting word. With our success we shall be able to take all of Korea regardless of the American forces. The threat of our atomic bomb will be of great power.

Mead spoke first, "So these are the clowns who directed the stuff at Kadena. Two things here: 'our atomic bomb' and 'Jeju Island'—where the hell is that? Now we've got Harm's location and the bomb's ... But what the hell can we do about any of it?"

Eli said, "I can start by giving *Force Three* a heads up. Maybe he's got more." He reached for Mikhail Lermontov's *A Hero of Our Time* written in 1840 and retrieved the key to the *straddling code,* beginning the tedious task of transcribing the numbers into letters—and into a message.

Mead paced the floor. Suddenly he stopped, turned toward Eli and said, "I don't like this. Finding Harm was too easy—There's more ... something more. Hold off on that message. It may be time we take some action on getting Harm back."

"You've got some ideas?"

"Not yet, Eli. But I wonder just how much the Russians—that is Khrushchev or even Stalin—know about what Shtykov is up to in Korea."

"And if they do?"

Mead began to pace slowly. "If they do, then Truman and MacArthur have a whole new problem ... but, if they don't know ... if Shtykov is a lone wolf ... maybe we've got leverage. Listen, Eli, what if we send the information to Glebov but say only an 'unidentified Russian' instead of naming Shtykov yet? See where it goes."

"Amos, I get the feeling you don't trust Glebov—"

"No, no. Well, maybe I don't fully trust anyone. But I also don't want information in our guy's hands that can get him in trouble—not yet. Can you hook me up with Washington—secure?"

Pyongyang, North Korea, Russian USSR Embassy

Colonel General Terenti Shtykov, the Soviet Ambassador to North Korea, sat at his desk reviewing the report of military goods shipped to North Korea since open war began with the Americans.

During the first month of the war, the Soviet Union sent 124 warplanes, 130 modernized T-34s tanks, 32 self-propelled guns, 310 mortars, 248 artillery pieces of various caliber, 84 antiaircraft guns, 50,000 rifles and carbines, 705 machine guns, 68,000 mortar shells, 82,000 artillery rounds, 15,000 tank rounds, and 122 radio stations for use by the army in command and control. As he slipped the report between the pages of a ledger he kept locked in his safe he thought, *this is getting lucrative ... but not as lucrative as what we can do with our new hidden asset.* A knock on his office door caused him to hurry his task. "One moment," he replied as he slipped the ledger into the safe and clicked it shut. "Come in."

A uniformed member of his house staff stepped in, saying, "Sir, you have visitors. Your guardsmen have returned from a mission." The General smiled broadly. "Send in Park-Liu."

A moment later the leader of the atomic bomb raiding party stepped into Colonel General Terenti Shtykov's office, stood at attention and saluted. "Stand easy, Park-Liu. George Huang reported that you have done exceptionally well in accomplishing your mission. I can tell you that you and your team will be rewarded well for this work."

Park-Liu said, "Thank you, General. You provided us with the right tools and training and we could not fail."

"I wish it was so easy to avoid failure," Shtykov said, almost to himself. How is George Huang?"

"We left him on Jeju Island, sir. He was well and sends his greetings. He said he will blend into the island quietly until his services are needed to complete the glorious mission."

General Shtykov smiled and stepped around to be seated at his desk. "That will be all, Park-Liu."

CHAPTER FIFTEEN

AP July 1950—United Nations Command created under General MacArthur. US 34th Regiment crushed by North Korean 4th at Chonan. Fifth Air Force destroys many North Korean tanks and troops at Pyongtaek. US troops retreat along the Seoul-Taejon road. US Eighth Army takes command of ground operations in Korea.

The Kremlin, Moscow, Russia, USSR

Ivan Ivanovich Glebov finished decoding and reading the message from Eli telling him of the trio who seemed to be the instigators of the theft of an American atomic bomb—including the 'unidentified Russian.' Before reading it he'd replaced the key to the *straddling code* in its secret spot. He sat thinking about his next move with this information. A knock on the door followed quickly with its opening and Lieutenant General Vladimir Paulovich Suslov stepped into Glebov's office. "Добрый день (good day), Ivan Ivan'ch. Do you have a moment to talk?"

Glebov rose and extended his hand to the general then indicated that he take a seat. "Of course, Comrade General. What can I help you with today?"

"I trust you received the information about our guest?"

"I did, General, and passed it on to the Americans as you wished. Now what is the next move for us? Have you positively confirmed that he is a CIA Director? I'm not quite sure where this goes."

General Suslov laughed. "First, Ivan Ivan'ch, we have so far hidden the fact of our presence in that part of Manchuria. We are not ready for the Mao government to know it—nor President Truman for that matter. But to your question, in truth, I still have doubts about his true identity—doubts that go both yes and no. At the least we may have a bargaining chip in the matter of the American's missing bomb."

Glebov asked, "What do you know about that matter?"

"Only that it occurred. Have you heard more?"

Glebov quickly thought *I'm not ready yet* and said, "Not yet, but Comrade Khrushchev will be putting me on the trail of information soon."

Suslov said, "Ah yes. I'm sure our Comrade will find the incident most useful to him as Chairman Stalin fades."

He rose and stepped to the door, turning to look at Glebov. "Ivan Ivan'ch, you will have a position of power one day the way you are able to play all the parts. *Dobryy den'*, my friend."

The door clicked quietly behind him.

Ivan Ivanovich Glebov's brow wrinkled as he rose and looked out the window at the cold, gray walls of the inner courtyard. *I wonder what he really knows—if anything.*

CIA Headquarters, Arlington, Virginia

The Director took Mead's call. "Hello, Amos. What have you got for me?" They both knew the line was not secure and probably tapped by KGB. Mead waited for the slight delay in the transmission then answered, "We've located our boy. I'll send you details by secure wire." The message that went out over secure diplomatic wire channel read, "*You were right about the Russian role. Harm's here in Moscow in KGB custody. This information came from Force Three with only the caveat that he knew the name was Wetmore—but not whether it is our Wetmore.*"

The Director dealt with the same delay. "Amos, you know we're way off script with this mission. There's no official sanction

... just a reminder. But I'm counting on you to make the next move—to get him home—without a total international incident."

"Understand, Director. No frontal assaults. Sir, we have information about the theft—we know the people who are the ringleaders of the—"

"We also have that information, Amos. I'll fill you in on secure wire also." The wire message read: *"It was acquired on the Mao train back to Beijing by Force Three China. Where did your intel come from?"*

The reply read: *"It is an eye witness account of the final decision to activate the Kadena Air Base raid.*

The Director continued, "You are working with *FTR* there?"

"I am, sir, and I've met *FTR* face to face as we acted out the first contacts with the Soviets. It went well, Director. But now I'm more interested in our boy—though the two go together."

"One last thing, Amos. Brigit is keeping the lines open with our other contact. She's damned effective ... as you know. And everything's fine at home. Keep me posted."

Both ends of the transmissions clicked off.

The KGB agents listening found nothing meaningful to report.

The Director asked Sarah to get Dr. Mead on the phone in California. "Hello Brigit. Just talked with Amos and he's sure they've located Harm in Moscow. Your observation was spot on. Now, I must ask you to run down to Rincon once more. I'll have them set up for you. And before you ask, yes it is to China. Here's what we need you to do ..."

Jeju Island, off the coast of South Korea

George Huang quietly blended into the life in the village of Seongsan on Jeju Island, knowing that it could be some time before he was called on to do more. He had made repeated visits to the cave where the bomb lay, studying its structure and mechanisms, and each time carefully placing the stones and rubble back over the opening that discouraged any casual entry into the space.

Today he sat in his room with the stolen nuclear insert that activated the bomb. His mission is to fabricate a time delay for the detonation sequence that will allow him to be somewhere else when—or if—they had to accomplish that extreme act.

George Huang believed in this mission, but he had no intention of becoming a pink mist fading into eternity to make it happen.

Metropol Hotel, Moscow, Russia, USSR

Amos Mead had the Marine driver take him to his hotel after talking with the CIA Director. He told Eli Jorgen that he needed some time to think through plans for the next move—a decisive move to rescue Harmon Wetmore. As he walked up to the ornate front doors of the Metropol he noted the two men loitering a few feet up the sidewalk, glancing his way in an awkwardly un-spy-like manner. Mead thought, *if this is the best they've got to shadow me I can't be considered very dangerous. Maybe that's something I can use.*

He went on into the hotel, slowed his step and, deciding he was hungry, walked into the café off the lobby. He ordered bread and cheese and tea—not his usual drink of choice. His mind was swimming. *Who all knows of Harmon? Force Three Russia, the KGB, who else? What's our leverage? Is Khrushchev in the know?* He sipped the hot tea and noted that his 'tails' had moved into the lobby. He decided to stretch out his meal break to make them as uncomfortable as possible.

After a few minutes Mead decided to use the early afternoon for a walk. He walked past his 'tails' and out the front door of the Metropol Hotel. He stopped and took his time looking across the street at the magnificent architecture of the Bolshoi Theater. Then he turned and strolled down the nearly empty sidewalk toward Red Square and the Kremlin, only a few minutes away. *I wish Brigit was here to see this with me—maybe someday,* he thought as he took his time enjoying the sights—and the awkward discomfort of his Russian followers. Slowly at first, and then rushing into his thoughts, a plan began to form.

Tokyo, Japan—Dai Ichi Life Insurance Building

In June 1950, North Korea attacked South Korea. The new United Nations authorized a military force be formed to aid South Korea. It also directed the US government to select the force's commander-in-chief. General Douglas MacArthur was appointed Commander-in-Chief of the United Nations Command. From his headquarters in the Dai Ichi Life Insurance Building in Tokyo, MacArthur immediately began directing aid to South Korea. He ordered the US Eighth Army to Korea. Pushed back by the North Koreans, the lead elements of the Eighth Army were forced into a tight defensive position dubbed the Pusan Perimeter. As the US forces were steadily reinforced, the crisis began to lessen and MacArthur began planning offensive operations against the North Koreans.

Military staff cars flying varying numbers of stars denoting ranks from their fender mounted flags began to arrive in front of the Dai Ichi building. From one of them, Chief of Naval Operations Admiral Forrest P. Sherman and Army Chief of Staff General J. Lawton Collins emerged. They had flown to Tokyo to represent the Joint Chiefs of Staff in meetings with General of the Army Douglas MacArthur and his Pacific area and Korean War commanders. Admiral Sherman and General Collins were escorted into General MacArthur's office.

"Gentlemen, I trust you had a comfortable flight. Though we all know how long it is to be sure," MacArthur said as he began to re-light his ever present pipe. "May I see that you get a stiff drink in you before we do this deed?"

"No, General, thank you, but Forrest and I are anxious to hear all you are planning before we relax," Army General Collins said. All of the lower ranked participants had already been escorted to a large meeting room when MacArthur, Collins and Sherman joined them—causing the assembled group to jump to stiff attention.

"Be seated, gentlemen," General MacArthur said as he proceeded to the front of the room and a chair more opulent than all the others. "Let us proceed with the agenda," he continued, opening the folder handed to him by an Aide. "I have here a plan that will reverse the tide of conflict in Korea."

Everyone in the room with a copy of the agenda eagerly read ahead of the General's measured tones. *Amphibious landing at Inchon ...*

Virtually all of the commanders in the room were skeptical of what was prima fascia an overly ambitious plan. It took two more days of discussion for the group to finally, though reluctantly agree that MacArthur's strategically inspired concept would be, if not easy to execute, at least "not impossible."

So the plans to make an amphibious assault on the captured and occupied capitol of Seoul's port city, Inchon, moved into high gear.

Spaso House, American Embassy, Moscow, Russia, USSR

Amos Mead had risen early and arranged to be taken to Spaso House to meet again with Eli Jorgen. "Coffee's on the sideboard, Amos."

Mead poured a steaming cup of the American coffee and took a seat across the desk from Jorgen. "Eli, I've got the germ of a plan I want to bounce off you," he said. "It's a bit far out—but I think it's the only way we can go ..." He paused as Mr. Chin entered the room and handed Eli Jorgen a folded paper.

"Please excuse, sir," Mr. Chin said. "This came in the morning vegetable delivery."

Mead knew what it was and where it came from as he watched Jorgen turn and take the Mikhail Lermontov book, *A Hero of Our Time* from its place on the shelf. He opened it to the middle and retrieved a sheet that held the key to the current *straddling code* and began the tedious task of transcribing the numbers into letters—and a message. Mead waited.

Finally Jorgen looked up and said, "Amos, we've got more news on Wetmore … he's being moved from Lubyanka prison to a gulag. Glebov will advise time schedule and final location."

Mead said, "Eli, as scary as it sounds, I think this will make my plan possible."

"I'm listening, Amos."

"Kidnapping—we snatch him while he's on route."

"You're kidding," Jorgen said. "Kidnap him from the KGB?"

"Yes! He's not a high value target—that is if they're not sure who he really is. So security may be light enough to pull it off."

Jorgen sat in silence, looking into space, thinking. "Okay, we get to him—then how do we get out of Russia?"

Mead was also pensive, his words measured as if he was thinking them out as he spoke—which he was, "How well do you trust Glebov? I hope I know the answer, but I need to ask you. Can he be trusted unconditionally?"

"I have no reason to say no. We've worked together for years … okay, yes. I trust him completely. Why?"

"Because I plan to take a big chance to make this work—and it will involve him deeply. First I must contact the Director …" Mead's voice trailed off as he began to write on a message pad used for diplomatic secure wires.

CIA Headquarters, Arlington, Virginia

The Director read the secure wire from Moscow, hardly believing what he was reading—especially from Amos Mead.

"Sarah, please get me through to the President."

Spaso House, American Embassy, Moscow, USSR

Eli Jorgen said, "Do you really think the President will green light your plan?"

Amos Mead answered, "If he doesn't, then I'm out of options. I really believe that if we move on three fronts—get Harmon, position ourselves on that Korean island, and ruffle up the bomb plot's apparent leaders we can put real political pressure on the leaders of the proxy war in Korea."

"Those are pretty high level thoughts, Amos," Jorgen said. "What brings you to call it a 'proxy' war?"

"Come on, Eli, you know we're really fighting the Russians and Chinese—not that bohunk North Korean puppet—"

"Whoa, Amos. That's way above my pay grade—"

"Yah, mine too for sure. But all I can see now is bold moves or no moves," Mead said as he paced the floor of Jorgen's office. Eli Jorgen leaned back in his desk chair, paused and said, "Amos, why did you ask me about trusting Glebov?"

Mead continued to walk toward the window that overlooked *Spasopeskovskaya площадь* (Spasopeskovskaya Square). "Lot of interesting history out there, Eli. Generations of intrigue, wars, power plays ..." Mead's voice trailed off as he continued to look out at the Moscow spring, deep in thought. Jorgen sat back and quietly waited for him to continue.

Spaso House where the two men sat is located not far from the ancient region of Moscow called Arbat, cut through by one of the oldest surviving streets in Moscow. Exactly when it came into existence is not known, but it is mentioned in a 1493 document describing a fire which started in the wooden *Церковь Николы на Песках* (Church of Nicholas on the Sand) and spread throughout Moscow, devastating large areas of the city. Located just one mile west of the Kremlin, the area surrounding Spaso House was inhabited in the 17th century by the Tsar's dog-keepers and falconers. Spaso House and the square on which it is located are named for the handsome Russian Orthodox Church situated on one side. Erected in 1711, the *Tserkov' Spasa-na-Peskakh* (Church of Salvation on the Sands).

Mead turned to face Eli and said, "I need Glebov to get me involved with Nikita Khrushchev."

"To what?!" Jorgen said.

"To get me in a position to bring Khrushchev into the plan—of course without compromising his work as *Force Three*." Mead stepped over to Eli's desk and leaned forward supported by his fists on the polished wood. "Really, Eli, think about it. When Lenin died Trotsky and Stalin competed for the leadership—a deadly serious competition. Now Stalin is in ill health, fading fast if reports are to be believed. Who wants to succeed him? The line forms with Malenkov, then Beria, and our friend Nikita—historic Russian power intrigue."

Jorgen stood up, a pensive expression on his face. He raised his gaze to stare at Mead and finally said, "Okay, all that is true. But I'm having trouble with why Khrushchev would not just throw you in the KGB guesthouse with Wetmore—"

Mead jumped in, "That's always a possibility, but I think that Mr. Khrushchev will have an interest in building some outside brownie points for his future. And with Korea bubbling over, we know, admitting it or not, the Russians will have a hand in it. Nikita will want to keep the potential drama lower than it would be if Truman started crying foul about the prisoner—or two prisoners as you so kindly pointed out. And he won't want Russia to be blamed for the bomb theft—whether they knew about their boy in Pyongyang or not."

Jorgen said, "So you're going to spring Wetmore, kidnap the Russian ambassador to North Korea and force the Chinese to help you recover the bomb—all in one blitzkrieg mission?"

"Hey Eli," Mead said, plopping down in the leather chair next to the window. "I've learned that Teddy Roosevelt was right when he said, *Do what you can, with what you have, where you are.*"

The White House, Washington, DC

The President of the United States, the Vice President and the Director of the CIA sat facing each other in the Oval Office. This was a meeting of the hierarchy of *Force Three*. "Mr. President," the Director said. "At first glance I thought Mead had lost his mind. But it began to make sense as I thought about it."

The President said, "Tell me the part that makes sense."

The Director said, "Well, sir, as Mead summed it up … if he succeeds we get the bomb and Wetmore, and Khrushchev quietly puts a chit in his pocket from us for further reference."

The Vice President chimed in, "And if he fails?"

"If he fails," The Director continued, "then there are two prisoners in Moscow that nobody's talking about—"

The President interrupted, raising his hand as he placed a call to his secretary, "Get SECDEF over here pronto." He continued, "I say we go with Mead's harebrained scheme. Give him the go ahead to talk with Nikita—if that goes well we're on our way, or, that is, he's on his way. When Defense gets here we'll run down Mead's wish list and get assets in place."

The Director stood, saying, "I'll go to your communication center and get the message to Mead—and I'll get Dr. Mead going on her part of this caper. Back here then, sir?"

"Yes, back here," the President said, "I'll need you to explain a lot of this to Defense." He leaned back in his chair and added, "I kinda wish I was going along on this mission—only kinda—too old for this."

The CIA Director left the Oval Office deep in thought. Downstairs in the White House communications center he had the embassy in Moscow called and the call put through to Eli Jorgen's office. "Eli, tell Mead it's a go. Set up his meeting with the big guy. I'll be back with the logistics later today—or tonight, or whatever the hell time it is there."

In Moscow an official call from the Embassy of the United States is placed to the Kremlin, to Nikita Khrushchev's aide, Ivan Ivanovitch Glebov.

In Washington, D.C. a secure and top secret message goes out to *Force Three* agents in China and Russia.

CHAPTER SIXTEEN

AP—SPECIAL REPORT—North Korean Sixth Army drives down the West Coast, capturing Chonju and Chinju, and outflanking the US Eighth Army. The North Koreans are positioned to drive to Pusan and cut off all UN forces in Korea. Eighth US Army orders withdrawal to prepared positions.
General Walker issues 'Stand or Die' order.

NAVCOMMSTA, Rincon, California

Brigit Mead sat at her now familiar place before the bank of Navy radios at Navy Communication Station Rincon. The call from the Director put her in motion, anxious to get back in the game as she waited for word about her Amos. Whatever he had set in motion she knew that she was now part of it. She carefully reviewed her notes—not a script, though based on the Director's urgent call.

The White House, Washington, DC

The President handed the list to Defense Secretary Johnson. He read it aloud, "MATS flight from Vladivostok to Tokyo … Squad of ROK Rangers. How'd he know about that unit?"

The Director, who'd returned just as the SECDEF arrived, answered, "Mead was OSS in WWII and served in Southeast Asia—he'd know. Wetmore probably knows them personally."

The President said, "We're well aware that these guys fought the Japanese in the war. They're veterans and we need them for the two main prongs of this mission—infiltration and observation on the Korean island where we suspect the bomb is hidden and infiltration into Pyongyang"

SECDEF said, "From the top, sir. Are we sure the bomb is there?

Director of CIA answered, "Not one hundred percent—but there are no governments with the capability of going airborne with it. Nobody else has a B-29. The Soviets haven't modified their heavies to carry nukes yet—and why would they steal what they've already got?"

SECDEF said, "Fair enough. Now what about this infiltration into Pyongyang stuff?

The President rose and walked to the window looking over the Rose Garden. He turned to face the two men and said, "For a kidnapping, of course. Kidnapping a Russian General."

The Kremlin, Moscow, Russia, USSR

Amos Mead followed Ivan Ivanovitch Glebov into the inner office, this time on his own. Eli Jorgen stayed behind at Spaso House to keep up on messages from home. Ivan Glebov stood next to Mead. Nikita Khrushchev rose from his desk and with a broad smile stepped around it, offered his hand and said, "Мы еще увидимся, товарищ Мид. Иван Иванович говорит, что у вас есть ко мне срочный разговор." Glebov translated almost simultaneously, "We meet again, Comrade Mead. Ivan Ivan'ch tells me you have need of an urgent talk with me."

"I do, sir. Thank you for allowing me this time," Mead answered, looking toward Glebov and listening to the translation. Glebov said to Mead, "It is okay, Mr. Mead. I will provide simultaneous translation for you and the First Secretary. Please proceed."

Nikita Khrushchev had taken his seat behind the large ornately carved desk, an obvious treasure left over from tsarist times. Mead noticed tapestries on two of the office walls reflecting similar heritage. He took the seat across from the desk that Khrushchev pointed to. "Mr. Khrushchev, I have a very important request to make of you. It will be a shock, I'm sure, so I hope you will allow us to discuss the meaning and importance of it in full."

The First Secretary of the Communist Party nodded thoughtfully as the translation moved smoothly over Mead's words. "Mr. Mead, I appreciated your knowledge of my history in the Great Patriotic War. I also understand that you served as a spy in the war. Is that true?"

Mead thought, *this guy's good—keep me in edge*, then said, "I served with the American OSS and tracked Nazi spies. My duties were more counterspy than spy, sir." Mead knew that the Russians would have done their homework on him so he continued, "Later I operated in the South Pacific and Southeast Asia, also counter spying."

"And, Mr. Mead," Khrushchev said, "you received a decoration for bravery in the Pacific."

Mead smiled. "You are well informed, Mr. Secretary. With all due respect may we get to my reason for being here, sir?" It was a little more direct than he wanted, but Mead wanted to keep some control over the situation if he could.

"Of course, Amos Natanovich. Of course we can—please proceed."

It took an instant for Mead to realize he'd just heard his middle name—and his son's name—Nathan used in the Russian familiar manner. *A good sign.* He continued, "First, sir, I'm sure you are aware of the theft of an atomic bomb from an American military base in the Pacific."

Khrushchev disclosed nothing in his face as the translation finished.

"But I quickly add, sir. We know the Soviet Union had nothing directly to do with the theft."

A slight smile appeared on Khrushchev's face then faded. He said, "You are a lawyer representing a trade interest, Mr. Mead. What do you have to do with international thefts?"

Mead answered quickly, "Mr. Khrushchev, I am a lawyer—but my client sits in a KGB cell as we speak and that fact becomes a critical part of my request."

Khrushchev looked hard a Glebov. Mead could not tell whether Khrushchev knew about Wetmore or not. Glebov nodded his head almost unperceptively.

NAVCOMMSTA, Rincon, California

Brigit Mead spoke into the microphone sitting on the ledge in front of her, "Calling *shandian yun*, calling *shandian yun*. This is *Glinda*, repeat, *Glinda*, in the clear. Over." She listened carefully, intent on the electronic sounds coming from the headset. Once more she broadcasted, "*Shandian yun*, this is *Glinda* calling in the clear."

The US Navy in Pearl Harbor had completed the link to China. Brigit heard, "Hello *Glinda*. This is *shandian*. We have no more word on your friend."

"It is not about my friend, *shandian*," Brigit cut in. "It is about the theft of an atomic bomb." She had been instructed to be direct—even blunt—about her message. There was a pause and then General Kuisong—*shandian*—said, "We have just been informed of what you speak, *Glinda*. But we have no knowledge of it nor any involvement."

Brigit replied, "I believe you, *shandian*. But there is one in your midst who is involved. We know who he is and we are prepared to act." Here voice was firm.

Military Headquarters, Dongchen District, Beijing, China

General Yang Kuisong, *shandian,* listened intently to *Glinda's* statement. He turned to look at the other generals in his office:

General Su Yu, General Tai Li, and General Gui Suen. He turned back to the microphone and said, "Are you prepared to name him, *Glinda?*"

The Kremlin, Moscow, Russia, USSR

Amos Mead watched the reaction between the two Russians, deciding that he should continue. "I do speak with the authority of my government, Mr. Khrushchev. But everything we say and do is off the record. Swift action and secrecy will serve us both."

Khrushchev nodded, rubbing his chin in thought, never looking away from Mead. "Continue," he said.

"The American prisoner in the custody of the KGB is the Deputy Director of the CIA. The KGB only suspect his identity. They have not been able to confirm it as fact. He was captured by them in Manchuria after an airplane in which he was riding crashed. His mission involved the Chinese—not the Soviet Union."

Khrushchev continued to nod, then said, "Why are you revealing this to me. You are taking quite a large risk, are you not?"

Mead answered, "I am indeed, sir. But if I am right about your appreciation of my plan—and my offer—then we quietly free the prisoner with no embarrassment to Russia—and gain the gratitude of my government in future relations. However, if I am totally wrong about this, then you, sir, have two American prisoners—or worse."

NAVCOMMSTA, Rincon, California

Brigit Mead heard him. She waited for a full three count, then answered, "Yes, if you desire. I can name him. I wish, however, to be sure it serves your purpose before I do so."

The scratchy radio reply in her ears was clear, "No, *Glinda*. At this time it serves no purpose."

In Beijing General **Yang Kuisong** knew very well who *Glinda* spoke of. General Su Yu sat near to him as they spoke. Though not part of the general's plot, he'd known of it since near the beginning.

What he didn't know was the motive. Mao had asked for a total report before he acted—if he acted.

Brigit continued, "That is as it should be, *shandian,* when the time is right. One question, *shandian.* This is idle curiosity from me. Do you know of a man named Tai Li?"

In Beijing, standing next to Kuisong, General Tai Li stiffened.

"I have heard the name, *Glinda.* Why do you ask?"

Once more Brigit waited for a count of three. "Tai Li nearly caused the death of my husband—at the same time I was helping you to avoid death. He was an evil man. I heard that he was arrested by the Generalissimo, so I wondered if he had survived the war—perhaps changed his allegiance to Mao."

Dr. Brigit Mead had a strong suspicion that Tai Li could hear her remarks—and that was good, and what she'd hoped for.

Kuisong spoke, "I shall keep a watch out for the name Tai Li, *Glinda.* Now, to the theft of your bomb. We believe the Koreans are to blame. I can think of no other motive … *Glinda,* you do know that Mao's forces have not entered the Korean conflict?"

"I am aware of that, *shandian.* Are you telling me that Mao will not interfere?"

"*Glinda,* you ask things that I cannot know. I trust we can continue in confidence and trust for each other?"

"That is my wish, *shandian.* That is all I have for now. Please contact me if you feel the need. *Glinda* out."

Military Headquarters, Dongchen District, Beijing, China

General **Yang Kuisong,** *shandian,* turned to the other generals in his office. If any of you have more to tell me, please arrange to come back. General Su Yu, General Tai Li, and General Gui Suen nodded and without a word filed from Kuisong's office. He remained seated at his desk and smiled at the discomfort this event had instilled in the troubled conscience of at least one man—maybe two.

The White House, Washington, DC

The President listened while the CIA Director updated him on the arrangements to support Mead's mission—a mission that had crept well beyond anything imaginable not too long ago.

"Sir the ROK Rangers have been flown to Tokyo. Two of them are receiving special briefings on Jeju Island and the man called George who we suspect has remained there. They have the photograph taken in Moscow. They will land as fisherman, blend in and observe. If they locate the bomb—all the better. The rest of the team is learning about Pyongyang. By now they know of the plans to land troops at Inchon in two phases—and of our plan to have them go in ahead of the second landing."

The President said, "And is Mead still planning to go in with them?"

"Yes, sir, Mr. President. And his sidekick with him—Harmon Wetmore."

"You know, Director, there are a lot of high level people who think this mission is pure folly."

The CIA Director answered, "May I quote General George Patten, sir? '*If everyone is thinking alike, then somebody is not thinking.*'"

The Kremlin, Moscow, Russia, USSR

Amos Mead continued to brief General Secretary Khrushchev on the many reasons why he should actively support his plans. The short time left for Stalin hung like the Sword of Damascus over the proceedings. He outlined the plan to take the prisoner from his escort and fly both him and Mead to Vladivostok. Glebov continued his continuous translation, showing no outward emotion as things he knew well were discussed. Khrushchev spoke directly to Glebov, "Is General Suslov in agreement with all of this?"

Glebov was surprised at his bosses apparent knowledge of his relationship with Suslov, but he showed no shock as he answered, "Yes, sir. He awaits only your blessing—and support for acquiring the logistics needed. He is stalling movement of the prisoner to the gulag by Arkady Lermantov until we notify him of your answer."

Mead did not understand the Russian conversation between Glebov and the General Secretary. But he heard the two names of the KGB generals and wondered if possibly the General Secretary's knowledge of their actions might be a surprise to Glebov. He, Glebov, had never told Eli—*Force Three*—of this link. Mead thought, *if he was surprised he's one cool character— no wonder he's lasted this long.* Mead was jerked back into reality when he heard Glebov translate Khrushchev's answer, "Proceed with the plan and arrange the transportation. Use the influence of this office, Ivan Ivan'ch. One more thing, I want our aircraft to take them all the way to Tokyo—a visible sign of our cooperation. Keep me advised."

Khrushchev turned to Mead. "Good luck, Mr. Mead. I trust we will meet again under less stressful circumstances—when I shall ask for payment of this debt."

Mead smiled and offered his hand, which the General Secretary took with a firm grip and a broad toothy smile.

"*До свидания*" (Good bye).

Ivan Ivanovitch Glebov led Mead out of the General Secretary's office and back to his own. Only after he'd closed the door to the secure office did he begin to show the tension he had so professionally subducted for the last hour. "Here's the plan, Amos. Suslov will have Wetmore escorted to the military train at Kursky Station. His escort is two KGB goons who will expect nothing. You just have Eli drop you at the station. The rest will happen around you—you'll know what to do."

"That's a lot of arrangement in such a short time, Ivan. I'm impressed."

Glebov smiled. "We've been working on this for a while—just needed the boss's okay. By the way, nice job in there."

"Well, Ivan Ivan'ch, funny how convincing you can be when it's your ass on the line."

CHAPTER SEVENTEEN

Spaso House, American Embassy, Moscow, Russia, USSR

Eli Jorgen said, "Glebov sent me the schedule in secret. We don't want too many knowing of our real relationship—especially KGB. He also sent information on the Soviet embassy building layout in Pyongyang for your planning."

Eli handed a sheet of paper to Mead showing a sketch of the front and of the interior—especially the office of Colonel General Terenti Shtykov.

Before Mead could say anything, Eli Jorgen continued, "Your ROK Rangers have this layout also and they've begun to plan until you get there. Two of them are already on their way to Jeju with your instructions to blend in, observe, and gather intel on the tall Chinese gentleman, George. Funny, *George* doesn't sound too Chinese to me."

The ornate grandfather clock standing in the hall outside of Jorgen's office chimed the hour. Mead noticed the chimes on his first visit—the same St. Michael chimes of the clock his father had in his den in Vermont. "Time to saddle up, Mr. Mead," Eli said. Amos Mead stood and straightened the black serge coat that only barely fit him. This suit of clothes had been given him on instruction from Ivan Glebov. Another similar suit awaited Harmon Wetmore.

Mead placed the black fedora on his head at a jaunty angle. "Okay—let the show begin."

KGB Prison: Lubyanka Square, Moscow, Russia, USSR

Wetmore heard the jailors walking toward his cell. When he looked up he saw two men standing stone-faced behind the jailor as he inserted the large key to open Wetmore's cell door. The jailor motioned for Wetmore to come out. Without a word the two burley men dressed in dark suits took positions on either side of him. It had been awhile since his captors had paid any attention to him—not since the drugging session. He wondered, *another new KGB experience?*

With nudges from his new escort the trio walked to the stairs that led up to the main floor of the classic old building. As they stepped into the hallway the parquet floors and pale green walls provided a stark contrast for Harmon Wetmore to the grey concrete of the world he'd now spent too much time shivering in its cold embrace. He actually shivered at the thought.

Fully expecting to be taken to another interrogation session—or worse—he was surprise, and a little confused, when the trio continued to walk to the large front doors, and on out to the street and a waiting car.

Wetmore lost track of time, but soon enough the car pulled up to the Kursky Train Station. As they exited the car Wetmore saw a military train a few tracks over—like the one he spent so much time on crossing Mother Russia on his way here. The trio began to walk toward the cross-over to the train. Suddenly three uniformed and armed Soviet soldiers moved directly toward them. Wetmore noted that their shoulder epaulets were not edged in red—they were not KGB.

His escort glanced at the soldiers and back at their destination, not paying any concern to the men who continued to move on them. Before the two KGB goons could react they were pulled aside by two of the soldiers holding their Makarov semi-automatic pistols low but menacing. The third soldier wordlessly took Wetmore's arm and turned him toward a Russian ZiS-111 limousine waiting at the curb with its motor running. Wetmore saw

143

the two KGB goons being hustled across the tracks by the soldiers to the waiting military train and placed aboard under Army guard for a long ride east. The train was destined for a base near Lake Baikal in central Russia.

No word of Wetmore's "escape" would get out until they arrived—and maybe not then.

The soldier shuffling Wetmore, an officer, opened the rear door of ZiS-111 limousine and gently pushed his head down to avoid a bump as he urged him inside and climbed in behind him. The limousine pulled from the curb headed toward the traffic-free middle lane reserved for Soviet elite. Harmon Wetmore raised his head for a casual look at the man seated across from him dressed in a black suit with a fedora sitting at a jaunty angle on his head. Recognition flooded him as a physical sensation. "Amos!"

"The very same, Harmon Wetmore. The very same—come to pull your bacon out of the fire one more time … How are you, old friend?"

"Too long a story," Wetmore said, sitting back in the leather seat and feeling a relaxation he'd not felt in many weeks.

Before he could say more, Mead handed him a folded suit of black serge clothes, complete with a black fedora—the twin to Mead's attire. "Climb into these, Harm. At least you'll smell a little better."

Wetmore eagerly shed his prison garb and struggled into the suit, thankfully a little large instead of a little small. He put the fedora on his head, matching the jaunty angle Mead had adopted. "Where is the parade headed, Amos?"

"To Chkalovsky Airport where an Antonov An-12 is ready to whisk us off to never-never land. Sorry to inform you, my comrade, but we are not going home. We're headed into a mission like none you've experienced before—or maybe you have, come to think of it."

"Goody. Seems nothing's changed in our world," Harmon Wetmore said, as he crossed his arms in front of his chest and let his heavy eyes drift into a relaxed nap.

CIA Headquarters, Arlington, Virginia

The Director read the secure wire from Moscow and picked up his new direct line to the White House. The President's secretary answered and immediately forwarded the call to the Oval Office. "Wetmore's free and he and Mead are on a flight to Tokyo—a Russian flight via Vladivostok courtesy of Nikita."

The Director smiled for the first time in a long time at the President's response, then said, "Yes, Mr. President. We'll put a chit in the file for Nikita in case he makes it to the top and needs our help." Then he took a serious tone, "So now, sir, the mission is on and we have to wait."

Over Russia

The Russian Antonov An-12 aircraft lifted off smoothly and climbed to cruise altitude headed east. The plane was outfitted for "executive" passengers. On this flight only three men settled into the large leather seats, Mead, Wetmore and their Soviet Army officer escort. No one spoke for a few minutes as the plane settled into level flight, then Wetmore looked at Mead and said, "Okay, Amos—what the hell just happened? How did you get here—how did *we* get here on this Russian aircraft—without armed guards?"

Amos Mead laughed. "It's a long story, my friend—but before I tell you … what the hell happened to you? Manchuria? Flight crew?"

Both men looked down at the deck shaking their heads. Wetmore spoke first, "Touché, Amos." He sat back deep in the overstuffed seat and continued, "I was in Korea because of the mission to bring out a Chinese defector … a general. It was an important first for our program of infiltration—"

Mead interrupted, "But I'm told you lost contact with all the groups you infiltrated into China—all but the last one."

145

"That's true," Wetmore said. "That's probably why I over reacted to make the last mission successful. Too much hope ... too little common sense in hindsight. One of the loadmasters fell off the rear of the aircraft at the last minute and broke his arm pretty badly. There was nobody else to send and I couldn't stand to see the mission scrubbed waiting for a replacement."

"So you pulled rank and elected yourself the replacement."

"Sure. Wouldn't you? Okay, maybe not. Anyway, I asked the other loadmaster if he could teach me the ropes. He said 'no problem' as he just needed a little help and some back up muscle— so I stripped out of my duds and got into a flight suit. I emptied my pockets of all ID—"

"But you failed to establish a false identity, papers and such."

"No time, Amos. We had a rendezvous time in Manchuria. We had to take off—and we did." Wetmore looked around the cabin. "Did you arrange a 'wet' flight, my friend? I can use a drink."

Mead reached into a nearby compartment and produced a bottle of *Пятизвездная* (Pyatizvyozdnaya vodka). "This is five star Russian Vodka—made in St. Petersburg. I developed a taste for it while I was waiting for you to finish your Russian holiday."

Wetmore accepted the glass Mead handed him and held it out for a pour of the potent libation. He took a sip, then a long draw on the vodka, ending with a sigh. "So we flew to Jilin Province in Manchuria—and got our asses ambushed."

Mead let the silence sit for a moment as Wetmore seemed to be reflecting on his experience, then he spoke, "Tell me about the ambush, Harm."

"It'll take longer to tell than it took to happen. We made our first pass over the site and dropped the pick-up gear. We orbited and went down for the pick-up pass—and my suspicions came to life in a roar."

"Your suspicions?" Mead said.

"Yah. On the first pass I spotted some mounds alongside the field. At first glance they looked like piles of dirt covered with snow. But they struck me as oddly shaped—too many sharp

146

creases or something like that. In the second pass the white covers came off of a whole batch of AA guns—which began spraying us with at least .50 cal—maybe bigger."

"My God, Harm. How did you miss getting hit?"

"At first I crouched back away from the open hatch, hunkered down and waited to be hit bad—nothing came. Then I saw that they were aiming at the cockpit. The poor bastards on the flight deck took it all. Fire erupted just below the wing ... probably from fuel. The other loadmaster and I couldn't move from the forces of the pitching plane. That pilot—or copilot—is a hero, Amos. He kept us in the air until we crossed some woods away from the Chinese and managed to stall it into a belly-flop into an open space. It was hard enough to break the tail-booms."

Mead just listened, watching Harmon Wetmore relive the crash in his mind. Wetmore continued, "My partner and I were thrown forward as the plane decelerated nose down. My safety strap held and stopped me about halfway along the cargo bay—the other guy's broke and slammed him into the forward bulkhead. He was just shaking it off when I got to him after we stopped. Flames were a blowtorch coming off the flight deck—we knew those guys were gone. We ran to the back of the plane ... the jump out of the open hatch was only a foot or two. I heard the Chinese yelling up a storm and crashing through those woods. I yelled at my partner to run— I took off for the woods to one side of our crash path and kept going ... sure the kid was behind me ... Amos it was like Burma all over ... just kept going until I got to a stream. I heard AK-47 firing, but it was back at the plane—nothing my way. Never saw my friend again."

Wetmore rubbed his chin then dabbed at his eyes. He took a good gulp of the remaining vodka in his glass. "So I started to climb this hill. Steep, but plenty of hand and footholds. Boulders and small scrub brush—kept in the shadows and watched my back-trail. Nobody came ... I kept climbing. Got to a kind of ledge area and rolled up onto it—out of sight of anybody coming up the hill. Damn, Amos, I was tired ... just sucked dry. Too old for this stuff."

Mead asked, "And the Russians? When did—"

Wetmore jumped in, "I was laying there in a daze—then I felt cold steel pushing against my neck and somebody saying '*Dobryĭ vecher, gospodin amerikanskiĭ*.' It didn't click at first—he was speaking in Russian—'good evening, American'—and that was it. He took me to a well hidden lookout post, telling me in English that his troops had watched the whole crash thing. I never let on that I spoke Russian—never did. We then hiked over a pass in the mountain, got on some kind of truck and went to a place called *Yanji*—then off to Vladivostok we went. Started out on a Russian military plane. The damn thing caught fire and we crash-landed at Vladivostok. Nobody hurt … just shaken up. After that we were on a military train for a long time." Wetmore seemed to drift back into his memories.

Mead said, "And you ended up in Moscow—in the KGB guest quarters."

"There's one other thing, Amos," Wetmore said. "Along the way I saw a train from China—a special train—carrying Mao Tse-tung they told me." He went back to pensive.

Mead waited.

Finally Wetmore looked up, reached out his hand with the glass for a refill and said in a jaunty voice, "So, Amos, how's Brigit?"

Filling the glass half full of the vodka, Mead answered, "Fine Harm—worried about you. More than that, she's got a piece of this action—actually been talking over Navy radio to an old acquaintance in Beijing—Chinese general she helped during the war while you and I were on our camping trip in the Burma jungles."

Wetmore asked, "What's that all about? China? Communist China?"

"Well Harm, that brings me to part two of why we're winging over Russia, ensconced in first class, drinking fine Vodka, dressed like European professors." Mead began his task of informing Wetmore of what had transpired—courtesy of *Force Three*—and the plans for their mission. He told a surprised Wetmore about the

148

theft of an atomic bomb, and their belief that it had made its way to Jeju Island off the Korean coast. "From what our people have ferreted out it was pulled off by a group of second tier officers tied to both Soviet Russia and Red China."

Wetmore listened, sipping on his vodka.

Mead added, "Our best information is that they acted for personal gain involving their cashing in on a North Korean victory."

Wetmore spoke, "How does that work?"

"Blackmail, Harm. If they lose the battle they hold the UN hostage to a hidden atomic bomb. But now the bad guys have two problems—both compliments of *Force Three*. We know where the bomb is, or nearly, and we know who they are."

Wetmore spoke again, "So Mead and Wetmore are going to swoop in on our Russian jet and save the day!?"

"Not far off, Harm—but with a little help. Oh, you asked about Brigit—she's talking with China using her best skills of psy-ops. Stirring up the stink in Mao's ranks." Mead continued to inform Wetmore of the ROK (Republic of Korea) Rangers and their role in the mission. He told him of the two who were on their way to Jeju to pinpoint one of the players and the bomb. Then he told Wetmore about the upcoming amphibious assault on Inchon by MacArthur's forces—and the fact that Mead's group would launch on the North Korean coast at the start of the second day of the planned two day Inchon mission.

One of the fears of many of the Army high brass was the fact that the extreme tides in the Inchon harbor would not allow MacArthur to land his entire force the first day. They would have to hold a beachhead until the tides returned and the rest of the force landed. Mead had figured that the shock of the invasion on the first day would provide them cover in the confusion to pull off their plans.

"And we hit the beach to do what?" Wetmore asked.

"We're going to Pyongyang, Harm—to kidnap the Soviet Ambassador to the Peoples' Republic of North Korea. That's all."

Wetmore just slowly shook his head—and took a long drink of the *Pyatizvyozdnaya* vodka.

The Antonov An-12 droned on in the clear Russian air. There would be one stop for fuel before Vladivostok. Plenty of time for Mead to go over the actual attack plans on the embassy. But he had one more agenda to discuss with his old comrade-in-arms. "Harm, the last time I heard from you was a call after we'd got home from Germany. You said you had another assignment for me. Was this it?"

Wetmore smiled and said, "No Amos. My China thing hadn't popped yet. My call was about more Nazi hunting in South America. We'd pinned down a location in Maldonado, Uruguay—a castle built by Humberto Pittamiglio in Las Flores near Maldonado. He was a Uruguayan architect, an engineer, constructor, Minister of Public Works and diplomat in the early and mid-20th century. He was also an alleged alchemist—which fits right in with his Nazi mentors and benefactors. We saw this place as 'Wewelsburg west' and—"

Mead interrupted, "You started with 'we.' Is that the royal 'we' or are you still working with our Israeli friends from Mossad?"

Wetmore smiled. "Yes, Amos, I was working with Devoŕah and Moshe Talon. Why do you ask?"

Mead sat back in the leather seat, his arms crossed on his chest and a serious look on his face. "Harm, I need to know what you and Devoŕah were doing when I confronted Hauptmann on the Black Sun in Wewelsburg Castle—and I need to know why Brigit thinks that there were other people involved in the Hauptmann chase … I need to—"

"Whoa, Amos, whoa. Where are you going with this?"

"Harm, where I'm going is … look, we've been friends and shared more dangers and laughs than any two human beings alive … but I've got to know—were you working with Mossad?"

Wetmore sat quietly, waiting for Mead to finish. "Amos, we work with rules and regulations and we pledge allegiance to those who make them. But sometimes the right thing to do is go with the one who is fighting for what you *really* believe in. I think we share what I believe in—justice … sometimes even retribution."

Mead's eyes never looked away as he said, "I can't deny that, Harm. I think I'll take you at face value—trusting—because we've got a lot of work ahead of us. Sorry I went off on you …"

"Forget it, partner."

Mead poured another round, this time offering some vodka to the Russian.

NAVCOMMSTA Rincon

Brigit Mead received the information from the Director that her husband had indeed freed Harmon Wetmore, and that the two were on their way to Tokyo for the next phase of their mission. A mission that involved her deeply—both by deep concern for Amos, and directly with her China connection.

"The connection has been made through Pearl Harbor, Ma'am. It's all yours."

General **Yang Kuisong,** *shandian,* knew well that *Glinda* was carefully playing him. *But for what purpose?* He thought.

"Thank you for hearing me out once again, *shandian.*"

Kuisong said, "It is always my pleasure to speak with you, *Glinda.*" This was not a lie. It harkened back to a different time. But now it was the intrigue of the present.

"It is time for you to act, *shandian,* if you intend to. We are aware of Su Yu and Tai Li. They are tangled in our problem. Things are moving rapidly that will make it unpleasant for Mao. If you take care of things it would be better—for us both."

The addition of Tai Li's name to her warning was her idea.

Brigit continued before Kuisong replied, "We also know of the two others involved with them. I'll leave that to you to learn for yourself. And, *shandian,* if you want a motive—look to the usual one of great profit and power."

Kuisong said, "Glinda, you have given me much to think about—and to discuss with Mao. You are aware that Mao and our country is not part of this cabal?"

Brigit smiled. She felt that there was movement here. "We do not believe the Peoples' Republic of China, nor any other government, is involved in this. That is why it is in your interest to take action in those matters that are near you." Brigit did not mention North Korea or the Soviet Union. Let Kuisong find out about ambassador Shtykov on his own. "That is all I have today, *shandian.* If you have nothing more for me we can end this—both the call and the trouble. Thank you once again, *shandian. Glinda* out." She gave the old finger across the throat signal to the sailor on duty to "cut" the connection.

Amos, stay safe and hurry home, her only thought as she headed back to Santa Barbara to wait.

Vladivostok, Russia, USSR

The Antonov An-12 descended for a smooth landing at the Soviet Air base at Vozdvizhenka. They were actually some sixty miles north of Vladivostok in the barren wastes of the Primorsky Krai region of Far East Russia. As they taxied to the main terminal, Mead and Wetmore saw the rows of Ilyusin Il-4 bombers of the Soviet 444th Bomber Regiment. Known to NATO as 'Bob,' the Il-4's were left over from WWII—but still effective for use in Manchuria, or North Korea.

But Mead was not gathering intelligence for NATO—part of his "gentleman's agreement" with Nikita Khrushchev. This was their last stop before the overwater flight to Tokyo. The stop was for fuel and equally as important, the special final clearances needed for the Soviet plane to enter Japanese airspace.

It was two hours later and the trio, Mead, Wetmore, and the Soviet soldier, re-boarded the aircraft. As the only active plane on the field they were cleared for immediate takeoff, climbing to an assigned altitude and rolling out onto the southeast heading that would take them to Japan—and a future that God-only-knows.

Jeju Island, Korea

The fishing boat landed with little fanfare, one of the many who frequented these waters. Earlier it made an unseen rendezvous at sea with a US Navy Destroyer to take on two passengers—who now stepped ashore to begin their mission.

CHAPTER EIGHTEEN

Tokyo, Japan

Mead led the way to exit the Russian aircraft. As Wetmore got to the door he turned to the Russian Army officer who had escorted them from Moscow and said in perfect Russian, "Спасибо. Счастливого полета." (Thank you. Have a safe flight.) The startled expression on the officer's face turned into a broad smile. He saluted Wetmore and reached for the door to close it, their return flight to Vladivostok cleared for taxi.

Two large boxes were unloaded from the Russian plane. Mead stayed close to them as they were brought to waiting vehicles. Safely loaded, and with Mead and Wetmore in the lead car, they were driven to the barracks where the ROK Rangers awaited them.

A senior officer from General MacArthur's Intelligence staff greeted them at the barracks. He relayed the General's greetings— and misgivings about why this mission carried so much clout with Washington. The staff officer told Mead with a chuckle that in truth the General was miffed that he wasn't running the show. The officer provided Mead with a folder containing a summary of *Operation Chromite*, code name for the Inchon Landings. Mead quickly scanned the key points and handed the folder to Wetmore. Mead had no questions so the officer excused himself and Mead and Wetmore went in to meet their team.

The Rangers snapped to attention as they entered the room. Mead said, "Easy guys. I stopped being an officer in the last war.

This time I'm your planner and back-up. You will run the show—let me tell you what that show is."

The team gathered around a large map laid out on the table—the coast of Korea, from Inchon to up river north of Namp'o. "Gentlemen," Mead began, we will be going ashore near Namp'o at night for a short river ride up to Pyongyang. North Korean partisans will be waiting for us—if we're lucky. We will have trucks to take us to our target—the Russian Embassy."

The Korean soldiers exchanged glances, some smiling, some seeming to be doubtful. Mead noticed. "Hear me out. Then we can talk about it." This time the expressions were indicating interest. "If we land at the right spot we'll have about a three kilometer ride. I figure about ten minutes, counting dodging contact with any DPRK troops."

The senior member of the Rangers detail, a *jungsa* (Sergeant First Class), asked Mead, "Sir, what is the timetable for this operation?"

"Good question, Sergeant," Mead said. "We are tied to the scheduling for the Inchon mission. We will land during the night between the first and second day of the landings. Our agents in Pyongyang are prepared to spread rumors of the American Marines moving rapidly north to Pyongyang from Inchon. We're counting on the North Korean government's panic—including our target. If our information on his movements and whereabouts holds up we should meet him in his office—with all the proof we need."

"Amos, I'm not as current on this mission as you are," Wetmore said. "Been sorta out of the loop—but just how reliable have your Pyongyang people been?"

The Rangers watched and listened to their two "white officers" with interest. They were experienced warriors, having fought as guerillas against the Japanese and then against the Kim Il Jung takeover in the north. Mead said, "They've been spot-on so far, Harm. Most are operating under the CIA, as you probably know. I'm confident in their reports." Then he added, "Have to be—my ass is on the line too."

Going back to the map table, Mead reported on what he'd been briefed and what was in the folder he'd received from Intelligence, "A couple of weeks ago a joint CIA and Military Intelligence recon mission put a team in Incheon Harbor. They landed on an island in the mouth of the harbor called *Yonghung-do* and sent intelligence back to U.N. forces." Mead stopped and picked up the folder, opening it to a page he wanted. He continued, "The team included ROK Navy Lieutenant Youn Joung and a South Korean counter-intelligence officer named Colonel Ke In-Ju."

The Ranger *jungsa* said, "I've worked with the Colonel before."

Mead nodded and continued, "They worked with local partisans—people like we are counting on for our mission—and pulled together information on tides, mudflats and seawalls. The tides at Inchon are similar to those where we will land at Namp'o. The tidal range of twenty-nine to thirty-six feet is one of the largest in the world—information important as you can imagine to our success. There's more, but it doesn't involve our route through Namp'o to Pyongyang."

Mead signaled to Wetmore and he walked over to the large boxes that had come in the Russian plane with them. "Christmas is early this year, my friends."

Wetmore tore open the first box and drew out a military tunic. Holding it up he said, "Dig in. There are uniforms for each of you."

Mead added, "These are the Soviet style uniforms of the security guard assigned to Soviet Colonel General Terenti Shtykov, Ambassador to the DPRK—and our target." He carefully watched his team of six experienced, battle- hardened ROK Rangers for reaction. But they sat quietly, waiting for him to continue. "Gentlemen, if all goes as planned we'll be guests of the US Navy until they drop us off near Korea Bay. We move toward the mouth of the Taedong River and meet up with the first of our partisan folks for the trip to Pyongyang. There we're met by two trucks—one driven by a partisan and one by one of you." Mead paused and looked around the room. "Who's the best driver?" His remark drew a chuckle. A few fingers pointed at a young man who just smiled and lowered his gaze. Mead said, "Okay, you're my man you and the *jungsa* will be in the second truck. Here's why two trucks—"

Mead laid out his plan.

Jeju Island, Korea

George Huang quietly blended into the life in the village of Seongsan on Jeju Island. The village was just large enough, and busy enough with itinerant fishermen, that neither George nor the two members of Mead's team were immediately seen as out of place.

The team's advantage was that they knew who they hunted. George Huang didn't know he was being hunted—at least not yet. A recent message from Su Yu worried him. The general told him that their enemies seemed to have knowledge of the plan—even their identity. But he was sure that George and Jeju Island were still a secret. George continued to stay to himself, working on the trigger mechanism for the bomb, which he had not yet been satisfied with his progress so far. He wanted to be sure it worked as a time delay—for his own sake.

He continued to make visits to the cave where the bomb lay, checking the fit of his detonation mechanism. He also used the time to study the bomb's workings—for his own scientific curiosity. He kept a journal of his findings and impressions for future study. As always, when he left the cave he was careful to place the stones and rubble back over the opening.

The third day after their landing one of the ROK Rangers was in the farmers' market buying ingredients for their meal. The two Rangers seldom traveled around together. Every day, Jeju's traditional markets bustle with people looking for fresh, local, specialty products like medicinal herbs, flowers, and traditional ingredients at low prices. The Ranger learned that Jeju had two types of markets: those that run every day, and those that run every five days. Today he was at the Jungmun Rural Market in the center of the village. Its fresh fish came from the nearby fishing port— the Rangers' cover. The smells combined in the sea breeze and fresh fish of many kinds reminded him of his boyhood home near Pyongyang.

The Rangers had already learned of another benefit of the five-day markets. Since so many of the villages have them, merchants move around the island selling their goods from one to the next. Because they are constantly traversing the island, these merchants play a role in delivering information from village to village—a fact that the Rangers intended to use if this search stretched out too far.

As the Ranger examined a fresh *mun-eo* (octopus) someone brushed by him, not unusual in the bustling market. But as he glanced at the man walking away he noted how tall he was. Leaving the *mun-eo* in its small tank, he slowly set out to get a closer look at the tall man.

Pyongyang, North Korean Capital

Kim Il-sung, Prime Minister of the Democratic Peoples' Republic of Korea, picked up the delicate tea pot and filled his cup. He reached out across the low, round, silver filigree topped table and filled the cup of his guest Soviet Colonel General Terenti Shtykov, Ambassador to the DPRK. Shtykov took a sip of the hot tea and spoke, "I find it fascinating that your city's history dates back to when the Goguryeo dynasty built its capital here in the year 427 AD."

Kim Il-sung laughed. "You find something to teach me every time we meet. Pyongyang has been ruined and rebuilt a few times by invaders over the centuries. Our interest now is to see that it never happens again."

"We share that concern," Shtykov said. "I have grown very fond of Korea and its people. After we win this war and push the western invaders into the sea I would like very much to retire here."

158

Again Kim Il-sung laughed, this time longer and heartier. "You have I'm sure made sure your nest is properly feathered for your future, General."

Shtykov did not respond. With a small smile he lifted his teacup to his lips and blew gently over the brim.

Any smile disappeared from the lips of Kim Il-sung. He set his cup on the table and leaned toward Shtykov. His voice carried a tone of rising anger as he said, "General, you must inform Comrade Stalin that we are in need of almost every supply for the army. We send the raw materials he demands, but he is slow to fulfill his side of the bargain."

Shtykov still did not respond, the smile remaining on his face.

As the silence continued Kim Il-sung grew restless. After a long moment he spoke, "General we have been receiving reports of men, large amounts of supplies, and ships obviously concentrating at Pusan and in many Japanese ports for a major amphibious operation, and the leader of our North Korean-Japanese spy ring was arrested in Japan as he was transmitting the plan he had obtained. He never completed the report, so we do not know where or when they plan to strike."

Staring straight at Kim, an insult in its own right, Shtykov said, "You know we have them struggling in the Pusan area just to survive. They cannot be planning anything but an evacuation of their forces. Do not worry about invasion."

The General knew about the incident in the Yellow Sea with an American task force led by their aircraft carrier Valley Forge. One of their F4U Corsairs had shot down a Soviet A-20 Havoc who was trying to bomb the ships. The United States Navy was indeed getting close. But he chose not to discuss it with Kim Il-sung as it would only create more demands for Soviet assistance.

Kim Il-sung replied, "We cannot be so sure, General, there are too many signs of activity—"

Colonel General Terenti Shtykov cut him off, "I am the one who will tell you what to worry about. Don't forget who is running this war of yours."

CHAPTER NINETEEN

AP—SPECIAL REPORT—*An armada of two-hundred-thirty amphibious and other ships conduct a surprise amphibious assault on the port of Inchon on Korea's west coast. Named Operation CHROMITE, the 1st and 5th Marine Regiments of the 1st Marine Division spearheaded the attack.*
Enemy and allied leaders alike had doubted that a major amphibious operation could be successful at Inchon, where the high tide ranged between twenty-three and thirty-five feet. At low tide, attacking ships faced the risk of being stuck in the mud and two fortified islands blocked access to the port of Inchon.

Taedong River, North Korea

Mead, Wetmore, and the team of ROK Rangers hunkered down below the gunnels of the LCVP trying to keep out of the spray-whipped wind as they moved into Korea Bay toward the mouth of the Taedong River. The barest sliver of a moon cast a pewter streak across the calm surface of the river. It was the only light to be seen in the early morning pre-dawn. Wetmore slid over near Mead and whispered, "This feels a little too familiar, Amos."

Mead chuckled, "Sure does—but at least we didn't have to jump out of an airplane to get here."

Just seven years before Mead and Wetmore had been on a mission to China and were shot down over the Irrawaddy River delta, beginning a long dangerous trek through Japanese infested jungle—beginning with a dangerous river journey hidden by natives. They never figured on being together again in enemy territory.

Their mission into North Korea was timed to be helped by MacArthur's landings on Inchon. The morning before, about 0630 local time, the US Marines stormed ashore at Inchon. The surprise invasion provided Mead's mission with the cover and the panic they sought. Partisans were even now spreading word out from Pyongyang that the Marines are turning north to assault the city. Truth was that the Marines were hanging on to their positions waiting for the second wave to come in on the high tide. Then their breakout would head for Seoul—not Pyongyang.

Mead's raiding party was aboard USS Wantuck (ADP-125) when she delivered 3rd Battalion of the 5th Marine Regiment on their raid on Wolmi-do Island off Inchon. The Marines stormed ashore on the island and quickly consolidated their position in preparation for the second phase of the operation—the invasion of Inchon itself later that afternoon. USS Wantuck then sailed a few miles up the Korean coast to deliver another, smaller raiding party. Mead and his ROK Ranger raiding party had endured the small landing craft's rough ride since being launched from USS Wantuck (ADP-125) off the Yellow Sea coast of Korea. The Gray Marine diesel engine that was moving the craft along at a steady ten knots suddenly became quiet, throttled down to an idle, as the coxswain noted his position and watched for the signal they expected.

Mead moved next to the coxswain and followed his extended arm to see the dim but distinct blink of a light near the shore. Mead knew the signal also and counted the blinks. Their boat, Navy PA-47-2 on its stern, answered the signal and came to a stop. After a tense few minutes a shape loomed from the darkness, low to the water with little silhouette against the darken shore. The craft was about thirty feet long with a shallow draft. A wheelhouse, set near the stern, the only superstructure, it was the fishing boat the partisans had promised Mead, and it was on time.

The bowman on the US boat threw a line to the fisherman. Together they pulled the crafts alongside. Mead signaled his team to cross the rails. "Bring all your gear and get low in the boat," he said in a loud whisper. He turned and shook hands with the coxswain. "See you tomorrow night."

"I'll be here, sir. Good hunting."

The two boats cast off, Navy PA-47-2 swinging her bow back toward the open sea and the safety of the two small offshore islands that faced the mouth of the bay. There they will wait out of sight of the mainland. The Korean fishing boat headed up the Taedong staying in midstream as she passed by the darkened Namp'o and proceeded toward their target— Pyongyang, twenty-seven miles upriver.

Pyongyang, North Korean Capital

Soviet Colonel General Terenti Shtykov pushed past the ceremonial guard and rushed into the office of Prime Minister Kim Il-sung. He stood in front of the Kim's desk and scowled. "I'm not impressed with your spy network—how did the Americans' landing at Inchon go unreported?"

The Prime Minister stood to his full five feet three inch height and spat back, "I tried to tell you last evening, General. You would have none of it. I was just informed that the Americans are swinging north. We have too little time to prepare a defense beyond the troops left here. Our main fighting force is in the south—"

General Shtykov interrupted, "You fool! I am in charge of that army—I know where they are. What do you plan to do now?" He did not wait for an answer as he turned on his heels and stormed out of the building to his waiting staff car. He spoke to his driver, "The Pyongyang Military Academy—hurry." Tires spit gravel as the car lurched through the gates and out onto the boulevard. Moments later he climbed out of the car in front of what originally was the Soviet 25th Army headquarters, now used by the Soviets to train Korean people's guards. He was met at the door by the commandant who led him into the building. They entered a room where senior officers, Russian and Korean were gathered. The General barked, "Your report."

"We have little new intelligence, General," the commandant answered. "All units are on alert and prepared to defend the city."

The group gathered around a map table and began to line out strategy to be conducted to counter the American force. But Soviet Colonel General Terenti Shtykov had little trust in any of it. He knew, but would not say it aloud, that his only course of action now is to evacuate to the north. It had grown late as he got back to his car and ordered, "To the Embassy."

Pyongyang, the Soviet Russian Embassy

Park-Liu, senior officer of General Terenti Shtykov's fifty man protection force for the Soviet embassy in Pyongyang, North Korea, directed his men to bring the trucks to the front of the embassy. He had been contacted by the general and was instructed to load as much of the records as possible—and all of the gold stored in the vault. It had been crated already for just such a case as this. Park-Liu had been the leader of the theft mission that provided them with an American atomic bomb. He wondered *what would be its use. How will it serve us now?*

Mead's raiding party landed near the old fishing wharfs on the river, their boat snuggled into a group of similar fishing craft. On shore two military trucks awaited them, provided by the Korean partisans. As the team moved from the vessel to dry land, Mead raised the radio strapped to his chest. High above and just off the Korean shore an aircraft orbited. Mead called, "Spooks calling Caps One."

"Caps One, Spooks—countersign."

"Roger Caps One—countersign Three Foxtrot."

"Roger that Spooks, go ahead."

"Debarking feet dry. Will advise when ready for the hammer."

"Roger, Spooks. Good hunting. Caps One, out."

Mead directed two of the team to the first truck. "You know your mission. Be careful … act like you belong there. If our information is correct—and it better be—the confusion will give you cover." He shook hands with each Ranger and watched them drive off. The rest of the team got into the back of the second covered truck. Mead and Wetmore joined them in the back. A partisan drove this truck with a Ranger beside him. Mead said to the team with him, "We'll go to the rear entrance. We keep it quiet unless we run into the wrong people—then take them out swiftly and quietly." He held up his Soviet *Pistolet Besshumnyj* (silenced pistol). "We will go up to the ambassador's office and wait for his arrival."

He passed around a drawing of the interior of the embassy, the office that was their target marked. They'd studied the drawing before, but Mead felt a refresher was in order. At least it was something to do during the short, dangerous ride to the embassy.

The first raiders' truck pulled up to the entrance to the embassy grounds and proceeded forward. The gate between the two massive stone entrance structures stood open as a line of the same type of trucks moved past the steps to the building's entrance, stopping as each was loaded. The embassy security people were in a hurry and focused on getting their job done and moving out—to the north and away from the American force they knew to be near the outskirts of Pyongyang. The partisans, skilled provocateurs, spreading the rumors were effective.

Without a glance from the working troops, the newly arrived single truck parked just to the side of the loading area and two uniformed 'security men' got out, walking erect and with obvious purpose to the front door. They entered and, unchallenged, climbed the ornate curved staircase to the second floor.

Two real security guards stood at each side of a large ornate door that led into the quarters and office of the ambassador. The two Rangers walked up to the sentries and the *jungsa* told them that they were relieved to help finish the packing of the

164

ambassador's convoy. "We have been assigned to stand the guard until the ambassador returns," the *jungsa* said with obvious authority. "Also, leave us your rifles—you will not need them for your loading duties."

The sentries handed over their Soviet made AK-47s and hurried away without question, anxious and relieved to be on one of the trucks leaving for the north. The pair of new 'sentries'— both members of Mead's raiding party dressed as embassy security guards—took up their positions at each side of the door, feeling relieved that their first ruse had succeeded.

At the rear of the large three-story building that housed the Embassy of the Soviet Union the other truck parked near the service entrance. The four uniformed Rangers exited the rear of the truck followed by Wetmore and Mead, also in the Soviet style uniform, their distinctive Russian style billed caps pulled low over their forehead—though there was no one to see their Caucasian eyes in the early morning misty greyness. The first raider went up to the rear door, tried it and finding it unlocked, slowly pulled it open and peered into the hallway beyond. He motioned for the others to follow as he entered the dimly lit hallway with his Soviet Makarov 6P9 *Pistolet Besshumnyj* (silenced pistol) in hand. Silently in line they entered the building.

Suddenly a security guard stepped into the hallway from a bathroom, his Kalashnikov AK-47 hanging loosely from his shoulder as he finished buttoning the front of his trousers. With only the sound of a muffled cough two rounds hit him in the chest and he dropped where he stood. The raiders stopped for an instant and listened. Hearing no reaction to the sounds they stepped around the dead sentry and the pooling blood seeping from his chest and moved to the door leading to the main foyer. They stopped again to holster their pistols and straighten their uniforms.

So far the diagram of the embassy provided by Eli to Mead in Moscow proved accurate. The first raider opened the door leading from the hallway to the large ornate rotunda-like foyer and stepped through—waiting only a second for the rest of the team to walk through and form up like a military detail on a mission—which they were. Mead and Wetmore stayed in the middle of the group as they walked to the curved marble staircase and climbed the twenty or so wide steps to the second floor. Recognizing the sentries as two of their own they approached the office door. Mead spoke in a low voice, "Has the ambassador arrived?"

"No sir. It's all clear. I've slipped the lock—door's free."

Mead turned to the others who were cautiously watching the activity on the ground floor near the open front entrance and said, "You know your jobs, let's go."

At the front of the embassy the ambassador's sedan slid to a stop at the bottom of the entrance stairs. Security people nearby set boxes down and stood at attention. The ambassador said, "Continue your work." Without slowing he walked up the steps into the building, his personal bodyguard one step behind him. The two men climbed the stairway and as the Russian general cum ambassador approached the door to his office the two sentries snapped to attention and saluted, the one on the right reaching over and opening the heavy door.

Inside the ornate office, decorated with fine art, paintings and tapestries from Russia and furniture from the tsar's palace, Colonel General Terenti Shtykov enjoyed the good life. He walked directly to an alcove and opened a full size steel safe door with practiced ease. He entered and came out with an armful of documents which he placed in a leather case sitting on his desk. His body guard stood quietly just inside the door.

Well hidden behind draperies and in the adjacent personal quarters the team waited for Mead's signal.

Jeju Island, Korea

George Huang walked steadily through the crowded market, deep in thought and unaware of the man who trailed him. He was still uneasy about Su Yu's message, though he trusted that he was still alone on the island. He arrived at his small quarters and opened the door. Foot traffic was thinner here and he saw a man stop and look away, then look back at him. George hesitated an instant and saw the man look down as if in thought, take a folded guide out of his pocket, look around and walk away. *Just a lost tourist ... must relax.*

The Ranger mentally kicked himself for the lapse, but figured no harm done. He returned to the market, purchased their meal and headed back to the small apartment on the second floor of one of the buildings lining the perimeter of the marketplace. His partner was waiting. The first Ranger said, "Got him. I saw him in the market and followed until I saw his face. Also saw where he stays."

"Tomorrow," the second Ranger said, "we get closer. Get on the radio and report this to Tokyo."

In Tokyo the message from Jeju Island was immediately forwarded to CIA headquarters in the US. The Director compiled his report and called the President. "Sir, Mead and Wetmore are ashore in North Korea and our agents on Jeju have located the third man in the bomb plot."

"It's hell waiting, Director. But *Force Three* is still in the fight after all these years," the President replied.

CHAPTER TWENTY

Pyongyang, the Soviet Embassy

Park-Liu, senior officer of the Soviet Ambassador's security force watched as the last truck loaded with the Ambassador's things joined the line up at the edge of the compound, all engines running. His own truck with a squad of men, also sat running. He waved to the driver of the lead vehicle of the convoy, standing beside his truck awaiting orders, to drive on.

As he turned to enter the building he saw one other truck remaining, but hesitated only a moment, thinking it may be one of the Ambassador's personal vehicles—no concern of his. He went up the entrance stairs and entered the foyer. His booted footsteps echoing, he walked straight to the curved stairway leading up to the Ambassador's quarters and began to climb. As he neared the top he saw the two sentries, and when he gained the top and stepped toward them he stopped. "Who are you?" Park-Liu demanded. He did not recognize their faces.

The nearest sentry, staying at attention and facing forward answered, "We were sent to guard the General. We were told the security detail would be leaving."

"I know of no orders for you to be here!" Park-Liu stepped between the guards and grasped the latch of the door, but it opened before he could push it—pulled from the inside by the ambassador's bodyguard. Park-Liu, recognizing the man, said loudly, "Something is wrong. The sentries ... I do not know them."

From somewhere in the room a voice sounded, "Show time!" Curtains flew back and doors crashed open. The bodyguard reached to draw his side arm, but his hands never left the holster before two round holes appeared in his forehead. He slumped to the floor where he stood, oozing blood soaking the ornate carpet. Park-Liu backed out of the door, his pistol drawn under cover of the dead guards falling body. The Ranger 'sentry' slashed at the pistol with his AK-47. It spun out of Park-Liu's hand, hitting the marble floor with a resounding metallic clang. But even before it hit the floor, the Ranger's AK-47 swung high for a butt-stroke into Park-Liu's startled face, crushing teeth and bone. He staggered around, hands on his bloodied face, backing up to the iron railing. In a roundhouse move the Ranger kicked him in the chest.

His hand still covered his blood filled mouth and battered nose so no cry was heard as he tumbled over the railing and fell to the marble foyer floor, landing on his head and crumpling in a heap. As the blood spread over the marble floor one of Park-Liu's remaining squad, standing just outside the entrance, saw his body and stepped in to peer up at railing—only to fly back outside as a burst of AK-47 fire raked his body.

Inside the office Soviet Colonel General Terenti Shtykov, Ambassador to North Korea, paled and stood stiffly at the side of the desk, the last of the papers still held in his hand. One of the Rangers looked toward the door as one of the "sentries" leaned in and said, "We've got some company. One down and I think only a squad left—the convoy has driven away."

Mead and Wetmore each held an arm of the ambassador as a Ranger secured his hands behind him. The remaining three Rangers moved to join the pair outside the office. The wide curving staircase provided cover from view and any gunfire from the entrance—if one stayed up against the wall. Easing down the stairs, sliding along the wall, the Rangers prepared to confront the remaining security detail. The Ranger *jungsa*, raising his arm to halt the team's descent, eased toward the rail. A burst of fire assailed their ears in the domed foyer. The *jungsa* grunted, but returned it with a burst from the AK-47 he carried. A scream came from outside the door. The *jungsa* motioned the team to proceed as he slumped down onto the cold marble step, a dark stain spreading around his chest. The team hesitated but he gestured forcefully for them to continue. As they reached the bottom they moved aggressively on the front door, pistols and the two rifles blazing.

The few remaining security men were not up for a fight. The sight of their leader's body and the others down and bloody sent the running for the last truck. The Rangers let them go, but watched carefully for any remaining troops—none were seen. All quiet. They rushed back to their fallen sergeant.

The *jungsa* was sitting up on the step, his hand under his armpit, his teeth grinding in obvious pain. The first Ranger to reach him pulled his hand away to inspect the seriousness of the wound. Removing his jacket, noting the jagged tear in the armhole, he saw the crease in the side of the leader's chest, now just oozing blood. "Give me an aid kit," he said. "It's just a flesh wound—no entry."

In the office above, **General Terenti Shtykov seemed to regain some composure at the prolonged silence that now filled the space. He glanced at the Rangers filing into the room, but quickly looked back at Mead and then at Wetmore, scanning up and down the uniforms they wore. "Who are you? What is the meaning of this?"**

As the Rangers took up positions by windows and in the outer hall, Mead turned to the General/Ambassador, smiled and said, "I bring you greetings from Moscow—and from General Su Yu and Mr. George Huang."

Shtykov's jaw dropped. He sank back against the desk and watched his tormentors gather up all the material that he had recovered and boxed up—all the evidence of his crimes.

"Have we got everything?" Mead asked his *jungsa* (Korean Sergeant First Class), now neatly bandaged and back in charge.

"You okay, Sarge?" Wetmore asked.

"All set to go, sir. Just a scratch," the sergeant answered.

170

Mead said, "Secure the general. We're going home … wait one. Take the general's uniform blouse off—and secure his cap." A Ranger untied the general's hands and pulled the tunic down and off of his arms. Mead nodded and said, "Okay, NOW we're going home. He was first out of the office, flanked by one of the Ranger sentries. They stepped across the space to the railing overlooking the ornate foyer. They saw the problem and recoiled as one.

An embassy security guard was coming through the front door below them, and more could be seen waiting outside.

At least a squad, Mead thought. *Hopefully that's all.* He put his finger to his lips, silencing the already quiet team who had stopped just inside the office and mouthed, "There's more."

Soviet Colonel General Shtykov yelled, "Stop them! Help!"

A gun barrel came down against his ear and he slumped back into a raiders grasp.

The security guard downstairs stopped. He saw the carnage, and, not sure of the cause, yelled back to his men, "*Iliwa, munje gaissda!* (Come here—there's trouble)." Kalashnikovs at the ready, two more embassy security guards, the last of the fifty man detail ran into the foyer, spreading out, looking up to the office door. They had been called to bring an extra truck but had arrived late.

Mead's group drew back into the office. Quickly he motioned for the general to be dragged into the adjoining room, then whispered to the Ranger at the door, "Call those guards to come up and help. Point them into the office." Then, to the rest he said, "Hide—we'll lure them in and take them down."

The Ranger at the door stepped out and shouted, "*Yeogie ol - ulineun dangsin-ui doum-i pil-yohabnida. jang-gunnim* (Come up here—we need your help. It's the general ...)"

The guards bounded up the steps two at a time and the Ranger "sentry" motioned them into the office—but one held back and said to the Ranger, "*Naneun dangsin-eul gieog haji anhseubnida. dangsin-eun nugu yo?* (I don't remember you. Who are you?)"

171

His answer came quickly as the Ranger heard the commotion inside the office. *"Dangsin-ui choeag-ui agmong* (Your worst nightmare.)" He spun in place, expertly high-kicking the guard in the face—grabbing his Kalashnikov in the motion. The guard backed away against the railing, holding his bleeding face as the raider used the rifle to slash stroke the side of his head and follow that with a butt stroke that reeled the guard back. With flailing arms the embassy guard flipped over the railing and fell to the marble floor below.

Inside, the first guard confronted the Rangers and was met with a silenced round to the chest. The last man in raised his Kalashnikov. Behind him the Ranger coming into the office gripped the man around the throat as the rifle fired into the ceiling. The Ranger twisted hard and the dull crack of the breaking neck joined the echo of the gunshots. He released him, dropping the guard to the floor in a heap.

Mead said, "Good thing these guys chose a fight. We can't take prisoners—except that one." He pointed at the revived Soviet ambassador. Then he added, "Now—is that all for sure this time?" He looked at his watch. *Still on time.* And said, "Load everybody in the one truck in back. We've got room."

Carrying their load of evidence and goading the Soviet Russian ambassador along, the team descended the stairs, watching out the front door for any more stragglers of the security guards. They moved toward the hallway leading out the back of the embassy to where the truck and its Korean partisan driver waited.

A shot rang out.

They froze.

It wasn't inside the building.

Mead crept up to the door and peered out. Standing next to their truck, the driver stood with a smoking pistol. On the ground a man lay, not in uniform. The driver turned toward Mead and lowered his weapon. "Embassy worker. Three ran out that door. This one pulled a gun. Bad move for him. The others ran around the corner of the building—through those trees."

Mead nodded and said, "Load up."

They didn't wait for a second invitation. Wetmore was the last to pile into the back—with the Russian. Mead, standing behind the truck, reached into his shirt and produced a whistle on a lanyard around his neck. Three short blasts on the whistle produced the sound of a motorcycle being started just outside the compound wall. In a second the motorcycle, a military style with its rider in a DPRK army uniform, slid to a stop next to Mead. Mead handed the rider the uniform jacket and cap taken from the Soviet general to the soldier who shoved it into an open saddle bag. Mead gave a salute to the soldier who returned it with one hand as he gunned the cycle to life with the other, spun in place and raced toward the wall and the road beyond.

Mead had one more task to do.

He clicked on the radio strapped to his chest, listened for an instant then broadcast, "Spooks calling Cap Two."

The radio answered, *"Roger Spooks, Cap Two requests countersign."*

Mead responded, "Roger Cap Two—countersign Foxtrot Three Three Plus."

"Roger that Spooks. You ready?"

"Roger. Mission accomplished. Departing location. Target convoy estimated a few miles on highway to the north. Come on in. Free fire. Watch for the bike. He's ours."

The radio crackled, *"Roger Spooks. Tally ho the convoy. We're inbound."*

Mead yelled for the driver to proceed and accepted strong hands helping him into the back of the moving truck. The Korean partisan driver slowly and cautiously moved the truck around the building to the front entrance road and entered the highway for the short—unpredictable—drive to the boat.

Military vehicles, similar to their own, moved up and down the roads. Some stopping at intersections to disgorge soldiers who set about putting up checkpoints. Wetmore said, "Looks like they got the word about the Inchon Marines."

Mead nodded, keeping his eyes on the activity as they sped by, too early in the process to be challenged. The Soviet Russian general also watched, hoping to see an opportunity to get help.

Suddenly a violent roar hit the startled Ranger team as a trio of Douglas A-1 Skyraiders flashed overhead, their Wright R-3350 radial engines becoming pulsating music to the men as they peered, best they could, from under the canvas cover.

The flight formation sported Marine Corps markings.

Mead's driver swerved, reacting to the sudden shock, but maintained control of their truck.

First the streaks of rockets, then the wing mounted cannons raked a gouge down a line of Korean trucks, the sound of the salvo of rockets and cannon fire reaching the startled ears of the raiding party. The lead Ranger shouted to Mead, "We will be lucky if we are not killed by Americans!"

Mead and Wetmore smiled and pointed toward the canvas top of their truck. Just visible as a silhouette through the backlighted canvas the men saw 무료 painted large. They began to laugh—
FREE.

"The Marines have instructions. If they see the figures on a truck, we're home free."

"Looks like it worked, Amos," Wetmore said. "This time."

CHAPTER TWENTY-ONE

Santa Barbara, California

Dr. Brigit Mead sat in her kitchen in the little Islay Street house, slowly offering little Nathan the next spoon of pureed peas. He actually liked them and opened wide. She was moving slowly, automatically, as her mind was halfway around the globe. *How are you doing, Amos? Where are you?* Her thoughts kept spinning to no answer. *No word in too long time, my love. Maybe I'll call the Director.*

The telephone on the kitchen counter rang.

Brigit jumped, and spilled the jar of peas as she reached for the jangling instrument. Nathan swirled his hand in the unexpected green puddle on his highchair, giggling.

Taedong River, North Korea

Mead, Wetmore, and the team of ROK Rangers with their captive stayed low in the fishing boat as it moved down the center of the Taedong River, maneuvering with the other river traffic and being as unobtrusive as possible. Only one military patrol boat came up river, powering along on the other side from the small fisherman. He took no notice.

Reaching the mouth of the river and entering into the bay the boat turned toward the sea. It took another fifteen minutes before they spotted the LCVP hugging the rocky shore, awaiting their return. The transfer was quick. Mead thanked the captain of the fishing boat and wished him well. His answer in broken English was, "It will not be long before your Marines come and take Pyongyang. We will be waiting."

Mead smiled and shook his hand, letting go as the LCVP edged away and moved to join the outgoing tide. The small landing craft provided a rough ride, but no one complained as they sailed out into the Yellow Sea and moved toward USS Wantuck (ADP-125), now steaming in their direction from Inchon.

Back aboard Wantuck with their team being fed and his prize secured in the ship's brig, Mead and Wetmore sat with the ship's captain over a steaming cup of coffee. They reported on the amount of activity in the North Korean capital and the great job the partisans were doing. The Captain filled them in on the Inchon landing—perfect results. He added details of the break out from the Pusan Perimeter by the UN troops and that Seoul was nearly recaptured after savage infantry fighting by the Marines. The surviving North Korean forces were being mopped up as they fled ahead of the ROK along east coast roads. "One more thing," the captain added, "General MacArthur has given permission for the troops to cross the 38th Parallel. We're going into North Korea."

Mead contacted Tokyo by radio and the message was forwarded to the CIA Director as instructed.

"Mission accomplished. Prisoner in irons. Next to Jeju. Love to the Doctor."

Tokyo, Japan—the Dai Ichi Life Insurance Building

Harmon Wetmore and Amos Mead sat outside the office of General Douglas MacArthur awaiting their audience with the Supreme Commander. Their prisoner had quietly been turned over to the CIA station chief in Tokyo to be held until further instructions. The boxes of evidence of the amassing of his illicit fortunes were also secured by the CIA. Mead and Wetmore had shed their North Korean uniforms and were back in the dark suits provided by Eli—with fedoras.

An aide answered an intercom call and motioned the pair to go into MacArthur's office. Walking into the spacious domain of the commanding general, they stopped two steps in front of his desk and stood at stiff attention, each reciting his name—a reaction left over from their military service in the presence of 'the man.'

"Stand easy, gentlemen." General MacArthur said. "Take a seat. I'd appreciate a brief update on your mission—if I'm privy to same. I'm well aware that you're the President's men—under his orders—and I don't give a damn as long as you stay out from under my feet. I'm not exactly the darling of our President, so I'll leave this to your discretion."

"Thank you, General," Mead said. "Our mission into North Korea was successful, sir. However, it was conducted under strict international concerns for secrecy of justification and its target—"

MacArthur interrupted gruffly, "Figured as much."

"However," Mead continued, completely unruffled by the general's demeanor. "Since the mission does have an impact on the theft of the atomic bomb from Okinawa we believe that we should coordinate, or at least cooperate with your commands in the next phase of our work."

The general stood and walked over to a large map of the theater adorning one wall—from Japan to beyond Korea in the Yellow Sea. "We have successfully moved through Inchon and relieved Seoul. I will be going there soon with President Syngman Rhee to see our success first hand. Our troops performed flawlessly—a glorious fight." He stood facing the map with a finger pointing to Seoul, his other arm behind his back. Mead and Wetmore sat quietly during the prolonged silence.

General MacArthur finally turned slowly, pointed directly at Mead and said, "Now how may we support you?"

Santa Barbara, California

Brigit picked up the telephone, ignoring her sticky hand. "Hello—yes, Director."

177

With growing relief she got the report of Amos's successful mission and his return to Tokyo—and that he and Harmon Wetmore were safe and sound. The Director continued, "Brigit, it's not over yet. We have the bomb to recover. But now I must ask you once again to go to Rincon and talk with your Chinese contact. The message I'm asking you to send is—'Su Yu's Korean contact is in our custody. He speaks eloquently about his Chinese colleagues—with exceptional detail. Chairman Mao may lose face on the world scene if the story comes out. It is not out yet. We will keep it a secret forever if he can control his people.' Does that make sense, Brigit?"

Brigit was taking notes as the Director spoke. She replied, "Yes sir, it does. I'll be at Rincon in a couple of hours. Oh, if you contact Amos again tell him I love him."

The Director said, "Will do. Oh, one more thing. I am arranging to contact *Force Three China* and ask him to support any reaction you trigger there. So good hunting and thank you, Brigit."

The phone went dead.

Brigit sat for a moment thinking about what she needed to do, like get Nathan cleaned up and over to Amy Sokol's house. Finally she thought, *I'll tell Kuisong about Su Yu—and Tai Li.* The latter, Brigit's addition to the message based on her hunch of his greedy involvement. As a psychologist she always looked deeper into motivation. She knew that Su Yu was a general who was charged with the invasion of Formosa—a mission found impossible by the other generals and Mao.

It must have crushed his ego, she thought. *Could well be why he agreed with the Russian's plot to build a kingdom on a united Korea.* She smiled to herself. *Not any more, boys.*

Tokyo, Japan—the Dai Ichi Life Insurance Building

Before Amos Mead could answer MacArthur's question, the general continued to speak, "My people tell me you two were OSS

178

in the War and even worked in China. I never held any trust in OSS. Nimitz used you, I didn't."

Mead interjected, "We were well aware of that, sir." MacArthur laughed out loud, his hands on his hips. "Okay, then. I'm going to tell you more than you should know—as civilians. But as you're the President's men ... here it is. The Joint Chiefs of Staff have issued orders for the retaliatory atomic bombing of Manchurian military bases if either their armies crossed into Korea or if the Chinese or North Korean bombers attacked Korea from there. Also, the Air Force Strategic Air Command is ordered to augment its capacities—and this should include atomic capabilities."

Wetmore and Mead sat and listened to the general with interest. They were aware of some of the message, but not that it had reached this level. The general continued, "You already know that the President ordered the transfer of nine Mark VIII nuclear capsules to the Air Force's Ninth Bomb Group. He has signed an order to use them against Chinese and Korean targets."

"Yes sir," Mead said. "That's where the theft came in. The President intended that we keep the news to a *Broken Arrow*" incident—not a stolen bomb, just a nuclear incident without detonation. So far as I can tell the order has held up."

"I agree," MacArthur said. "That is our orders. But did you know that he's publicly talked about use of the A-bombs?"

Mead said, "No sir—"

"Then read this."

General MacArthur grabbed a newspaper from a nearby table and shoved it at Mead. The headline read:

President Truman said today that his government is actively considering using the atomic bomb to end the war in Korea. The first line following: *The President said that only he commanded atomic bomb use.*

All Mead could think about was, *I hope nobody makes any mistakes in judgment or about the intentions of the other guy.*

Spaso House, American Embassy, Moscow, Russia, USSR

Eli Jorgen finished reading the wire from the Director, through the *Force Three* connection. He sat back in his chair, feeling a sense of relief from the tension of wondering what Mead and Wetmore had discovered. *I need to get this to Glebov,* he thought and reached for his copy of Mikhail Lermontov's *A Hero of Our Time* and retrieved the key to the *straddling code.*

The Kremlin, Moscow, Russia, USSR

General Secretary Khrushchev told Ivan Ivanovitch Glebov to enter. "You said you have news of our Korean problem," he said.

"Yes, sir," Grebov said. "The American ambassador reports that our plan worked without flaw. The Americans Mead and Wetmore conducted a successful raid on the embassy and took Colonel General Terenti Shtykov into custody. They retrieved evidence of his plans including bank records of his thefts—"

Khrushchev interrupted Grebov, "Have the Americans kept their word?

Grebov said, "They have, Comrade Secretary. All is under full secrecy and Shtykov will be given to our custody when we work out the plans for the best way and time. No one but you and I— and our American friends—will know of this."

"One more thing, Comrade Secretary," Glebov said, a sly smile rising to show in his eyes. "I received this from our mission in Pyongyang—a top secret wire."

He handed a printed copy to Khrushchev.

With regrets we report the finding of the remains of Colonel General Terenti Shtykov found in convoy attacked by American warplanes. Body burned, but scraps of his uniform with insignia and some identification papers survived. Contents of convoy seem to be his property. It was headed north out of Pyongyang. More as available.

Nikita Khrushchev smiled broadly with his signature toothy grin. "Clever. Clever indeed. Now, Ivan Ivan'ch, how have our KGB friends taken the mysterious loss of their prisoner?"

"As one might expect, Comrade Secretary—by keeping it a KGB secret to avoid embarrassing themselves."

Khrushchev held his smile, appearing to stifle an urge to laugh out loud. "Secrets are good—sometimes."

CHAPTER TWENTY-TWO

AP—SPECIAL REPORT—A *United Nations sanctioned general assault sends troops across the 38th Parallel to begin reunification of Korea. The American 1st Cavalry Division led the fight.*

China begins support of North Korea.

U.S. Army Combat Intelligence reports that the lead elements of the Communist Chinese 38th Field Army has crossed the Yalu River.

It is reported that the North Korean capital of Pyongyang has fallen to the United Nations Forces.

Tokyo, Japan—the Dai Ichi Life Insurance Building

The conversation came full circle to address Mead's needs for a raid on the island of Jeju—if that were needed. Mead said, "General, my plans are in an early stage as of now—too many critical variables to tie up. I will need continued access to the ROK Rangers—"

MacArthur interrupted, "Damn fine fighters, those Korean Rangers. Damn fine, indeed."

Mead exchanged a glance with Wetmore, then answered, "Agreed, General. That's why I want them with me again. But, sir, I also need to have access to Air Force technical people—and the Navy for transportation—"

"Say no more," the general said, stepping on Mead's words. He hit a button on the intercom on his desk. "Colonel, Mead and

Wetmore are on their way out there. Get them whatever they want."

The pair rose from their seats. "Thank you, sir."

"Just clean this damn thing up—I've got a war to win. Good day, gentlemen."

Mead has the reports from Jeju that their "tall Chinese man" is under surveillance. He has to assume that means the stolen weapon is on the island. The first order of business is to learn what they may be facing from the bomb. A select group of Air Force senior atomic weapons experts, summoned at Mead's request, gathered quickly at MacArthur's headquarters. Joined by Wetmore and the ROK Ranger sergeant, Mead opened the session, "The theft of the bomb is kind of an open secret among you folks." Nods of agreement met his gaze. "But it does not, I emphasize *not*, under any circumstances, go beyond us—orders of the President. It is a "*Broken Arrow*" event to the press and the world. My information says we've been successful so far."

"Gentlemen, it is not our intent to keep it secret to avoid blame or undue fear—it's simply to allow us to complete the mission of locating it and recovering it without interference by foreign powers. How long it remains secret is anybody's guess. With some luck we can have it back before it becomes an issue and get on with the business of this war."

One of the Air Force colonels spoke, "You sound like you have more information on this that we do."

"I'll give you that, Colonel," Mead answered. "What I need from you is ... what are the dangers we face if we lay hands on this thing? For all we know it could have been dumped at sea—it certainly hasn't flown anywhere. So if it is hidden on land somewhere and we find it—what then?"

Mead walked over to where his briefcase stood open on a table, retrieved a paper, scanned it for a moment, and finally said, "One more thing. The person who we have reason to believe is with the bomb, a Chinese scientist named George Huang, has a PhD in

Physics from MIT—specializing in nuclear physics. We must assume he knows what he's doing with the bomb."

The Air Force Colonel rose and walked to the blackboard. "Let's hope he does, Mead. Or we may be seeing a big bang." He drew a crude oval shape on the board and began to speak, "The basic bomb is a metal case that holds the shaped explosives and the nuclear core. Without the nuclear core it's just a big dumb bomb—"

Mead interrupted, "And that very essential nuclear core was stolen with the bomb."

"Correct," the Colonel responded, turning back to the drawing. "Now, in a two-stage thermonuclear weapon the energy from the primary impacts the secondary. An essential energy transfer modulator called the interstage is located between the primary and the secondary and protects the secondary's fusion fuel from heating too quickly—which could cause it to explode in a conventional heat explosion before the fusion and fission reactions get a chance to start."

"Whoa, whoa, Colonel," Mead said, "We've got to get this down to my level—like how to be sure we don't blow up an island. I appreciate your lesson—maybe even understand some of it—but we've got to get tactical for this mission."

"I understand, sir," the Colonel said, laughing. "But I'll need to share just a little more before we break it down." He paused and looked at Mead before turning back to the drawing. "The interstage and the secondary are encased together inside a stainless steel membrane to form the canned subassembly—we call that the CSA. The interstage material is doped with beryllium. Beryllium moderates the flux of neutrons from the primary and absorbs and re-radiates the x-rays." The Colonel walked away from the drawing and stood in front of the group. "I won't ask for questions—time to get to your concerns, Mr. Mead."

Amos Mead stood and walked to the front. As he began to speak he noticed that Harmon Wetmore had slipped out of the room. "Let's call a biological break. Then I want my team in here to prepare for the mission."

The officers scattered to coffee, donuts and the latrines. Mead sent word for the Ranger team to assemble in the room. In a few minutes the room filled with the Air Force people and ROK troops. Mead opened, "Colonel, these four ROK Rangers are our mission security team—and our backup. I'm asking you to assign one technician who can actually understand what we find with the bomb to join Mr. Wetmore and me on the team. We already have two Rangers on the island who have ID'd one of the thieves, the Chinese nuclear physicist. They're keeping him under surveillance and hoping to locate the bomb's hiding place. I've not received word of success there yet."

Mead saw Wetmore slip back into the room and quietly take a seat. "Colonel," Mead continued, "Please take us through the arming scenarios."

The Air Force colonel stood and faced the group. "By way of definition, gentlemen, the *arming system* of a nuclear weapon is that portion of the weapon which originates the signals required to arm, safe, or re-safe the firing and fusing systems. Also it actuates the nuclear safing system. The *fusing system, however,* is that portion of the weapon that originates the signal which triggers the firing system. The fusing system normally consists of radars, baro switches, timers, impact crystals, antennas, and baro sensing elements. Since the bombs at Kadena Air Base were intended for air burst the one you're looking for has a radar proximity fuse. You also need to know that we usually employ more than one type of fuse in each warhead—for example, a contact fuse doubles as a backup to a radar fuse. When a contact fuse is installed to back-up a radar fuse we term it *salvage fusing*."

"Makes sense," Mead interjected. "If you don't get an air-burst, it'll explode when it hits the deck. We don't want an intact weapon in unfriendly hands that can be turned against us—or disabled or disassembled and copied. This is what we've got, colonel—an intact weapon in unfriendly hands. We think we know

185

it's not being used to steal secrets—but to steal a victory in Korea by blackmail."

The colonel continued, "That's why we need to be able to recognize the level of danger that enemy has established. Will the bomb be fused—or worse, booby-trapped? Also, there's the possibility this scientist can rig a time delay detonation—unless he's suicidal."

Mead said, "So far these guys have acted more like petty thieves, looking for survival when they're caught. We can only hope the scientist follows suit."

The Air Force colonel nodded and continued, "Our weapon is a capsule bomb, meaning that the nuclear material for the bomb is kept in a special capsule separate from the rest of the device for safety's sake. In normal use that means that just before the bomb is to be dropped from the aircraft the capsule is inserted into the bomb casing to arm the weapon. But I must stress that our situation is not normal. There is no delivery vehicle. The bomb is stationary—but the same rules apply. The Chinese scientist must insert the special capsule … which, I'm told, he possesses. To arm the bomb, he must insert the fissile nuclear materials into the bomb core through a removable segment of the explosive lens assembly—which is then replaced and the weapon closed and armed."

The colonel motioned to the group to come up closer to the diagram pinned to the wall. He pointed to various elements as he spoke. "This easy to remove cartridge is the electrical and electronic heart of the weapon. The batteries, radars, and switches of the fusing system are readily accessible. The detonator contacts of the unit are on the face of the cartridge, and the detonator distribution system is inside the weapon. When the cartridge is inserted into the weapon, pressure contact provides the connection between firing system and the terminals of the detonation system."

For the next hour the Air Force officers discussed a variety of possible ways that booby-traps or delay fusing might happen. The combat and guerilla experienced ROK troops on the team asked pointed questions and took notes, fully aware that their own lives were on the line with a mistake. The ROK Sergeant asked, "Can you be specific about the arming system—what we're going to face out there?"

The colonel looked at Mead, who nodded and sat back to listen. "Well, Sergeant, the internal neutron initiator, code name *Urchin,* is a neutron generating device that triggers the nuclear detonation of an atomic bomb—once the critical mass has been 'assembled' by the force of conventional explosives." He walked back to the board and pointed. "The detonator is located at the center of the bomb's plutonium pit, which consists of a beryllium pellet and a beryllium shell with polonium between the two ... more than you need to know. As I told you earlier our bomb probably has a radar fuse—but you can expect to find a contact fuse as a backup— remember, we called that *salvage fusing.* Hit that with something hard and heavy and you go bye-bye in an instant."

"Thank you, sir," the sergeant said. "I can work with that."

All the questions got specific answers and explanations in return. They knew as well as Mead that their collective butts were on the line. Success was the only option.

During the session, Wetmore motioned for Mead to join him in the hall. "Amos, I was just in touch with Suen—"

Mead interrupted him, *"Force Three China.* I assume he was happy to be back in contact with you."

"I'll assume so," Wetmore said. "He's pretty busy—and on edge—at the moment."

"On edge?" Mead asked.

"Yah, lot's going on. I've already sent what I heard to MacArthur's Intel Chief—so here it is. That 38th Army incursion by the Chinese was a feint. The 39th—about thirty thousand Chinese troops—are pushing the UN troops back to the Chongchon River."

Mead looked puzzled. "So what has him on edge?"

Wetmore looked at his notes and said, "Mao has sent four Chinese Armies to attack the 1st Marines and 7th Infantry at the Chosin Reservoir—but here's the weird news. Our old friend General Tai Li was ordered to be in the front ranks of the assault. At least we know that Mao does not approve of individuals on his staff trying to line their pockets."

Mead could only laugh and shake his head. "So we've got the Russian branch in the bag and the Chinese branch in the heat—at least part of it. That leaves us with the scientist—and the bomb."

"Not quite, Amos, Wetmore said. "There's one more thing. When Mao's people went to get Tai Li and Su Yu—General Su Yu was missing, along with an unknown number of his personal body guards. Not the people I want to see loose in the shadows right now."

Shaking his head, a hand rubbing his chin slowly in thought, Mead said, "Harm, this adds a whole to element to our planning for Jeju Island."

"I'd say so, Amos … oh, he also said that Kuisong would not tell Brigit about the two generals. Do you know what he means by that?"

"Sure do, Harm. When we get a minute I'll tell you what Brigit's been up to. But for now we've got some contingency plans to get to. Our opposing force scenario may have changed for the worse. Let's go back in and get the team working on it."

Mead and Wetmore quietly rejoined the session, and after a moment he addressed the Air Force Colonel, "Colonel, earlier I asked you for a technician—but how about *you* coming along with us? Our Intel on Jeju Island seems to be solid based on what we've learned so far. Good probability we'll be faced with the bomb—one way or the other. How about it?"

The Colonel smiled and replied, "You get orders cut from my general and I'm game."

Mead said, "I can get orders cut a lot higher than that. Welcome aboard, Colonel."

CHAPTER TWENTY-THREE

AP—SPECIAL REPORT—Communist Chinese Forces have surrounded Marines at Chosin Reservoir. President Truman threatens use of atomic bombs against Chinese Communist Forces.

Jeju Island, Korea

One of the ROK Rangers followed George Huang on his almost daily walk out from the village. Huang carried a walking stick and moved through small groups of tourists with a smile and greeting when he met them on the popular walking trail. The trail led up the slope of the volcanic mountain called *Hallasan* that dates back to the Pliocene epoch, but has not erupted since the year 1000.

The mountain is a massive shield volcano that forms the bulk of Jeju Island. Eruptions of basalt lava built the island from the continental shelf about three hundred feet below sea level to the mountain now towering over six thousand four hundred feet and visible from everywhere on the island, though the summit is usually adorned in clouds. A large crater with two lakes crowns the heights and over three hundred sixty parasite cones—*oreum* in the Jeju dialect—cover the flanks of the mountain. Most of them are cinder cones, but some are lava domes near the coastline. The lava domes contain miles of lava tubes—caves of varying proportions and depths.

Huang finally reached a small trail that branched off the tourist route and wound down the slope, disappearing around the base of a jagged basalt dome. The Ranger stayed back far enough to mingle with tourists or otherwise be occupied. But this move of Huang's caught him in the open and closing on the Chinese man too fast. He slowed and took out a tourist hiking map he kept. Huang stopped a few steps down the side trail, then turned and retraced his steps to the main trail—and the Ranger.

"May I give you directions?" Huang asked the Ranger.

"Thank you. I'm looking to find the trail to the lakes," the Ranger answered, holding out the map he held in his hand.

"Just stay on this trail, sir. It is a long climb." Huang turned and strode back down the trail toward the village. The Ranger was forced to continue—at least until he was out of sight.

In the village the second Ranger had easily picked the simple lock to Huang's quarters and looked around, careful not to touch or disturb anything. He saw the tools on the small table and the complicated device he seemed to be working on. There was no sign of the special insert to arm the bomb. He carefully backed out and locked the door. As he turned up the street he spotted the Chinese man coming down the trail at the edge of the village. Wondering if he had been seen at Huang's door, he slipped down the first narrow alley between the houses and hurried into the shadows, wending his way back to their quarters to wait.

It was some time later that the second member of the team arrived. "I ran into Huang on the trail," he said. "Rather he ran into me. I think he was worried about me. I can't tell any more—except that he turned around and came back to the village."

"I know," the second Ranger said. "He damn near caught me coming out of his place. I also do not know if he actually saw me or suspected anything."

The first Ranger said, "What did you find in his rooms?"

"A lot of tools and the early makings of a device I couldn't identify without more study—"

"And what of the arming device?"

"Nowhere to be seen. Maybe it's hidden there somewhere, or maybe it's with the bomb. In the meantime, we have to check in and give Tokyo what we've got—which is not much."

The Rangers set up their radio and called Mead's special code.

USS Wantuck (ADP-125), Korea Strait, East China Sea

Amos Mead, Harmon Wetmore, and the ROK Ranger raiding party were once again aboard USS Wantuck. This time the party included a contingent of ROK Marines as security—and an Air Force Colonel, expert on the a-bomb. In light of the news that General Su Yu and his goon squad were on the loose, it only seemed a prudent move to Mead to add the Marines.

Their high-speed transport, USS Wantuck, combined the hull of a warship and a destroyer escort with the superstructure of a troop transport. It was designed to both carry and launch amphibious landing forces. Sailing from Yokosuka Naval Base, Japan, this special mission involved a much smaller force than usual for USS Wantuck and her crew.

The nearly eight hundred mile sail took over three days at sea, long enough to produce interesting relationships among the American Navy crew and the Korean Marines. The Marines discovered what the ROK Rangers had already reluctantly accepted, how the American galley crew "ruined" perfectly good rice. To avoid a mutiny of sorts, Mead and the captain of the ADP came up with a plan to deal with the cultural sensitivity—they allowed the raiding party to cook their own rice. But Mead and the other Americans asked for something in return—the ROK Marines had to move their large crocks of *kimchee*, the fermented, pungent mix of vegetables and garlic onto the ship's fantail, as far away from American noses as possible. Though *kimchee* is common to Korean meals, it exudes a powerful odor that stuns the American sense of smell.

Mutiny avoided. The ubiquitous, 'Steaming as before,' is entered in the ship's log.

Gosan Village, Jeju Island, Korea

Mead had decided to land his party on the far side of the island from the village of Seongsan where his two advance party Rangers were watching George Huang. The Rangers had been told of Mead's scheduled landing, and about Su Yu's disappearance from China. They understood the potential for trouble.

The landing at Gosan Village went smoothly. The captain of USS Wantuck had commented about finally being able to drop troops off without ducking incoming fire from the beach. Mead agreed and hoped it would stay that way for him and his team for a while.

A group this large landing from a warship could not be considered discrete and Mead wondered how long word would take to cross the island to Seongsan village—and George. A small nearby Korean Naval Base provided adequate quarters for the team of ROK Rangers and Marines and their *baeg-in* (white people) leaders as they prepared for the mission ahead.

An advance party of two of the newly landed Rangers was sent to Seongsan to connect with the two Rangers already there. More intelligence was vitally needed before Mead was comfortable with any action of scale. Besides, he didn't know for sure if there were any "hostiles" on the island besides George Huang. As planned the pair dressed in fishermen clothes—their call sign, *Checkmate Scout*.

Mead met with the *Jungwi* (First Lieutenant) who commanded the small contingent of South Korean sailors manning the small base on Jeju Island. "My men are in need of some food, Lieutenant," Mead said.

The *Jungwi* responded, "Sir, we have only a small *sigdang* (mess hall). But I'm sure our cook can accommodate you. I will call her." A few minutes later a woman covered in an obviously well used apron came into the commander's office. "This is Mrs. Yun-seo Kang, Mr. Mead. She is our cook and very much in

192

command of our dining facility, such as it is. Isn't that correct Mrs. Kang?"

"That is so!" Mrs. Kang bellowed, an uncharacteristically loud voice for a Korean woman. "Come with me … I show." Mrs. Yunseo Kang walloped Mead on the shoulder as she pointed the way. It was supposed to be an affectionate cuff, but the cook, a solidly built woman in her fifties, very nearly threw Mead off his feet. He laughed, but while following her he covertly felt his shoulder for damage.

The women of Jeju have a reputation for strength. The island is famous for its *haenyeo*, female divers who gather abalone and other seafood for up to five hours a day in the cold sea—without scuba gear. Mead was learning more and more of the unique culture of the island.

A couple of hours later the team sat down to a meal as they waited for word from their advance party. Much to the delight of the Korean troops, the creative Mrs. Kang proudly served the Jeju version of *yukejang*, which is more like comforting beef gravy than the traditionally spicy hot broth. She also had *samgyetang*, a soul-warming chicken soup that contained an entire chicken, ginseng, Chinese dates, and abalone with so much rice in it that it's practically gruel. Mead and Wetmore and the Colonel agreed the latter was more to their liking. After a few minutes Mead said, "Harm, this doesn't feel right … just sitting here enjoying a meal as if we were on a holiday."

Wetmore, wiping a morsel from his lips, answered, "Just take the moment, Amos. We need intelligence from our guys. We can't just march across the island—unless we want to announce our mission to Huang and company—or maybe even Su Yu. Wherever the hell he is now."

Mead looked around the crowded mess hall at his men making small talk and enjoying a home cooked meal, then put his head down and resumed devouring the hot food.

Outside the sky darkened, clouds scudding out of the East China Sea, large rain drops beginning to announce the changes on the metal roof where the men sat eating.

Seongsan Village, Jeju Island, Korea

The two Rangers who had been living in the village, tasked with finding and tracking Dr. Huang, met Mead's advance party outside of Seongsan and passed on what they had observed. George Huang had kept to his usual routine and movements around the village, but had not gone back onto the mountain since encountering one of the Rangers on the trail. He reported, "We don't know if the cessation of his hikes is connected to the meeting or whether we've been discovered for what we are some other way."

The second Ranger said, "I went back to the mountain as I was interested in the caves and walked through the largest one, called *Manjanggul*, from end to end. It's over a mile long and cold and wet."

One of the advance party asked, "Did you see it as a hiding place for the bomb?"

"No ... too many tourists ... a very public place. But I heard that there are many such caves so I believe it is where we search, or follow, Huang. Come. We will take you to our rooms. From there you can contact Mead. We will walk near to Dr. Huang's."

The four men, dressed in clothing similar to the local fishermen, walked toward the village. The darkening sky and rising wind had already begun to fling waves of rain over the group. They hunkered into their jackets and, bowing to the rain gods, quickened their pace toward shelter.

Fifty yards from the door to Huang's rooms they saw a Chinese man step out onto the street—it wasn't Huang.

The two Rangers who had been following him for days stopped suddenly, the other two looking puzzled while they mimicked the move. "Follow me," the first Ranger whispered as he veered off the path and moved toward the waterfront. Glancing back, he watched as the stranger reacted to the rain and stepped back into the building, emerging quickly with a jacket around his shoulders and a hat pulled low. Another Chinese man followed the first, and then another, as they turned toward the mountain trail.

"Looks like we dodged a bullet," one of the new Rangers said. "But we can't follow those guys ... no cover. Let's get to your place and put a plan around this situation—Mead needs information, and quick."

One of the Rangers stopped at the corner of the first building that shielded them from the view of the Chinese, peering around to watch them depart. He turned and caught up to the others. "Maybe a problem ... that last guy was carrying some kind of package."

The rain began to drive in steady sheets, turning the usually dusty road of the small village into a slippery challenge. The Rangers reached the meager quarters of the advance party and radioed what they'd observed to Mead.

CHAPTER TWENTY-FOUR

AP—SPECIAL REPORT—1st Marine Division fighting through encircling Communist Chinese Forces at Chosin. First elements reach American 3rd Infantry Division lines.

CIA Headquarters, Arlington, Virginia

The Director read the secure wire from Mead. Routed through Tokyo, it was Mead's first report from Jeju Island since landing his raiding party:

Advance element located Chinese in village of Seongsan. Three spotted, but exact number and ID unknown. Raining hard with low visibility. Main force remains in Gosan village awaiting further Intel from advance group.

The Director picked up his phone to the White House, reporting Mead's message to the President and adding the conclusion that no contact had yet occurred with the targets. "But, Mr. President, the sight of additional Chinese can only tell us that General Su Yu has made it there and brought reinforcements. He may be getting desperate." The call ended with the usual request to be kept informed, and he called to his secretary, "Sarah, get Dr. Mead on the line, please."

Santa Barbara, California

Brigit Mead leaned back in her desk chair after replacing the telephone on its cradle. The call from the Director did not leave her with any comfort—even though she now knew where Amos was. She called Amy and told her she'd be a little late picking up Nathan, told Frank Sokol she was going out, then walked quickly to her car, heading south for Rincon. The Director had given her a mission.

NAVCOMMSTA, Rincon, California

The duty staff at Navy Communications Center Rincon was only too familiar with Doctor Brigit Mead. The Director of the CIA had contacted them earlier with instructions, so the line through Pearl Harbor to Beijing was already open when she arrived.

Sitting at the radio and adjusting the headphones, Brigit was thinking of her approach to this task. After getting the go-ahead from Navy in Pearl Harbor she began, "Calling *shandian yun*, calling *shandian yun*. This is *Glinda*, repeat, *Glinda*, in the clear. Over."

Brigit quietly peered down at the ledge in front of her, intent on the tiny electronic sounds coming from the headset. She was familiar with the process. Once more she broadcasted, "*Shandian yun*, this is *Glinda* calling in the clear."

The crackling static in her ears increased, then a voice, "*Glinda*, this is Pearl Harbor. Wait one. Your target is just coming on line." After an interminably long second she heard, "*Glinda*. To what do I owe the pleasure of your call?"

Brigit marveled at the skill of the Navy's simultaneous-translation services in Hawaii.

She answered, "Good day, *Shandian*, I'm sure this is anything but a pleasure, but it is necessary. You seem to have lost a general, my friend."

There was a pause on the air, just an electronic hum continued. Then the Chinese general spoke, "Can you explain that, *Glinda*?"

"Of course I can, *Shandian yun*. You know by now that I only speak of what I know. Such was our talks during the war that kept you from confronting the Japanese."

197

Another pause, then, "Please. Tell me."

"We have seen General Su Yu."

"Where have you seen Su Yu, *Glinda*?"

"That must remain only for me to know—for now. Is there more you wish to share with me?"

"Only this. Chairman Mao would very much like to know the whereabouts of the general, *Glinda*. Very much, indeed."

"I shall see what I can do for Mao, *Shandian yun*—when the time is right. I see that Mao is quite busy in Korea, and that it is not all success."

"*Glinda*, you know I cannot speak about that. Please contact me when you have more to say about General Su Yu."

NAVCOMMSTA Pearl Harbor came on the line, "Ma'am, Beijing is off the air."

Brigit slowly slid the headset onto her neck, rubbing her ears. She had wanted to ask about the young airman—but this was not the time.

Her mission to infuse turmoil took precedence. She would report to the Director.

Spaso House, American Embassy, Moscow, Russia, USSR

Eli Jorgen sat reading the deciphered message from *Force Three Russia*. Earlier he had sent a message asking to be advised when the Soviets might enter the Korean conflict. With the Communist Chinese now in the fight he'd acted on the request of the President who *wanted no more surprises*.

Ivan Ivanovitch Glebov's reply read:

No ground troops to be committed. But trainers will remain active and possibly some of the MIG's will have Soviet pilots.

This was news because MIG aircraft had not yet been encountered. Jorgen left his office in search of the CIA station chief. This news was for him to report through proper channels. As he walked down the long hall his thoughts went to *I wonder how Mead is doing.*

Gosan Village, Jeju Island, Korea

When Mead got the radio call reporting that the Chinese had headed toward to mountain carrying a package he made a quick decision. "Harm, we've got to go—now. If that package is the critical core—"

Wetmore interrupted, "And if it's not there's still no downside ... I agree, we go."

Mead asked the Colonel, "What do you think about the report?"

He answered, "The initiating core is a tiny item—could well be in a small package carried by one man. I agree that there's no time to waste if they're going to mate it to the bomb."

The team was called together in the mess hall, dripping wet from the short run from their quarters. They slipped their ponchos off over their heads, shaking them in a futile effort to shed water. Under the rain gear the ROK troops wore the olive drab quilted cotton uniform jacket with a cross-stitched quilt pattern and a pair of large breast pockets, and US style olive drab woolen trousers. They're U.S. style pile caps had devices of *yang* and *yin* symbols.

The storm intensified, the crash of sheets of rain on the metal roof and the window rattling wind causing Mead to think *monsoon*. A map of the island was laid out on the plank table and Mead began to make assignments. He had three small trucks supplied by the Korean Navy, barely room enough to carry them all. His advance team of two Rangers had ridden to Seongsan to meet the pair who had been trailing Huang in a merchant's truck. The merchant was returning to his village from an unsuccessful market flooded out by the storm.

Palm trees bent to the winds and waves of yellow mustard pulsated across the lowlands of Jeju Island, while less than one hundred miles away on the mainland of Korea a war raged. These thoughts and more went through Mead's mind as the last of his men crammed themselves into the trucks and he stepped up into the front seat with his driver. "Stay on the coast road," Mead said.

The trucks moved off into the storm, canvas tops already leaking on the miserable soldiers. Wetmore had the radio in the second truck, a frequency open to the advance party in Seongsan. He knew the thousand year old Mount Hallasan loomed ahead of them—but the scudding clouds and sheets of wind driven rains obscured its bulky presence.

Seongsan Village, Jeju Island, Korea

The two Rangers who had been tasked with finding and tracking Dr. Huang carefully, but quickly, started off in pursuit of the Chinese headed up the mountain. As they left the village and the cover the small buildings provided they had to stay well back and use the sparse cover of lava rocks and shrubs to avoid detection. The rain helped—but also hindered their ability to maintain contact with their targets.

The Rangers from Mead's team, call sign *Checkmate Scout*, stood watch on Huang's dwelling, trying to determine how many other Chinese were in the fight. Doorways and dripping canvas awnings provided some shelter, but they were already soaked and cold. "Did you see that?" A ranger said to his partner. "A light— just a flicker."

His partner nodded and said, "Looks like it was in a back room. So we know somebody's still home?"

The first Ranger started to speak but was interrupted by the radio strapped to his chest. He listened. "They've turned off the main trail—a small path to the left. This is the turn Huang took when he spotted me earlier. We're giving them time to get ahead further, then we'll follow."

"Roger that," the Ranger said. "We see at least one more in the building. Suspect more. Out." The Ranger switched the channel and called, "*Checkmate Leader*, this is *Checkmate Scout*, over."

Almost immediately the radio squawked, "*Checkmate Scout*, this is *Checkmate One*, over."

"Roger, *Checkmate One*. Small group headed up the mountain. Two of ours are following and we have an unknown number in quarters."

Wetmore thought for a moment then replied, "*Checkmate Scout*, continue to observe. Try not to make contact. We are one half hour ETA your position. *Checkmate One*, out."

The Ranger put the radio on standby. "We wait," he said.

From their vantage point on Mount Hallasan the trailing Rangers watched the three Chinese men climb between two cinder cones and disappear over a drop on the other side. These *oreum* (cinder and lava cones) cover the flanks of the mountain. The lava domes contain miles of tubes—caves.

The Rangers hurried to the spot where the path dropped away from the cones and spotted movement well ahead through the driving rain and dim reflected light. A black basalt boulder field spread out between them and the Chinese—who had just disappeared from sight.

Stopping to adjust their ponchos against the rain—almost a useless endeavor—the lead Ranger knelt down, leaned over his radio like a Condor over its prey, and pressed the switch, "Calling *Checkmate Scout*—we've lost visual. They may be into their lair by now. We are proceeding with caution—over."

Checkmate Scout responded, "Roger—understand lost visual. Our instructions are to avoid contact until *Checkmate Leader* arrives—ETA about twenty, over."

"Roger, avoid contact—but we're going to move ahead and try for visual again. Out."

Mead's caravan stopped to clear some large rocks from the road that had washed down from a steep cut face. One was moved far enough off the track for the trucks to proceed as Wetmore updated Mead on the radio call. Leaning toward Wetmore, he pulling his poncho hood back enough to speak, "Okay, Harm.

Advise them that we're arriving between the village and the mountain—if this damn map is right. Get a current status on those guys left in the village—how many."

Harmon Wetmore just flashed a thumbs-up and turned to climb into his truck. Sliding and scraping paint on the rocks the caravan moved off.

On the mountain the advance Rangers eased up to the last point they'd seen the Chinese. They saw that the path dropped steeply toward an opening in a large lava dome. The opening was closed nearly to the top by fallen debris from further up the slope. It appeared quite natural, but the men knew otherwise. As they scanned the face of the dome a flicker of light beamed out from the gap on top of the fallen rocks. The Rangers looked at each other, and then carefully picked their way down the slippery path. Evidence of others having lost footing on the path showed in the slick mud. The lead Ranger placed the earpiece of his radio in his ear—taking no chance of noise this close in.

The rain continued, sheeting like waterfalls off the larger basalt blocks as the wind whipped in whirls through the lava and cinder cones.

In the village *Checkmate Scout* and his partner squeezed back into a doorway as the light in their target building reappeared and grew brighter. The front door, just fifty feet away, opened suddenly and a Chinese man appeared, an AK-47 rifle slung barrel down over his olive drab cape. He stopped and looked both ways, then motioned for others to follow. In line, three more men, obviously military, appeared and headed after the first—toward the mountain trail. There was no light left lit in the room after the men left, closing the door behind them.

The Rangers waited a moment then rushed across the space up to the wall of the building they'd been watching. Easing to the window, *Checkmate Scout* peered in. Seeing no movement he motioned for his partner to take a position at the other side of the door. With a quick look in the direction the Chinese went, he tried the door—it opened. He hesitated an instant in case of outgoing fire. None came—he entered. On the table the light from the window showed him that the tools he'd seen in his earlier visit were placed neatly back in a box. The mechanism that was on the table was gone. The two Rangers checked the back room. All clear. He keyed his radio mike, "*Checkmate Leader*, or *Checkmate One*. This is *Checkmate Scout*. Trouble, sir. Four more Chinese have left the village headed up the trail. That's the last of them. We're following. We can be sure that General SU Yu is among them—considering the number of Chinese goons added to the party. Will try to warn our guys—they may be trapped between the groups. Your ETA? Over."

"*Checkmate Scout. Checkmate One*. Village in sight. Meet you outside the village in five. Out."

"Let's move," *Checkmate Scout* said. "Our reinforcements are inbound."

They set off toward the mountain.

The rain continued its relentless barrage.

CHAPTER TWENTY-FIVE

AP—SPECIAL REPORT—General Walton Walker, 8th Army Commander, has been killed in a jeep accident.
General Matthew Ridgway assumes command of Eighth Army.

Seongsan Village, Jeju Island, Korea

The two Rangers watched the tiny caravan emerge from the driving rain, and flagged them down in the waning light. The ROK Marines and Rangers emerged from the back of the trucks looking bedraggled and cold. Which they were. To a man they were looking for a fight—just as a change of pace.

But some of the group, including Mead and Wetmore knew that a fight is the last thing they want—with a live atomic bomb lying around somewhere up ahead.

"Mr. Mead," the first advance Ranger, *Checkmate Scout*, began, "There's the trail." He pointed to the muddy track that now ran like a river down the lower slope. "I have not been able to raise the advance team on the radio. They are between the first Chinese group and the second one. If they don't spot those last guys, they're in trouble."

Mead asked, "Is there any other route up there?"

"Not from this side, sir. A lot of those caves and tunnels in this mountain have more than one entry, but we don't even know which one we're looking for yet."

"Options?" Mead asked, looking around the team standing close in the rain.

"Just this trail, sir. And staying ready for a fight—or worse."

"Okay. Sergeant, tell your men to not bunch up. We go with combat spacing. Be ready to move into skirmish or defensive— depending what those Chinese folks decide to do." With a wave of his arm, the Mead force moved out up the muddy track, wondering how so much of his old Marine training was kicking in—and thankful that it was.

At the cave, half crawling, half climbing, the two advance ROK Rangers reached the opening in the mountain at the top of the rubble pile and carefully peered in. Shadows of weird shapes moved around the dark basalt as men moved across a single light source deep in a large cave. But only shadows, nothing specific, could be seen. From their position, the Rangers began to see that the rocks that appeared like rubble from below were carefully placed—and moved more than once.

The Ranger triggered his radio, but could not get a response to his call. Water or a simple loose connection was feared. As he hunkered over the microphone trying to keep it out of direct rain and find the problem, his partner rolled back, peering through the rain, checking the route below them that they'd just ascended— and saw movement. He tapped his partner's leg and pointed. "We've got company. We've got to move—now."

They looked to the side of the pile, deciding the left side had larger rocks for cover, and hurriedly climbed down the slippery route. The driving rain and whirling gusts of wind provided the only cover for the pair until they could snuggle in behind the basalt jumble below them.

The small group of Chinese men moved closer, intent on not slipping in their climb up the rocks. The last man in line was taller and struggled the most, huddled beneath his military style cape.

The two Rangers recognized him at once—Dr. Huang.

Slowly bringing their weapons, M-2 Carbines, to bear, the Rangers clung flat to the slick basalt block that hid them from the trails view. A shadowed crevice between two blocks gave them a view down the muddy trail.

Suddenly the Chinese group stopped. George Huang reached into his pocket and drew something out, placing it to his lips—the Rangers heard the three sharp tweets—then a pause and three more pierced the gloom. Peering intently at the Chinese on the trail the Rangers did not see the head of a man appear in the opening over the rubble. But the man saw them—and slid his PPS-43 sub-machine gun over the edge.

Shooting down at them, the first burst from the rifle twanged and scraped off the boulder just above the nearest Ranger. A grunt came from the second Ranger as rock fragments sliced his face and head. Blinking through the blood seeping into one eye, he raised his M-2 and fired at the silhouette in the faintly lighted opening. A scream came in reply—and more gunfire as others slid into position.

Down the trail, George Huang and his guards dropped down in the mud, sidling to the side for the small cover of trailside rocks.

The first Ranger slid around the basalt block, choosing more cover from the nearer cave opening, and fired first into the opening and then quickly down the trail as he saw the Chinese guards kneeling and raising weapons. The lead guard went down. The two ROK Rangers barely had cover from the two directions of the incoming fire. Sending carefully spaced return fire down range—one in each direction—was the only way the Rangers could defend themselves.

Coming up the mountain, having already made the turn from the main trail onto the path to the cave, Mead's party heard the sounds of the firefight coming from over the crest of the pass ahead of them. The Ranger *jungsa* moved up next to Mead and said, "We will take the lead. The Marines will stay with you. Follow slowly, listen for the fight."

"Okay, Sergeant. Good luck," Mead answered.

The *jungsa* and his ROK Rangers moved as quickly as the slippery path allowed, weapons ready, anxious to make contact and protect the advance party. With the ROK Marines leading,

Mead, Wetmore, and the Air Force Colonel moved along the path, barely keeping the Rangers in sight through the swirling rain.

The *jungsa* eased over the crest of the path and dropped below it to the military crest—avoiding being silhouetted. Below him the path bottomed out in about fifty yards, then climbed toward a rubble filled opening in the dome. Nothing moved, no sounds. Peering intently through the waves of wind-whipped rain he spotted movement between him and the dome.

Then the unmistakable sound of an M-1911 .45 caliber round made a muffled echo. The figure he'd seen moving across from him dropped and laid still, his sprawling position and sub-machine gun sliding back down the muddy path said he was out of the fight. Flashes erupted from the dark slit he could see at the top of a rubble pile up the edge of the dome. Answering flashes came from below it among the dark shapes of the basalt rock fall—*our guys*, he thought, hearing the familiar burst of an M-2 Carbine. He motioned to his men and moved in a low crouch down the sloping path. Reaching the bottom they still had not been seen.

But they had been seen—by the Rangers outside the cave opening. Seeing the Chinese guard go down under the advancing Ranger's fire, the pair slipped around for more cover from the opening. Another burst of PPS-43 fire pinged off of the rock face over their head. They returned the favor with their M-2 carbines. Below, another Chinese guard raised up—only to go down with the fire of at least three M-2's.

Two dark shapes remained on the path—one slowly standing with his hands held high over his head, the other huddled in a ball in the mud. The Rangers advanced to the pair, wary of the dark hole above them. The Chinese guard's weapon was kicked aside and he was roughly pulled to a kneeling position, hands on his head. The second man was dragged to a kneeling position—and George Huang stared up at his captures, raw fear in his eyes.

From the cave another burst of machinegun fire roared, but fell ineffectually around the group. It was immediately answered by fire from the nearby Rangers—this time advancing toward the dark opening, M-2's firing in short bursts. The ROK Marines, followed by Mead and the others, crested the hill and saw the hand signals from the Rangers to advance with caution.

Above them, standing at the dark opening in the side of the dome, a Ranger waved for them to advance to his position. Securing their two prisoners, the Air Force Colonel took personal command of George Huang, and the party moved slowly and cautiously up to the dark opening. A Ranger with the medical kit worked on the face and head wounds of his comrade.

Led by the ROK Marines, fondly called *gwisin jabneun haebyeongdae* (Devil capturing Marines), the party eased into the cave, slowly moving down toward the bottom, spreading out as the cavern grew in size around them. A dim light cast a yellow glow on the bottom of the cave. There were no sounds besides their own footfalls. Reaching the bottom they stopped, weapons at the ready.

There before them—a wheeled carriage—empty.

The atomic bomb was gone.

CHAPTER TWENTY-SIX

AP—SPECIAL REPORT—UN Naval forces are evacuating X Corps from Hungnam. UN Assembly has passed a Cease Fire Resolution. MIG-15 Soviet made jet fighters are attacking UN aircraft over North Korea for the first time.

The Volcanic Mountain called *Hallasan*, Jeju Island, Korea

Mead held the radio receiver tight to his ear, speaking into the small microphone, "That's correct, sir. The bomb is gone. We captured Huang, but not the *pit device*—as far as we know the bomb is an atomic weapon. But even if it is not, it's still dangerous as high explosive. Sorry, sir, we just don't know."

His radio call to Tokyo, patched through to CIA headquarters in Virginia, had a weak signal—but enough to get the job done for him. Mead had already reported to General MacArthur, so he knew the message would be coming to the President from a couple of directions—*Force Three* did its job—but came up a little short. A dangerous MK-VIII bomb that the world did not need to know about was loose in the hands of unknown people—or governments.

While Mead answered more questions for the Director, Harmon Wetmore gathered the team and said, "We've got to sweep this place clean—find anything they left behind."

The only light in the cave came from the lower entrance and didn't carry far into the lava swirled cavern. The battery-operated light the Rangers had seen on first contact had long since gone dim and faded out. Only their handheld flashlights now guided their search. The only smooth spot on the floor of the cave was nearly filled by the empty bomb carriage. A film of mud made walking a challenge—but also provided a record of what came and went. Large chunks of the lava ceiling were strewn about, especially near the walls. The men spread out, their lights sweeping around the darkness like the searchlights from an auto dealer's grand opening in Los Angeles. An ROK Ranger called out from behind the largest smooth sided boulder, "Over here, sir. It looks like a small workshop."

The Colonel led the way followed by Wetmore and Mead. They could hear the surf not far from the lava dome—and see the tracks leading from the bomb carrier out through the seaward opening. There were other tracks, truck tires—and boot prints. A crude work bench leaned against the side of the rock. Parts of unknown purpose lay haphazardly, while small tools were carefully lined up in a low box. An unfinished contraption sat in the middle, only a bit more refined than a classic Rube Goldberg assembly. The Air Force Colonel said, "Looks like it would have been a booby trap—or a delay mechanism to set off the bomb."

"It's the latter."

The voice came from a short distance away—from the tall Chinese man under guard by an ROK Marine—Dr. George Huang. "I was preparing the delay trigger ... but General Su Yu had other ideas. Look under the bench ... a box."

Wetmore knelt and swept his light under the bench and saw the box. He slid it out. It contained two pieces of paper with diagrams of some sort. Dr. Huang, his arms bound behind him and escorted by the Marine, walked over to Wetmore, then looked at Mead and said, "He took the rest. Su Yu took all of my detailed notes with him."

The Colonel asked, "What were they about?"

Dr. Huang looked at him and answered, "I've been learning about your bomb since we got it—"

Wetmore interrupted him, "Where is it—the bomb?"

"Gone," Dr. Huang said, "since yesterday. I assume. General Su Yu knew of your landing on the other side of the island. Su Yu had become very nervous since Shtykov's death—and then you arrived. He had the means to get the bomb back to the boat. It was an alternate plan anyway—I believe he panicked."

Wetmore suddenly found his voice, "Good God, Amos—the Navy is standing off the coast right now! If they confront Su Yu … in a panic as he is … a firefight could blow this island into eternity."

USS Wantuck (ADP-125) at sea off Jeju Island, Korea

Two miles off the island USS Wantuck and two small boats bobbed in the after storm swells. One of the boats, a Higgins (LCVP) launched from Wantuck, pulled abeam the other boat, a fisherman with an unusual cargo visible over her gunnels.

As USS Wantuck stood off from the other two, she kept her 5" deck gun trained on the fisherman, the ship's captain peering through the "big eyes" binoculars from the wing of his bridge. Protruding from the aft hold of the fisherman was a large gray whale-like object. He caught sight of some men ducking out of sight—wearing uniforms.

The LCVP with Wantuck's boarding party threw a line to a sailor in native fisherman's garb standing on the bow. Two other fishermen appeared on deck and the boarding crew drew weapons.

Suddenly an explosion—a deep throated *whump*—raised the stern of the fisherman out of the water. She settled by the stern and kept going down—scuttled. Small arms fire came from the area near the strange grey cargo directed toward the ship. On the bow the native fishermen cast off the LCVP and then dove over the side, swimming away from their boat. More small arms fire came from partially hidden uniformed men in the fisherman's stern. Wantuck's captain stayed under cover until he saw the LCVP pick up the fisherman and churn away on a course to take her away from the fishing boat and around the far side of her home ship.

A word from the captain—and the 5" gun roared.

The fishing boat, already shipping seawater over her stern, exploded in a massive ball of fire. The heat and shock wave swept across Wantuck's bridge as the ship rolled and righted itself. The captain and bridge crew, already under cover from the small arms, were not hurt.

On the island, the Mead team heard the report of the 5" deck gun followed by the large explosion. They rushed to the mouth of the lava cave, keeping close to the walls where the footing was firmer, arriving in time to see the water spout and smoke cloud settle near a large ship—their ship, USS Wantuck. The Air Force colonel spoke first, "Mr. Mead, I believe we just found our bomb—but we're still here, so, no nucl—"

Dr. Huang said, "It is true. Su Yu was taking it away on the same boat that brought it here. He did not know that it was inert. I was coming to retrieve the detonator—the *pit device*—from my own secret place of safekeeping when you came along. I will show you now. It is secured behind where you found my delay fuse." Huang looked out toward the sea and said, "General Su Yu and his men are on that boat."

Wetmore walked out in front of the group and quietly said, "They *were* on the boat, Doctor. There is no more boat, no more bomb—and no more Su Yu and company."

EPILOGUE

AP—SPECIAL REPORT—Communist Chinese Forces renew offensive: Seoul is abandoned again. General Ridgway stabilizes the UN lines along the 37th parallel and counterattacks with "Operation Thunderbolt" over a virtual carpet of dead Chinese Communist soldiers.
UN issues a resolution to end the Korean War.

The White House, Washington, DC, the Oval Office

Amos Mead and the Director of the CIA had driven as closely as possible to the White House. The historic building was undergoing extensive reconstruction, gutted to the outside stone walls and being reinforced with concrete and tons of steel. The exterior stone walls are those first put in place when the White House was constructed two centuries ago, and their protection was so important that workers dismantled a bulldozer and reassembled it inside to avoid cutting a larger doorway out of the walls.

The President's residence was no more. The Truman's lived in the Blair House and the President walked to work each day across Pennsylvania Ave. Only the West Wing, including the Oval Office, remained open.

Amos Mead and the CIA Director sat on red brocade arm chairs, moved to a place across from the desk of the President of the United States. The vice-president sat in a similar chair to the side of the desk. As they awaited the President's arrival Mead gazed around the room. In contrast to the chaos they had walked through to get to the West Wing it was *quiet and civilized* he thought. Green drapes framed the tall windows, while the walls were adorned with framed pictures of WWII aircraft. A large globe sat in front of a sealed off fireplace and a large portrait of a standing George Washington hung over the marble mantle.

The door opened and President Truman walked in and headed straight for his chair behind the elegant desk. No other officials joined them in the room.

This was a meeting of *Force Three.*

The President tapped his hand on a stack of papers on the desk in front of him. "I have your report here, Mr. Mead. But I want to hear it from you."

Mead hesitated a moment, finding his voice in this awe-inspiring surrounding, then said, "After we found the bomb missing from the cave, George Huang helped to clear up what had happened. He became very compliant when it was clear that he had no other choice. The big news was that General Su Yu took both the bomb and the detailed study notes that Huang had prepared."

The Vice President asked, "Doesn't the sinking of his escape boat put an end to all this?"

The Director said, "Maybe not. It seems that the group's original plan was to blackmail the warring governments with just the threat of the bomb. But after Colonel General, cum Ambassador, Shtykov "died" in an Allied air raid near Pyongyang—and his close escape from an unhappy Mao Tse-tung—General Su Yu decided to take the bomb for himself. One thought is that Su Yu figured he could bring it to Mao and make amends."

Mead continued, "So he got the bomb and Huang's notes, but not the pit detonator. Apparently when he was caught by our ship that had been cruising offshore awaiting our call, he decided to end it all by picking a fight with a 5" gun—and setting off his scuttling charges. Our Air Force expert is sure the explosion was from the bombs HE core—that's High Explosive—"

The President interrupted him, "I know HE well, Mr. Mead—remember, I was an artilleryman in the 'war to end all wars'."

Mead smiled and continued, "So any remnants of the bomb went to the bottom with the boat. Su Yu's body was retrieved along with a couple of his bodyguards. They were ID'd, then buried at sea."

The President said, "So you took your prisoner and the bomb's detonator and went aboard the Navy ship—"

Mead's turn to interrupt the President, "One more thing, Mr. President. While we were in the cave we found rivets and some bits of bent metal in a box, along with a pry bar and hand drill. At that point Mr. Huang told us that he had opened the bomb and studied it in detail. The Colonel confirmed the rivets probably came from an Mk VIII bomb."

The President said, "You're telling us that Huang knows a lot about the bomb."

"Yes sir," Mead said, and his expertise allows him to truly know and understand what he saw inside it."

The Vice President said, "It's a good thing he's in our custody—and not home in China." The President nodded and turned to Mead, "Go on with your report."

"Yes, sir—so we sailed from Jeju on USS Wantuck to Pusan where we were expecting to get a flight to Tokyo. But for some reason General MacArthur sent two aircraft to pick us up. Two Convair C-131s. Here's where it gets strange. When we arrived at Pusan, Harmon Wetmore announced that he had specific orders to deliver Huang and the detonator personally—and that he was flying directly via Europe to DC and the CIA."

The CIA Director interjected, "Mr. President, Wetmore had no such instruction from my headquarters."

President Truman nodded, a frown on his face, and turned back to Mead.

Mead continued, "I was in no position to argue—nor wanted to at the time. I boarded my plane with our Air Force colonel—and the detonator. Wetmore was upset, when the colonel would not agree to leave the device with him. It was Air Force property and it was going back to Kadena. Wetmore had no leverage—though he tried—so he left with Doctor Huang on his flight. The colonel and I flew to Tokyo to debrief General MacArthur, and then I came straight to Washington."

"May I interject something here, sir?" The CIA Director asked.

"Certainly," the President said.

"Mr. President, while Mead was en route home I instructed Doctor Brigit Mead to establish contact with her Chinese general friend, Yang Kuisong. She reported to him simply that General Su Yu would not be coming home. Her analysis of the conversation when she reported back to me was that she felt that Kuisong knew that they had lost a chance at getting the bomb technology. Sir, it was only her interpretation—but we've come to trust this lady's judgment over the years. She also reported that Mao has decided to ignore his American prisoner as if he did not exist, and he will not be returned. *Force Three China* has verified this, but thinks it is actually Kuisong's doing."

"I've heard that," the President said. But what of the Russian Shtykov?"

The Director smiled and said, "We kept our promise to Mr. Khrushchev. The ambassador was delivered to a KGB detail in Berlin and is now enjoying a long stay in Siberia. *Force Three Russia* reports that Khrushchev is happy that we all avoided the embarrassment that would come with disclosure of the plot."

We're happy to oblige," the President said with a broad grin. "So where the hell are Wetmore and Dr. Huang?"

The President answered the ringing phone, the one from his secretary. After listening, he said, "Have it brought in." He hung up the phone and turned to the Director. "There's a message coming in for you."

The door opened and an aide stepped in, looked around the Oval Office and, spotting the CIA Director, handed him an envelope. The CIA Director opened the message and scanned it. He stood and looked at Mead then back to the President and said, "Mr. President, I've been waiting for this confirmation of a report we just received—and, Amos, you haven't seen this yet—Harmon Wetmore's flight disappeared over the Arabian Sea."

Mead and the vice president leaned forward from their seats as the Director added, "Mr. President, the last transmission heard from the flight was overheard by a British plane flying from New Delhi to Cairo. He heard the flight officer asking for re-routing instructions to Tel Aviv—to Israel."

AUTHOR'S NOTES

As with the earlier books in the Amos Mead Adventures series, there is a thread of historic events and people running through the story. But with the usual disclaimers, the book is a fictional creation of my imagination—and love of a good story. However, I will point out a few of the historic bases for my tale.

Japan ruled the Korean peninsula for thirty-five years until the end of World War II. At that time, Allied leaders decided to temporarily occupy the country until elections could be held and a government established. Soviet forces occupied the north, while a small contingent of U.S. forces occupied the south.

The planned elections did not take place. The Soviet Union established a communist state in North Korea, and the U.S. set up a pro-western state in South Korea—each claiming to be sovereign over the entire peninsula.

This standoff led to the Korean War in 1950, ending in 1953 with the signing of an armistice. To this day the two countries are still technically at war with each other.

The opening events in Chapter 1—the crash of the CIA aircraft and the capture of the two crewmen is based on a true event that happened on November 29, 1952, when a C-47 aircraft (the C-119 transport is mine), assigned to a covert program called 'Third Force,' intended to create a resistance network within China, was carrying CIA paramilitary officers John Downey and Richard Fecteau. Their mission, as described in the chapter, was to pick up a person by "air snatch" from the ground. They were ambushed and shot down over Jilin province in Manchuria and, initially, all of those on the aircraft were presumed by the U.S. Government to be lost. And in fact, the pilots, Robert Snoddy and Norman Schwartz did not survive. Downey and Fecteau were captured by the Communist Chinese (Wetmore's capture by Soviets is my creation—although they were in the area at the time).

In Chapter 29 it is reported that the CIA airman would not be released. In fact, Fecteau was not released by China until December 1971, and Downey in March 1973—twenty years after the Korean Armistice. They were released only after President Richard Nixon publicly acknowledged Downey's CIA connection.

Chapter 5 telling of Mao Tse-tung's train ride from Beijing to Moscow is historically reported, as is his conversations with Stalin (Chapter 10 and 11). I found them in recently released KGB and Chinese histories.

Some of the Chapters are headed by a fictitious "AP news announcement." The items are real and in sequence of events, but not necessarily on the true time line. I included them to give a small sense of what was happening on the Korean peninsula.

Another place my story crosses into historic events is in Chapter 23. North Korean partisans did help the Allies at Inchon, but that was not the limit of their service. Shortly after the war began in June 1950, Far East Command began a secret guerrilla campaign behind enemy lines in North Korea using thousands of Korean fighters opposed to the communist regime in North Korea.

The 8240 Army Unit comprised of Rangers and other soldiers with unconventional warfare experience from World War II was one of those Korean partisan units headed by American officers who served in leadership and advisory roles. The unit was dubbed the *White Tigers.*

Histories of the operation indicate that for the most part the units were trained on islands off the western coast of North Korea. The existence of these units was not declassified until the 1990s.

I bring up the Atomic Bomb in the Introduction as it was actually discussed by the President and Joint Chiefs. It comes up again in Chapter 6 in the transcription of a meeting of Chinese Communist generals. The transcription is authentic, acquired from CIA historical records.

The theft of an Atomic Bomb from Kadena Air Force Base is my creation. (Chapter 13) The term *Broken Arrow* is accurate. By US Military definition *Broken Arrow* refers to an accidental event that involves nuclear weapons, warheads or components, but which does not create the risk of nuclear war. While my event is fictitious, there have been eleven actual *Broken Arrow* incidents in history, most involving the crash of a B-52 aircraft.

The mention of basing the bombs at Kadena Air Force Base in the Introduction and Prologue are true. In 1950, the A-Bomb was only five years old. A scary thought, but it was assumed then that atomic weapons would be part of any future conflict—like the Korean War. The Joint Chiefs of Staff did order the use of the atomic bomb against China if it sent troops or bombers into Korea. China ignored the threat. Ultimately, the United States promised to use atomic weapons in Korea only to prevent a "major military disaster."

The "technical descriptions" of the atomic bomb and its components came from declassified material and I truncated some areas for readability. Basically though, it is accurate. It was necessary to change the details of the bombs stored at Kadena from the real MK- IV to a fictional MK-VIII—because the MK-IV is too big for my trucks and fishing boat to handle.

Jeju Island, Chapter 17 and elsewhere, is a real Island off the coast of Korea. The volcanic mountain with its caves is true—but all the action is mine, as are the descriptions and locations of the villages named.

In Chapters 17 and 18 the history "lessons" about Nikita Khrushchev are factual. But his participation in Mead's plans in Chapter 21 is my creation. While Nikita Khrushchev espoused and truly believed that Communism would prevail over capitalism, his behavior after becoming President of the Soviet Union strongly indicates that he enjoyed the U.S. way of life. (I personally remember his stop in Santa Barbara, California during his west coast train trip) Khrushchev was not afraid to allow Soviet citizens to see Western achievements. He let Soviets travel (over 700,000 Soviet citizens travelled abroad in 1957) and allowed foreigners to visit the Soviet Union, where tourists became subjects of immense curiosity.

A Khrushchev biographer described the mercurial leader:

"He could be charming or vulgar, ebullient or sullen; he was given to public displays of rage (often contrived) and to soaring hyperbole in his rhetoric. But whatever he was, however he came across, he was more human than his predecessor or even than most of his foreign counterparts, and for much of the world that was enough to make the USSR seem less mysterious or menacing."

Nikita Khrushchev's son, Sergei, eventually migrated to the United States.

The last scene in the story hints of nuclear secrets headed to Israel and is fiction. But Israel's involvement with the bomb is fact-stranger-than-fiction. The first Prime Minister of Israel, David Ben-Gurion, was "nearly obsessed" with obtaining nuclear weapons to prevent another Holocaust being brought upon the Jewish people. He is quoted as saying, "What Oppenheimer, Einstein, and Teller—all Jews—made for the United States could be also done by scientists here in Israel ..."

He recruited scientists even before the end of the 1948 Arab-Israeli War that established Israel's independence.

Adding Dr. Huang to the mix (possibly!) is my own ending. Whether or not he and Harmon Wetmore survived the loss of his airplane—is a tale for another time.

ABOUT THE AUTHOR

Tom Gauthier is a retired business executive with degrees in Business Administration and Psychology. He served in the US Army as a combat intelligence analyst and in the US Air Force Reserve as a C-119 Loadmaster.

Tom lives in rural northeast California with his wife of forty years, Marlene. Merging a family in 1975, Tom and Marlene enjoy their four children, thirteen grandchildren, and fifteen great grandchildren.

He began writing novels in 2008. His first work, *Code Name: ORION'S EYE*, was an outgrowth of his studies with the Long Ridge Writers' Group. It also began the "career" of the character of *Amos Mead*. His second novel continued the Amos Mead Series with *MEAD'S TREK*. In 2011 Gauthier was signed by Patriot Media, Inc. publishers and the first two Amos Mead Adventure books were reissued as second editions in 2011 and 2012. The next Amos Mead Adventure followed in 2013 with, *DIE LISTE: Revenge on the Black Sun.*

FORCE THREE RISES is the fourth—with more to come.

Though not a part of the Amos Mead Adventure series, Gauthier's novel, *A VOYAGE BEYOND REASON* is a factual record of "Coach" (CBS TV *Survivor*) Ben Wade's solo kayak voyage down the west coast from upper Baja California, Mexico, to Colombia, South America.

Wrapped in a fictional story that drives the suspense of the feat to a climactic ending, it won an international award in a Writers' Digest competition for Literary Fiction, and is listed in the Library of Congress. It is available on Kindle.

www.tomgauthier.com

ToMar Associates Publishing   **Janesville, California**

Other Gauthier Novels

Code Name: ORION'S EYE
Available on Amazon.com, Kindle, and from PatriotMediainc.com

"Author Tom Gauthier has woven together a compelling story, mixing historical fact with fiction in "Code Name: Orion's Eye." The result is a riveting tale of military intrigue and espionage from World War II, involving the Nazis' desperate attempt to steal American radar technology."

Military Writers Society of America Review

MEAD'S TREK
Available from Amazon, Kindle, and Audible Audio Books

"Here's a voice that's original, animated, and refreshing. Tom Gauthier definitely knows what he's writing about—and it shows. You're there, amidst the action, feeling, hearing, even smelling the tension. Enjoy the adventure."

Steve Berry, *NY Times and International Best Selling Author*

"Gauthier weaves a compelling story of intrigue, action and romance …"
Lis Wiehl, *FOX NEWS Legal Analyst and author of* SNAPSHOT

DIE LISTE: Revenge on the Black Sun
Available on Amazon.com, Kindle, and from PatriotMediainc.com

"You won't want to put it down …The cast of characters is believable, and the action keeps you turning pages."

TH Handy *reviewed the kindle edition*

"5 stars for an exciting read. Loved this novel. It has everything a reader wants—well rounded characters, fast paced action and adventure with a sprinkle of revenge.

Reviewed by author **Angela Townsend**

www.ingramcontent.com/pod-product-compliance
Lightning Source LLC
Chambersburg PA
CBHW071310200626
46813CB00015B/1228